Roisin
MEANEY

It's That Time of Year

HACHETTE
BOOKS
IRELAND

First published in Ireland in 2020 by HACHETTE BOOKS IRELAND

1

Cataloguing in Publication Data is available from the British Library.

Trade paperback ISBN 9781529375183
Ebook ISBN 9781529375176

Typeset in Book Antiqua by Bookends Publishing Services, Dublin

Printed and bound in Great Britain by Clays Ltd, Elcograf, S.p.A.

Hachette Books Ireland policy is to use papers that are natural, renewable
and recyclable products and made from wood grown in sustainable forests.
The logging and manufacturing processes are expected to conform to the
environmental regulations of the country of origin.

Hachette Books Ireland
8 Castlecourt Centre
Castleknock
Dublin 15, Ireland

A division of Hachette UK Ltd
Carmelite House, 50 Victoria Embankment, EC4Y 0DZ

www.hachettebooksireland.ie

In loving memory of Colm O'Mahony, a sweetheart

Your heart knows the way.
Run in that direction.

RUMI

Friday,
20 December

Annie

THE FLANNERYS HAVE FORGOTTEN TO TURN OFF THE lights on their holly bush again. Off and on they flash, throwing tiny soft bursts of blue and red and green into the night. The tail end of the night really, already a faint lightening in the sky, smudges of grey breaking up the darkness when Annie looks east towards the school and the church and the chipper. The school closing today for the holidays, traffic on the road last evening, parents and children travelling to and from the annual Christmas concert.

All the concerts she has attended over the years, never a year without at least one of her children involved. Helping out with preparations beforehand in noisy classrooms, attaching cardboard wings to white dresses, clipping tinsel halos to shining hair, drawing ripped seams together with safety-pins, bending to tie laces, to wipe noses, to reassure anxious little performers with a hug and tell them they were going to be wonderful.

Her heart in her mouth as she watched them onstage in case of a stumble, or lines forgotten. Stepping into the aisle to take a photo that invariably came out blurry: thank God for Cora, who was a far better photographer. Clapping till her hands were sore when mishaps were avoided, and when they weren't.

She flicks through them in her head, all her children. All the precious, unlucky, sad, mixed-up, lonely little creatures who were never really hers, just loaned to her for a while. All the tears she dried, the tantrums and rages she tried to quell, the sorrows she did her best to mend, to melt away with toys and treats and singsongs, and happy bedtime stories.

Finished now, no more children. Packed it in two years ago, when her body ran out of the energy it needed to cope with a house full of young children. These days she drives the meals-on-wheels van around the neighbourhood each weekday lunchtime, and helps with events in the community hall, and does the readings in church every fourth Sunday, and gives the garden the attention it was craving. These days she takes Keith

Burke's little dog for a walk when Keith's hip is at him, and brings Ruthie, who is about to become her stepdaughter, to the cinema in Ennis every Thursday afternoon. These days she gets through more books, and takes long, lazy baths, and lies in bed an extra hour in the mornings.

Most mornings.

She stands in the lee of the porch, shoulders hunched, hands deep in the pockets of her winter coat, breath turning white as it meets the frosty air. Nothing beneath the coat except her nightdress, not nearly enough protection against this early-morning chill but she woke abruptly, going from sleep to full awareness in the space between one heartbeat and another, and something nudged her down the stairs and outside.

She turns her gaze to the sign that Joe Dineen erected six weeks ago, its wooden post attached to the gate pillar with plastic ties, and she feels the same belt of dismay that the sight of it always prompts. She can't make out the lettering in the faint light, but she doesn't need to read it. For Sale, it says, and Joe's number underneath. For Sale. Come and buy my home, come and pay for my refuge, my sanctuary, with euros and cents. It won't be the same without you in it, people tell her, and it won't, it won't. The loss of it, even before it's happened, causes her to weep inside. How can she possibly let it go, even as she knows the impossibility of keeping it?

She tilts her face to the sky. She turns it this way and that to take in the sweep of dimming stars. The threatened snow has yet to make an appearance, the days dry and bright and cold as

the year moves to a close. Perfect December weather really: no icy roads to torment the traveller, no stormy gusts to rip tiles from roofs and push trees sideways, no sleety showers to make even the shortest of walks a challenge. So far so good.

Her feet in their slippers tingle with cold. She shifts her weight to wriggle her toes, and turns her attention to the astonishing fact that today is the last day of her fifties. How did that happen? How has she become a woman with almost sixty years of life lived? In the mirror she sees the lines in her face and the pockets of skin beneath her eyes and the multiple white strands laced through her mud-brown hair that tell her it must be true, but inside, in her heart and in her soul, it seems the greatest of travesties, a miscalculation of epic proportions. She's never that age – she's nowhere near it.

Oh, she knows it's not old. In these days of extended life, sixty is middle-aged, maybe nudging towards elderly, but nowhere near old. We're in our prime, Matt tells her, his sixty-second birthday in another few weeks, and she laughs and agrees with him – and yet, and yet, the thought of sixty, the idea of it, makes her want to run and hide from it.

Then again, this milestone birthday is also going to herald a new beginning for her, and for Matt. Tomorrow they start on their journey together, years later than most but with as much anticipation and love, she's sure, as any couple heading for the altar. They may have taken longer to get there, but maybe the delay makes their destination all the sweeter.

She shivers. She draws the heavy coat more tightly around her without taking her hands from her pockets. She should go

in, find the redness in last night's ashes in the stove and coax it with firelighter and kindling to a fresh flame. Boil the kettle, make sourdough toast, begin the day as she always does. But still she lingers, reluctant to leave this quiet space, this time of waiting and wondering, this time of not-doing.

She thinks of the three people, strangers to one another, who will embark on their separate journeys sometime today. Making their way back to her, covering the miles that separate them. *I know it's really near Christmas, but I'd so love if you could be here*, she'd written to each of them. *I'll have a bed made up for you. Stay for the weekend, or as long as you want. Stay for Christmas if you can!*

She hadn't been hopeful that any of them would make it, hadn't been sure that they could leave work commitments or partners or whatever on such short notice, or that they'd even want to travel at this time of year. She'd braced herself against the possibility that none of them would be able to come – but they are able, and they're coming, all three. *Wouldn't miss it for the world*, Julia wrote, and *Delighted, great news*, Eddie wrote, and *See you then, looking forward*, Steph wrote.

It wasn't difficult to settle on the three she chose, with maybe a hundred – no, well over that – to pick from. First, because these three had left the deepest imprints, these three she finds tiptoeing into her thoughts more than any of the others. And second, because some feeling, some impulse, whispered to her that each of them needs her in some way, each of them is bringing a hurt for her to mend, just like she used to.

The tip of her nose stings with every frosty inhalation.

She can't feel her toes anymore. Come on, move. She takes her hands from her pockets and pushes the front door open. She enters the house as the morning edges in and the night recedes, and the lights on the holly bush flash on and off and on again.

Annie, then

THREE TIMES THEY CIRCLED THE BLOCK BEFORE locating the turn they were seeking. 'Honestly,' her mother said, 'you'd think there'd be a sign.'

'There it is,' Annie said. 'See? On the side of that corner house.'

Her mother tipped her head to look through Annie's window. 'There's no sign there.'

'It's under the ivy. The end is sticking out.'

'Oh, for goodness sake – how is anyone supposed to see that?'

Only the final *ry* of the street name was visible, which wasn't much help if you were new to Limerick and trying to locate the house that was to be your home for the foreseeable future.

'What number is it?' Her mother was peering now over the steering wheel at the red-brick terraced houses as they crawled past. 'Half of them don't even have numbers.'

'Fourteen – watch out for that bin. Look, there's twelve. It must be nearby.'

Number fourteen was right next door to twelve, the odds on one side of the narrow road, the evens on the other. Her mother cut the engine and eyed the house doubtfully. 'It's nothing much to look at.'

It wasn't. Its coat of mustard yellow paint was coming off in patches, the scrap of lawn in front of it overgrown and filled with thistles. The railing and gate that cordoned it off from the road were stained with rust. Two bins, one blue, one green, were positioned directly outside the only downstairs window, in which a dingy net curtain hung.

Annie saw it all, and didn't care. She'd secured her place in college and was leaving home for the first time, on the way to realising her dream of becoming a teacher. She couldn't wait for this part of her life to begin, and she didn't give a damn what kind of a roof was over her head. She'd happily have taken possession of a garden shed, or a tent on someone's back lawn. You won't look at us when you're a posh college girl, Matt McCarthy had said when she told him she'd been accepted for teaching. He'd have a good laugh now if he saw where she was proposing to live. Nothing remotely posh about it.

'You don't have to come in,' she said – but her mother was already getting out of the car, so together they hauled Annie's cases from the boot and made their way up the cracked concrete of the short path, her mother tut-tutting at a giant thistle that sprang up from the edge of the lawn. Weeds never lasted long in their garden at home.

Annie pressed the doorbell. They waited without speaking. Someone nearby was listening to Freddie Mercury singing about Moët et Chandon; again she was reminded of Matt, who was a big Queen fan.

Even this late in the afternoon it was hot, their third sunny day in a row. She peeled her shirt away from her back and tucked her hair behind an ear, and wished for a glass of ice-cold water.

'This is ridiculous. Are you sure you weren't to call to the college for the key?'

'I'm sure. I was told my housemate would be here.'

'Well, if she is, she must be deaf. Press it again.'

Annie obeyed, and when there was still no response she rattled the letterbox flap, which didn't produce much in the way of noise. There being no knocker, she gave a tentative thump to the door with the side of her fist, then a harder one – and the music cut off abruptly. Another few seconds passed, during which her mother sighed and shifted her weight, and looked at her watch. Finally, they heard the soft pat of approaching steps, and the door was opened.

'Hello! Sorry, I was out the back. I hope you weren't waiting long.'

Light brown curly hair, a wide gap-toothed grin. A grey,

well-worn Fleetwood Mac T-shirt. Tiny denim shorts that Annie prayed her mother wasn't frowning at. No shoes.

'Were you ringing the bell? I think it's broken.' The girl stepped forward and pressed it, frowning. 'Yup, stone dead. Anyway,' the smile returning, 'I'm Cora.'

'I'm Annie, and this is my mother.'

Hands were shaken. They were ushered into the tiny hall and given a tour of downstairs, which consisted of a poky sitting room that led to an even smaller kitchen at the rear of the house, and a tiny bathroom at the foot of the stairs, with a shower stall instead of a bath. 'This is it, I'm afraid,' Cora said. 'Just the bedrooms upstairs.'

The furniture was cheap and drab throughout, the carpet in the hall and sitting room threadbare. One of the kitchen cabinets was missing a door. The bathroom sink was chipped, the plastic toilet seat cracked. It was all a little sad and in need of attention – but there was what looked like a working fireplace in the sitting room, and the kitchen led to a surprisingly sizeable paved courtyard that was splashed with September sun.

A shiny pink bedspread was thrown onto its paving stones. Two pillows sat on it, along with a splayed book, and a tape recorder with a tumble of cassettes, and a tube of sun cream. A half-pint glass filled with orange peel stood by the wall. The place smelt of coconut.

'I stole your pillow,' Cora told Annie. 'I promise I'll give it back before bedtime.'

They'd been placed together, after Annie had added her name to a list of new students looking for accommodation.

House with two others, she'd written in the column that asked for her preferred option. Three seemed like a good number: any more might be too many, any fewer and you ran the risk of being stuck with someone you'd have to spend the year trying to avoid.

But preferences weren't guaranteed. A week or so ago she'd received a letter telling her she'd been placed in a two-bed house with one other female, and since then she'd been praying that the female would turn out normal, and easy to get along with. So far, things looked hopeful.

Cora bent to pick up the glass. 'Tea for anyone?' she enquired.

'Not me,' Annie's mother replied. 'I need to get back home. Can you show us Annie's room, so we can drop off her cases?' Wanting to see it, of course. Wanting, probably, to check the mattress, to scour the walls for signs of damp.

'Well, I've thrown my stuff into the room on the left of the stairs, but I don't mind which one I have. As far as I can see, there's not much between them.'

The stairs were narrow and steep, and uncarpeted. The bedroom to the right smelt a little musty. It ran the length of the house, with a window to front and rear, and it held a single bed, a small wardrobe, a dressing table with two drawers, and a wooden chair. No pictures on the walls, which were covered in pale blue paper scattered with tiny cream triangles.

While her mother was unpacking sheets, Annie peeped into the other room, and found it, as Cora had said, to be pretty much identical in size and layout, and smell. An enormous case, almost twice the size of Annie's two, lay open on the bed, something

red and frilly spilling from it. A rag doll with yellow plaits and a freckled face sat on the rear windowsill and beamed into the room. Jeans lay crumpled on the floor, a tower of paperback books on the dressing table.

The mattress on Annie's bed looked new, thankfully. Annie's mother pronounced it too soft, but otherwise acceptable. They made the bed with the clean sheets Annie had taken from the hot press that morning; she felt a surprising lump in her throat as they tucked in corners and settled blankets and eiderdown on top. It was really happening. She was really leaving home.

'You'll have to wait until you get your pillow back to put this on,' her mother said, dropping the pillowcase onto the bed. 'I hope she won't make a habit of that kind of thing. Make sure you don't let her walk all over you. And give a good scrub to that bathroom when you get a chance – God only knows when it was cleaned last.'

Annie was terrified her new housemate would overhear – but just then Queen started up again in the courtyard. She struggled with the catch in the back window until it released, and attempted without success to prise open the window – stuck fast, she guessed, with layers of paint. She'd have to find a way to free it. The front window opened more easily so she lowered the top half all the way, letting the warm air pour in.

Her mother pottered about for another few minutes, opening drawers, bemoaning the lack of hangers in the wardrobe, frowning at the flimsiness of the curtains, reminding Annie that they'd be expecting her home on Friday: 'I'm doing roast

chicken, so don't be late. Let Ivan know what time to pick you up at the station.'

'I will.'

This would be as much a change for her mother, Annie realised, as for Annie herself. The first of her two children to leave home, Ivan at twenty-three showing no sign of wanting to move out, happy to commute to his civil service job in Ennis in the old car he'd bought a year earlier. Annie was the one on the move – and who knew if she'd ever live at home again? The thought was at once exhilarating and terrifying.

Downstairs they found Cora sprawled on her bedspread in the courtyard. She waved a cheery goodbye to Annie's mother. 'See you soon,' she added, which Annie thought was unlikely, unless her mother was planning to return with a bucket of cleaning solutions and a mop.

They hugged at the car. 'I'll ring tomorrow sometime,' Annie promised. No sign of a phone in the house, but there was bound to be a payphone somewhere nearby, or in the college.

She stood on the path until the car disappeared, then made her way back into the house to find Cora in the kitchen, in the act of taking a tall brown bottle from the fridge.

'I figured I should wait till she left before I produced this – wouldn't want her to think you were sharing a house with a wino. Grab two glasses – I think I saw some in that corner press, or the one next to it. Isn't this house dire? We'll have to fix it up a bit, or we won't be able to bring anyone back. I'd say your mother was scandalised, was she?'

'Well …'

'Mine would have hit the roof if she'd seen it but she had to work, thank goodness – she's a teacher – so my brother brought me, and he wouldn't notice if the place was on fire. Are you any good with plants? I thought a few pots in the yard might be nice, but I haven't a clue – and maybe we could rig up some lights there too. I was thinking we could eat outside on a fine evening – better than in this horrible kitchen.'

She talked on, yanking the cork from the bottle and filling two glasses, spilling crackers onto a plate, cutting slices from a block of Cheddar. Annie had never tasted wine, or any alcohol apart from a small glass of sherry her father had poured for her the previous Christmas. She took a cautious sip, and found that it tasted slightly less sweet than the sherry, and was very cold.

'Isn't it awful? I hate Liebfraumilch, but it was all I could get for under a tenner at the off-licence.'

'No, it's fine ...'

'We can stock up on decent stuff when we do a shop in Quinnsworth.' She moved out to the courtyard, Annie following. 'We should probably start a kitty. We need loo rolls anyway – there's only one there, and it's a real cheapie. Where are you from, by the way?'

Annie named her village. 'It's in Clare, ten miles outside Ennis.'

'I've heard of it. I'm from Galway – well, between it and Salthill. Not a million miles from Clare.'

They arranged themselves on the bedspread. 'I asked the landlord for a toilet brush and a new shower curtain, and a door

for that cabinet. Have you checked out the state of the couch under that blanket?'

'No.' Annie wasn't inclined to check out the couch. 'What's he like? The landlord.'

Cora made a face. 'Youngish ... well, early thirties, I'd say. No wedding ring, but I'm not surprised – the smell of BO from him would knock you out. He lives in County Limerick, I forget where, so I'd say we'll only see him when he's collecting the rent. He says no parties, which is a bit rich – I mean, is he afraid we'll do damage to his lovely house? When's your birthday?'

Annie could hardly keep up. 'Er, not till December.'

'OK, mine's next month, so that'll be our first party. We'll have a bit of time to check out the college crowd, see who's worth inviting. And we can always ask the neighbours too, so they can't complain.' She reached for the sun-cream tube and squeezed some of its contents into her palm. 'You want some?'

'Thanks.' Annie pulled her skirt up past her knees and applied the cream to her skin, inhaling its coconut scent. She wouldn't dare wear shorts like Cora's – she'd feel far too self-conscious with so much skin on show. The two pairs she'd left at home were longer and baggier, and were worn only in the back garden on the hottest of days.

Cora raised her glass. 'Cheers, Annie. Here's to a good year. Tell me if I'm talking too much – everyone says I can't shut up. And if I ever do something that annoys you, you have to tell me instead of suffering in silence. Deal?'

'Deal, as long as you promise to do the same.'

'Oh, you needn't worry – I will.'

17

The house was awful. No way would Annie's clothes fit into that wardrobe: she'd have to leave half of them in her case, even with the dressing-table drawers. If she needed the toilet in the middle of the night, which she always did, she'd have to negotiate those narrow stairs half asleep.

But it was ten minutes' walk from the college, and lights and a few plants would be lovely in the courtyard, and their first party was already being planned. And she was free to live as she chose here, and already her new housemate felt like a friend.

Cora ejected the Queen cassette and riffled through the others. 'Supertramp or Janis Ian?'

'Janis Ian.'

Annie took another sip of wine. It tasted slightly better. They ate crackers and cheese in the last of the sunshine as Janis Ian learnt the truth at seventeen, and Annie was brimming with hope.

Julia

SHE CROSSES THE ROOM AND OPENS THE BALCONY
doors, feeling the immediate inrush of crisp early-morning air.
She ties the belt of her dressing gown and steps out, and looks
up as she always does to marvel at the magnificent curved
sweep to the heavens of the Tour Eiffel, just a handful of streets
away. So privileged she is to have this unimpeded close-up
view: little wonder she'd paid a small fortune for the penthouse
apartment. She'd balked when she'd heard the asking price
– how on earth could she justify it? – but her manager and

her accountant were all for it. You are a star now, Lucien had declared. You must have an apartment that deserves you. Such nonsense, typical Lucien – but her accountant had said it would be a good way to invest the almost comically large royalty payments that kept landing in her bank account. And here, perched a storey above the other buildings in the vicinity, she has the peace she craves. Yes, she'd happily pay for the peace, appreciated even more than the view.

She returns inside and closes the doors. She sits at the baby grand piano – a Steinway, another wild extravagance Lucien had insisted was her due, but the pure sound of it is magic. She runs her fingers lightly over the keys, playing again the minor chords she's chosen for the lines that have been repeating themselves in her head for over a month. She sings softly:

Little girl in a red coat, red hood,
Makes her way through the dark wood, scary wood,
Doesn't know there are wolves there, out there,
Every day there are wolves there, out there—

And after that, nothing. Nothing else comes. No further lyrics or tune, no chorus, no bridge. She's searching for sinister: she wants a song full of fear and dread and danger, a song that's inches away from a scream, something to make the listener shudder and thrill. She can feel it, she can almost taste it. She finds snatches of the rest, phrases darting suddenly into her consciousness, but they skitter away before she can grab onto them, before she has a chance to capture them in her recorder.

She's blocked. For the first time she's seriously blocked, and it's terrifying. What if she's lost whatever ability she had? What if she never manages to write another song? With the new CD releasing in January to coincide with the tour, there's no immediate pressure, but Lucien likes to see ongoing new material. Your fans adore you, he says, but you can never become complacent. You need to stay creative, stay producing. She knows he's right, he's always right about these things – for all his melodramatic pronouncements he's an excellent manager – but what can she do when it just won't come?

She leaves the song behind and drifts into the kitchen, and looks in the fridge to regard the two uneaten fillet steaks. She'd been about to prepare a marinade the day before when the phone call had come. I'm so sorry, Jean-Luc said, and told her of his older son's earlier fall from a swing that necessitated a trip to a medical clinic for an X-ray. We're here now, he said. Claudia is in with him – and Julia flinched at the casual mention of the wife he kept promising to leave. I'll arrange a night next week, he said, forgetting that next week was Christmas week, and his family would claim him, and his mistress would once again be left alone.

She could have fried a steak for herself but she didn't, so there they both remain, and she doesn't fancy letting them sit in the fridge all weekend. She'll donate them to Madame Frossard's pair of little pekinese on the floor below before she goes to the airport – better that than throw them out.

And what of the gift she'd wrapped? What of her Christmas gift to him of a signed first edition of Colette's *Nudité*? Bound

in beautiful green Moroccan leather, title in gilt on the spine, gilt-edged untrimmed endpapers, as much a work of art as of literature. He loves Colette; she was so happy to have found this for him. Nothing to be done now but save it until they meet again, until he can make his escape and come back to her.

She returns to the sitting room and retrieves Annie's most recent letter from the beautiful little antique bureau that was her aunt's housewarming gift when Julia bought the apartment three years earlier. She reads the words she knows pretty much by heart, and they calm and comfort her in the same way that thoughts of Annie always do. At the other end of this day she'll be back in Ireland, back with Annie, and staying with her for two precious nights. It's been far too long, eight months since her last visit, and she can't wait.

Thoughts of Annie, and the bond that's still so strong between them, bring the inevitable twinge of guilt about Aunt Karen, the only sister of Julia's dead father, and her closest living relative. Karen wasn't in a position to care for a young child when Julia was orphaned but she claimed her as soon as she could, and brought her from Ireland to her home in France, and supported her until Julia found work as a music teacher, and could manage on her own.

Aunt and niece had always got on perfectly well while they lived together in Karen's far more modest but perfectly adequate apartment in the twelfth *arrondissement*, and they still meet up when their separate schedules allow it – Karen is now a partner in the multinational finance company she joined in her twenties, and spends as much time out of France as in it – but for whatever

reason they never achieved the emotional tie, the communion of hearts that bloomed between Julia and Annie in the years they lived together.

Julia recalls with such clarity her first encounter with Annie. She a frightened three-year-old, her universe turned on its head by the death of her parents a week before. She remembers clutching the hand of the social worker who had brought her to Annie's house, and Annie's immediate kindness, the way she'd crouched in front of Julia, the gentle tone she'd used. The words were long forgotten, but the warmth of her foster mother's welcome remained.

She drops the letter onto the bed and slips off her dressing gown and nightdress. She showers and dresses, tucking old jeans into short fur boots, gathering hair into a simple side ponytail, wrapping a heavy navy wool shawl over her pink cashmere sweater. Applying no make-up, looking as unlike Julia M as it's possible for her to be. In the hallway she steps into her private lift and pulls its door closed. Down it glides, smooth as silk, noiseless as a whisper, through the seven floors.

If Jean-Luc had stayed the night, which had been the plan – Julia never enquired about the excuses he offered his wife for not returning to the family home on the nights he spent with her – they would still be in bed now, with Julia happy to forgo breakfast in exchange for another hour with him. Hungry instead for tenderness, for softly spoken words, and promises she wants to believe – but now, after missing dinner, she craves the comfort of food, and good coffee.

In the lobby she nods to Tristan, who lowers his newspaper

and lifts a hand as he always does to touch his temple solemnly with an index finger. *'Bonjour, Madame,'* he murmurs, and the orphaned little girl in her, the fostered little girl in her, wonders as she always does if he's slightly mocking her. Does he see through her? Does he sense, as she herself does, that she doesn't really belong in this place of plush carpeting and original artworks, and residents who were born into wealth, unlike her?

She steps into the bubble of the revolving door and steers it around to the street. Outside she sets off briskly, pulling up her shawl to mask the lower half of her face. Always the disguise now, always the armour between her and the rest of the world.

The *boulangerie* isn't far. In less than a minute she sees the light from its window spilling onto the pavement. The vanilla scent of fresh-baked pastries wafts towards her as she approaches. She enters the shop, the inward motion of the door triggering the little bell above it, and Monsieur Moreau emerges immediately from the back, aproned and smiling, wiping his hands on a small blue towel. She pulls down her scarf and greets him in the French that has become as natural to her as English in the twenty-eight years she's been living here. The baker returns her greeting and plucks with his tongs the *pain au chocolat* she requests, and places it in a small white carrier bag.

'Café crème, Madame?' he enquires.

'S'il vous plaît, Monsieur.'

She returns to the apartment, her face once again masked by her shawl. Ironic how her fame, while making her and her music known to so many, has also served to separate her from

them. In the five years since her first CD placed her quickly and decisively in the spotlight, she hasn't grown comfortable with strangers approaching her, wanting to talk with her, to touch her, to take a selfie while they stand too close. *Sign this!* they demand, thrusting menus or envelopes or supermarket receipts at her. *Sign my arm! Sign my sleeve! Wait till my friends hear!* And Lucien, when she tries to explain how unnerving she finds it all, just doesn't get it – or pretends not to.

Julia, he says, the French version softening and sliding out the j, how can you complain about this? You are where so many want to be. It's the price you pay, *chérie*, for all you have gained – and, really, it's just people being friendly. You must learn to accept it, Julia.

Easy for him to say, with nobody attempting to clip a shank of his hair with nail scissors (it happened once; the man was hustled away before he succeeded, but still she shakes when she thinks of it). Easy for him: he doesn't have to walk onto a stage in front of thousands, doesn't have cameras thrust constantly into his face, doesn't always, always, wish it were somehow otherwise.

She enters the lobby of her apartment block. Tristan glances up from his newspaper and gives her his usual salute. She unwraps her shawl as she crosses to the alcove that houses the penthouse lift. She presses the button for the only floor it visits, and up it glides to her sanctuary.

Steph

FINALLY, THE CLOCK RADIO TELLS HER IT'S TIME.

Quietly she inches to the edge of the bed. She slides a leg out and follows it with the other, her feet touching down in turn on the thin cotton mat that protects her from the stone floor. There's a dense feel to the air, the window closed against the chill of the night.

In the darkness she dresses, every sound she makes – the whisper of cloth on skin, the soft upward slide of a zip, the minuscule snap of a fastener – seeming magnified in the near

silence of the room. If he wakes she'll say she couldn't sleep, she's going for a walk before breakfast, although the lie will add fuel to his later displeasure – but he doesn't wake, the rhythm of his breathing remains unchanged.

She tiptoes in bare feet down the narrow back stairs, fingertips trailing over the cold roughness of the whitewashed wall. In the kitchen she puts on her flat-soled everyday shoes, their leather uppers thin and soft as velvet. She drinks water and takes an orange from the bowl, and draws aside the curtain below the sink to lift out the backpack she filled yesterday before he got home from taking the guests on a cliff walk. From the front pocket of the bag she takes the note she wrote, asking for his understanding. She slips it into one of the boots that sit by the door, so he won't find it until he's about to leave the house, nearly two hours from now.

Outside the air is cold, with a smell of rain and ocean in it. Her cotton sweater is thin but she'll wait till she reaches the port to put more on. The sky is dotted with stars, their reflections hopping like sparks on the surface of the sea, far below to her left. The moon slides towards the horizon. The white paving stones in the courtyard gleam softly.

She closes the door quietly and hitches the backpack onto her shoulders, feeling the weight of Annie's wedding gift, which Stavros let her have for half the marked price, and which she has wrapped carefully in most of the clothes she's bringing along. Hopefully she can keep it intact till it reaches Ireland.

Ireland. The thought of it, of seeing it again, prompts a small

rush of nervous excitement. Six years and two months since she stepped onto the ferry in Dublin, eighteen and desperate to get away, and determined never to return – and yet here she is, answering Annie's summons without thinking, the pull back to the country of her birth taking her by surprise.

She crosses the yard, praying that none of the others are awake. She braces herself, all the way along the drive, for the creak of a window being pushed open, a call to give her away, but thankfully no such sound comes. Enough wine or ouzo last evening maybe, at the local *taverna*, to keep them slumbering till Gareth rings the breakfast bell.

She thinks of him laying out the food without her, and feels a stab of worry. Leaving him to the breakfast isn't the problem – he's perfectly able to slice bread and chop fruit and spoon yogurt into dishes. The problem will be his reaction when he reads her note, and discovers what she's done.

No point in dwelling on that now. She'll ring him from Athens airport, after he's had time to get his head around it. She picks her way in the half-light over the steeply descending rutted path, passing the straggle of low houses and ramshackle sheds and chicken coops that have settled themselves into the hillside. She makes out a thin curl of smoke rising already from the Frangopoulos' chimney, and inhales the scent of burning wood that mingles with the mint and rosemary and eucalyptus that grow all around.

Further along the path she smiles at the blow-up Santa in the window of the wooden cabin owned by Deirdre and Steve from Bristol: how incongruous it looks, one of the few

dwellings on the island to acknowledge the imminent arrival of Christmas.

She peels the orange as she walks, flinging the rind into the bushes on the sea side of the path. She hears the clanging of goat bells further up the hill, a sound that always strikes her as vaguely mournful. When she first moved here the bells would wake her in the early hours; now she dreams right through them, unless she's got a reason to be up before dawn.

The orange is wonderfully sweet. When it's gone she licks its juice from her fingers. She rounds a bend and sees the little ferry, lit up and waiting at the harbour. Although she knows she's in good time she breaks into a slow jog, causing the rucksack to give a little slap against her back with every touchdown, making her wince each time it nudges against the bruise on her left hip that hasn't quite healed.

By the time she reaches the port a thin strip of light has appeared at the horizon: in the rest of the sky there is a small paling of the dark. The moon has vanished; the last of the stars are winking out. It feels slightly surreal to be up at this early hour. It feels, she decides, as if she's dreaming, lying asleep beside Gareth in the olive mill, soon to wake and rise and begin the day.

There are few about. Some out-of-season tourists pull cases on wheels in the direction of the ferry; a couple of farmers set up their vegetable stalls. A clutch of old women in black stand on the steps of the church across the street. Behind them a banner is strung across the front of the building, spelling out a message in the Greek script that Stavros has told her means Happy

Christmas. A young man in shorts and sweatshirt pushes a baby's buggy rapidly down the prom with a shaggy little brown dog trotting alongside.

She pulls her second sweater from the rucksack and puts it on. She asks in Greek for coffee at the little kiosk by the ticket office. The man smiles as he hands it over – she knows his face but not his name – and tells her to have a good day in English. After two years here they still see her as a tourist. The coffee is hot and strong. She sips it slowly as she watches two wooden crates being loaded onto the ferry.

I know you didn't want me to go, she said in her note, *but this is something I need to do. Please don't be cross, please try to understand. I'll phone you later and explain better.* But how can she explain it any better? The weekend before Christmas won't work, he'd said when Annie's letter had arrived at the beginning of the month. We'll be in the middle of a retreat. Tell her you're needed here, I'm sure she'll understand. We can both visit in the new year – but instead Steph had accepted Annie's invitation, without his knowledge and against his wishes.

He doesn't mean to hurt her. Creative people can be fiery, everyone knows that: she should be better at recognising the signs, and staying out of his way. His anger never lasts long, and he's always sorry afterwards.

Just like her mother was always sorry.

She finishes her coffee. She tips the dregs onto the cobbles and crumples the cup, and deposits it in a nearby bin. She buys a ticket for the ferry and boards. She stands at the rail while the sun rises slowly, while the gulls circle and swoop and shriek.

She looks down into the dark water. She hears the soft wet slap of it against the ferry, and she's reminded of how she and Gareth met two years earlier, the day after arriving on the island that had been recommended to her by a girl she'd waitressed with in Croatia. She'd been woken early by the goat bells, so she dressed and went to check out her new surroundings. After walking for twenty minutes or so she found the charming little sandy cove.

Nobody about, the turquoise water looking clear and inviting, so she stripped to underwear and walked into the sea, relishing the shock of it on her warm skin. She remembers plunging down into the cool saltiness, striking out parallel to the shore with the amateurish breast stroke she'd taught herself in the lake near Annie's house. After a dozen strokes she was breathless. She flipped onto her back to smile up at the pale blue sky, loving the rise and dip of the incoming waves, unaware of the current until she turned her head and saw with a heart lurch how far from land it had swept her.

She swung around and struck out for the shore, but quickly realised she was still being pulled strongly in the opposite direction, rendering her inexpert and increasingly desperate strokes useless. She began to tire, arms leaden with the effort of fighting with the sea, and properly frightened now. A wave came sideways at her. She went under, and took a mouthful of water in the muffled darkness. She pushed back up, coughing and disoriented, barely able to draw breath before another wave sent her under again – and suddenly, out of nowhere, she felt something grab her hair and yank her roughly and painfully to the surface.

'Climb on!' a loud male voice commanded, and she saw the white bulk of the jet-ski she'd failed in her panic to spot approaching, and the figure that was leaning towards her. 'Climb *on!*' he repeated, transferring his grip from her hair to a wrist, and she clambered up, scalp stinging, gasping and coughing and sobbing with relief as she leant against him and held on tight.

He saved her. He was literally her knight in shining armour: how could she not be dazzled by him? Gareth the writer, the most glamorous and interesting person she'd met since leaving Ireland. Older, cultured, confident, sexy. He took her back to her lodgings on his motorbike. She clung to him as her wet hair flew out behind her. She asked if she could buy him breakfast, or a drink, or anything, to say thank you. He seemed amused by her. Within weeks she'd moved into the converted olive mill, completely enthralled by him, scarcely able to believe he could possibly be interested in her.

She turns from the rail, from the thought, and goes to sit inside.

At Piraeus she finds the bus stop for the airport and joins the straggling queue. By now the sun is higher, the night chill softening. She stuffs her second sweater back into her bag. She'll need it again this evening, heading straight into the heart of an Irish winter.

A movement catches her eye, ahead in the queue. She watches a man, a youth really, slide his hand into the pocket of the woman in front of him. A pickpocket, trying his luck.

Without thinking, she shouts, 'Stop!' in English, and again in Greek: '*Stamáta!*'

32

Heads swing towards her as the youth whips out his hand and darts away, lost within seconds in the busy street. 'A pickpocket,' Steph says, pointing in the direction of his flight, but she doesn't know the word in Greek, and she must have been the only one to witness his action because nobody responds, nobody comments. Instead they shift their feet and edge away, maybe thinking her deranged, and given to sudden inexplicable outbursts.

She takes a breath and hitches her rucksack higher on her shoulder. The incident has quickened her pulse. It has caused something not unpleasant – adrenalin, she supposes – to zip and dart inside her. It has reminded her of her younger, wilder self, when she used to be afraid of nothing, and nobody. That Steph was someone to be reckoned with. That Steph would have given as good as she got, if anyone had dared to raise a hand to her.

The airport bus arrives. She shuffles forward with the rest.

Eddie

THE PHONE ALARM, LOW AND INSISTENT, PULLS HIM slowly from a dream that dissolves and vanishes as he wakes. He checks his screen, sees 8:10. He presses snooze and turns onto his back, and lets his eyes close again as he tunes in to the sounds of the morning. The ebb and flow of traffic in the street outside his window, the intermittent *peep* of some urban bird, the gush of water through the pipes of the building, the distant slam of doors, the low rumble of his flatmate's snores from the next room.

It had been the small hours before he got to bed, the restaurant forced to stay open an hour later than usual to accommodate a work group of a dozen on their Christmas night out, who arrived late and got progressively louder as the evening wore on. As usual, the manager turned a blind eye: as long as they wanted another bottle of the plonk that masqueraded as house wine they weren't going to be turfed out. By the time Eddie could get away the tube stations were closed, leaving him with no option but the night bus, or rather three night buses, which definitely took the scenic route through London: close to two and a half hours before he finally reached home.

It could have been worse. A few of his colleagues were heading to a late-night bar, and were trying to get him to go with them. He was sorely tempted, particularly as Alison, the newest and prettiest waitress, had made it clear to him that she was up for it. You coming? she asked but he said better not, he had an early start. Going to a wedding in Ireland, he told her. We might grab a drink when I get back – and she laughed and agreed that they might. Tricky sometimes having a fling with someone he sees every day at work – Jodie's definitely been cool since their night in October, clearly looking for more than that – but Alison, he thinks, will be happy with a brief encounter.

At eight thirty he gets up. He pulls on the boxers and shirt he wore the day before and heads to the kitchen, skirting the forlorn-looking tree in the corridor that Colin dragged home from the market last weekend. Draped so far only in strands of last year's ragged tinsel – can't find the lights, Colin said, and

I think the baubles broke. Eddie doubts that it will look much better by Christmas: Colin's good intentions have a habit of running out of steam.

They're out of milk again, the empty carton sitting like a taunt in the sink – second time this week Colin's done that to him – so he pops the tab on a can of Colin's Fanta lemon and adds a dollop to his cornflakes.

His teeth feel furry. His eyes have matter glued into their corners. He eats the odd mixture without pleasure, losing heart halfway through. He scrapes what's left into the bin and deposits bowl and spoon in the sink, next to the milk carton. In the shower he scrubs his teeth and shampoos his hair. He climbs out and inspects himself in the mirror above the sink, and is not cheered.

Dark shadows under his eyes, the whites bloodshot, the strain showing of too many late nights and rushed meals, and not enough money. No closer now to realising his dream than when he came to live in London, eight years ago this month. Good on paper with his qualifications, a special commendation from the catering college, two years working as second-in-command in a small but successful Dublin eatery, and employed pretty much without a break in London since his arrival – but time and again he falls down in the interviews that matter. No problem chatting up a female, great success in that department, but give him a shot at getting a job he would actually love, and he reverts to a nervous, mumbling idiot. And with his thirtieth birthday behind him since September, he's increasingly conscious of newer competition snapping at his heels. Will he ever make it

here? Is he destined to live out his days in the wrong kitchens, outside the coveted neighbourhoods?

Don't think about it, not now. Not this weekend.

He dresses quickly. Getting on for half past nine, time to pack up. He grabs his bag and brings it out to the Jeep. Parking right outside the gate – one advantage of living in Watford. Great parking, not so great when your work commute to Whitechapel takes at least seventy minutes on a tube – or rather, on three tubes. Just as well his stop is the last on the Metropolitan line, with him regularly falling asleep on the way home.

He returns inside for the cake. Colin was banished from the kitchen for the two mornings it took Eddie to produce the three tiers. When he'd offered to make it as his wedding gift, Annie had demurred. How on earth would you get it home from London? she'd asked, and he'd told her to let him worry about that. Well, only if you promise not to go to too much trouble, she said. All anyone needs is a taste – but it was a wedding cake, and it was Annie, so he did go to some trouble.

He chose lemon and elderflower for the top tier, and rich dark chocolate in the centre, and light fruit at the bottom, each tier iced appropriately. Not assembled yet, not until he lands at Annie's. He stores them in their separate boxes, side by side in the Jeep's small boot, along with the plastic container of tissue-wrapped fondant flowers that he'll add at the finish.

He returns to the apartment for his jacket, and finds Colin in the kitchen. 'You took my Fanta,' he says, scratching an armpit.

'You finished the milk.'

'Fair enough. You for the off, then?'

'Yup.'

Colin jerks a thumb in the direction of their rooms. 'Anyone left behind there that I should know about?'

Eddie grins. 'Not this time. Could have copped last night, but I decided to be sensible.'

'First time for everything.' Colin swigs the leftover Fanta. 'Have a good one, mate. Tell the Irish I said Happy Christmas.'

Colin works chiefly from home, translating books and various documents from English to Spanish or French. Occasionally he's called on to attend court cases, to interpret for witnesses or defendants. He and Eddie met through a mutual friend when Eddie was casting about for a new place to live, around the time that Colin's former flatmate was leaving to get married. In the seven months they've been sharing the rather poky but affordable ground-floor flat, they've established an amicable co-existence.

Colin also happens to be Hollie's older brother. Eddie made her acquaintance soon after his arrival, and it wasn't long before he felt like getting to know her a little better. At the time he wasn't sure how Colin would feel about it – maybe he was protective of his sister, maybe he didn't fancy her getting involved with Eddie, who'd already had his share of overnight company in the apartment – but he needn't have worried. Colin made it plain that his sister's love life was none of his business, and Hollie remains an occasional, and welcome, visitor to Eddie's bed.

Traffic is light as he negotiates the streets that lead west out of the borough. Seven hundred pounds the little Jeep cost him

two years earlier, his entire savings plus a small loan from his stepmother Francey. The car is ancient, almost as old as himself, and spotted with rust, but so far serviceable. It comes in handy for getting out of London on his days off, taking him to the likes of the Cotswolds and the Wye Valley and Windsor, but it stays put the rest of the time, Eddie having no desire to negotiate London traffic on his commute. Coming into its own now though, with the cake too large for hand luggage on a plane, and too fragile to risk checking it in. Hopefully it'll survive the road trip to Annie's.

He reaches the turn for the motorway and joins the drivers heading out of the capital. With less than a week to go before Christmas, traffic is heavy but moving well. He slips into the centre lane and allows his mind to wander across the Irish Sea, all the way to Annie's house and their last meeting there in September, when Eddie had been home for a weekend for the fortieth birthday of his oldest brother.

Come and see me if you can, Annie had said on the phone. I have a bit of news that I'd love to tell you in person, so he'd borrowed Francey's little car and taken a run over the border from Limerick to Clare. I'm getting married, Annie told him, showing him her modest ring, looking as pleased with it as if it were the Hope diamond. No date set yet, but I hope you'll be able to come.

Annie's getting married. No way he'd have missed it, even though he'd had to lie to get the time off. My sister's wedding, he'd told the manager, because it sounded more credible than telling him it was his old foster mother's. I'll make it up, he'd

said. I'll do more hours over the next while, and the manager had grumbled and eventually agreed. It's for Annie, so it's worth a bit of —

Without warning, the van directly in front of him makes a sudden swerve into the fast lane, revealing to Eddie a slow-moving car that he's now set to ram into. A lightning glance in his wing mirror shows another vehicle racing up in the outer lane, cutting off that option for him. He utters an oath and slams on his brakes – and immediately feels the Jeep drifting off to the left, across a mercifully empty slow lane but heading straight towards an embankment that rises up steeply from the edge of the motorway. He curses again and tries desperately to correct the skid, slamming the gearstick into third and lifting his foot as much as he dares from the brake. Somehow, miraculously, he manages to avert a collision and steer the Jeep instead along the hard shoulder.

He brings it to a gradual halt, legs trembling so badly when he stops that his calves thump against his seat. His heart is batting in his chest, like a creature trying to hammer its way out; there's a loud buzzing in his ears. Something seems to be swimming around in his head, making him feel as if he might faint.

He's unable to switch off the engine, so tightly have his hands glued themselves to the steering wheel. He drops his forehead onto them, trying to collect himself, trying to calm his breathing as the Jeep rocks heavily with every vehicle that flies past. Did nobody see or care that he almost crashed, that he could have died?

He loses track of time. Is he in shock? His phone rings on the

passenger seat, causing him to start violently. He manages to peel a hand from the wheel to answer it.

'Yes?' His voice sounds far away, and like someone else's.

A beat passes. 'Martin?' An English accent, female.

'No.'

He disconnects, quelling an impulse to laugh, suspecting it might tip into hysteria. Several deep breaths later he begins to feel more composed, and at length he pulls out warily and rejoins the flow of traffic.

So quickly it could happen, a life snuffed out in an instant. Road fatalities on the news every day – but until it happens to you, or nearly happens to you, there can be no real understanding of the horror. He imagines his father getting a call to say Eddie had been killed. Would he regret that they hadn't been closer in life, or would the loss of his youngest son, the son who had cost him his first wife, mean all that much?

He's careful to keep his speed well within the limit as he continues his journey. He crosses the country, passing from England to Wales as the clouds gather and grow dense. Rain on the way, or maybe hail, getting colder the further west he goes. He turns the heat up to full, not that it makes a lot of difference, and follows signs for Holyhead when they appear, reaching the port just in time to see the ferry sailing off without him.

Annie

CORA SMOOTHS THE SHEET, TUCKS IN CORNERS. 'Nothing like fresh bed linen.'

'No.' Annie plumps newly covered pillows, tweaks them straight.

'So – are you all set?'

'I am, I think. I have a casserole made for dinner, just needs reheating.'

Cora pulls a crease from the bedside rug with her foot. 'I don't mean for this lot, you foolish woman, I mean for your wedding tomorrow. Have you everything done? Do you feel ready?'

'Oh ...' Annie takes a folded bath towel from the bundle on the chair and places it at the end of the bed. 'I'm ready. Yes.' Running a hand along the towel, back and forth. 'I'm all set.'

'Annie.'

She looks up.

Cora, arms folded, is regarding her through narrowed eyes. 'Is everything OK?'

'It is. Why wouldn't it be?'

'You seem a bit deflated.'

'Ah no, I'm not. I'm just ... It'll be a big change, that's all.'

'You're not having second thoughts about getting married?'

'No.' She shakes her head. 'No, of course not.'

'Because you know you can tell me if you are.'

'I'm not. Honestly, Cora.'

'Well, I'm very glad to hear it. You and Matt McCarthy were made to go together. The only mystery is why you took so long.'

Annie smiles. She lifts the towels. She'll say nothing about not wanting to leave the house; practical Cora will tell her it's only bricks and mortar, and she doesn't want to hear that. 'Come on, one more bed.'

They prepare the room she's earmarked for Eddie, the small one next to the main bedroom where she moved him when he got too big for his cot. Doors always ajar, his and hers, in case he woke in the night and called out, or came looking for her. Eddie, whose baby smell and perfect tiny fingers pierced her heart a thousand times a day, who reminded her – poor lamb, not his fault – of what might have been.

He rang her while they were making Julia's bed. I missed the

ferry, he said. I have to wait for the next one, and she told him not to worry, to take his time and get here safely. The prospect of seeing him and the others again soon is wonderful.

They're descending the stairs when the front door knocker sounds. 'They couldn't be here already,' Cora says. 'Could they?'

'No, Joe's bringing back that couple, the ones who came to view the house last week. The solicitor and her husband.'

'For God's sake, what's he doing bringing them today? Did you not tell him you were expecting company?'

'They won't stay long.'

A second viewing, Joe said, as if it was a good thing, as if Annie should be thanking him. The Johnsons, they're keen. It might be sale agreed by Christmas, he said, and every word was like a nail into her chest. The Johnsons don't fit in this house – but then, she doesn't think anyone else fits in this house either. She can't imagine anyone but her living in it.

'I'll make myself scarce,' Cora says, pulling on her coat as she heads for the back door. 'I'll be here bright and early in the morning. Ring if you think of anything you've forgotten.'

'I will.'

Cora, who'd been there when nineteen-year-old Annie's universe had shattered into smithereens, who'd held Annie's hand while she'd cried a river. Faithful Cora, who'd had the good sense, a few years afterwards, to marry a farmer who lived a mile up the road from Annie, putting her within easy distance of her best friend. Annie, of course, had paved the way there, arranging encounters between Cora and Dan, putting in a good word for Cora when a job had come up at the local school.

'Annie, there you are.' Joe's cheeks and the tip of his nose are pink with cold, but he looks well pleased with himself. 'You remember Hugo and Olive?' Stamping his feet on her doormat, rubbing his gloved hands together. All but dancing a gleeful jig, his cut of the selling price no doubt mentally lodged already in his bank account.

'Hello.' Annie steps back to let them in, Hugo with his expensive-looking navy coat and tartan scarf, Olive in her red suit and matching nails, and improbably lifted eyebrows. God only knows what changes they're thinking of making to the house. 'I'll leave you to have a look around,' she says, and moves to the kitchen without waiting for a response. Let them think her ill-mannered: their opinions don't interest her.

The kitchen smells pleasantly of the casserole she cooked earlier. She stands at the window and looks beyond the old paving stones to the long sweep of lawn, the line of beech trees hemming it in at the bottom. How many picnics and doll tea parties did she set out on that grass over the years? How many children climbed those trees, or flew through the air on the swing her brother Ivan had suspended from a sturdy branch? Two lengths of rope and a slab of wood for a seat, all they needed.

She imagines Hugo going at the trees with a chainsaw – no, he wouldn't: he'd pay a man to do it. She can see paving slabs where the lawn is, a hot tub and a barbecue, and one of those silly swing seats. And the old wooden shed would go for sure, replaced with some monstrosity.

Her phone rings. She takes it from her pocket and sees *Matt*. She lets out the breath she didn't know she was holding.

'Well,' she says, pulling out a chair and settling into it.

'Well,' he says. 'Are you all ready?'

'As ready as I'm going to be.'

She can't remember a time she didn't know him. Up through school together, hanging around in the same gang every summer. Never a romance, not quite – although there was a time when she thought they might – but always a strong friendship between them, you could call it a kind of love, down through the years. She could never imagine life without him somewhere in it, even though they'd often been on the periphery of one another's journeys, intersecting briefly before drifting away again.

And look at them now.

'You're glum,' he says.

'I'm not.'

'You are though.' He can see into her, even on the phone. That might be one of the things she loves most about him.

'I'm just a bit busy.' Busy, with her meals-on-wheels lunches all delivered, and her house clean and her beds made, and nothing at all to do but wait for the interlopers to leave, and her three guests to arrive.

'I should let you go so.'

'Ah no, stay awhile.' Making a lie out of her claim to be busy, but he lets it go.

'Forecast isn't great for tomorrow,' he remarks.

'Isn't it? I didn't catch it.' She turns to look out the window again, and this time notices a sky layered in grey.

'Snow, they're saying.'

'Cold enough for it alright. We might have our white Christmas yet.'

'We might.'

Pause. She conjures him in her head, the solid lovely shape of him. The green eyes, the spatter of pale freckles underneath, the grey almost taken over in the bit of hair that's left to him. She sees him standing at the worktop, feet braced, phone wedged between cheek and shoulder while he polishes a shoe, or cracks the shell on a hard-boiled egg for Ruthie. He can never do just one thing at a time.

Postman Matt, the village children call him, and he knows every one of them by name. Knew all her children too, even the ones who didn't stay that long with her. She remembers some of them watching out for him in the mornings, waiting for his whistle coming up the path. Sometimes he'd call even when he had nothing to deliver, just to say hello to them.

And tomorrow … A delicious something licks up through her, leaving her lighter, happier. 'It'll be good,' she says.

'It will.' He rarely needs anything explained to him.

She hears footsteps on the stairs. 'Right, I'd better get going. See you in the morning. Don't be late.'

She hears the soft music of his laugh. 'Don't *you* be late, Annie O'Reilly, or I'll come and get you.'

'I'll be a small bit late. Wait for me.' She disconnects. She brings a smile to her face, and prepares to be pleasant.

Annie, then

'JASON O'DONNELL,' HE SAID, 'AT YOUR SERVICE.' Tipping the bottle a little too enthusiastically in the direction of her paper cup, causing a slosh of wine onto her wrist. 'Oops.'

She'd noticed him earlier, pretty much as soon as she and Cora had walked into the room. Short, stocky, curly dark hair. Leaning against a wall in the company of two females, both of whom were laughing – and his pleased grin suggested that he'd been the source of that laughter.

It wasn't Annie's first sighting of him. In the six weeks or

so since the start of the term she'd spotted him around the college, usually with one or two others of his group. The grads, they were known as, a cohort who'd already furnished themselves with arts degrees elsewhere and who were now, for whatever reason, taking the extra year that would achieve the qualification they needed to teach in primary schools. Older by a few years than the general student body, they tended to hang around together.

And out of their twenty-odd number, Jason O'Donnell had come to Annie's particular attention, had begun featuring on her radar. Within a few days of her first sighting she found herself searching the common areas in the college for a sign of him. Was it the open, friendly expression he usually wore, or the overall look of him, the faded jeans and rumpled T-shirts, the slightly dishevelled, stubbly aspect of him that suggested he'd not long got out of bed? Was it the hazel eyes, or the full bottom lip, or the small sweet plumpness below his chin? Was it all of those things that had made her more aware of him than of any other male student?

She'd said nothing to Cora, who had set her sights on Noel, a third year from Kerry, and who had dragged Annie along to tonight's house party, hosted by a trio of other final-year students, in the hope of finding him there. Cora was great – in the time they'd been living together, she and Annie had found much happy common ground – but by her own admission, discretion was not her strong point. I'm the world's worst at keeping a secret, she'd said cheerfully. I really try, but I never seem to manage it. Don't ever tell me anything you don't want

to travel further – so if Annie mentioned her crush, or whatever it was, it would definitely have done the rounds. It might even – the thought alone made her face hot – find its way to him.

And now here he was, turning up beside her as she stood at the window and waited for Cora to complete her round of the house in her search for Noel. Here Jason O'Donnell was, formally, if a little drunkenly, introducing himself to her.

'The wine,' he said, only slightly slurring, 'is crap, but it's free so we won't complain. Apologies in advance for the head you're going to have tomorrow.'

She laughed, pinching herself that he'd singled her out, willing him to hang about. 'You're forgiven.' Her own head was swimming slightly: she and Cora had split a bottle of Blue Nun between them before leaving their house. This wine was warm with a bitter aftertaste, but she didn't care.

'So who are you?' he asked, and she told him, glad to be wearing the dress Cora had made her buy in Todds, still more expensive in the autumn sale than anything she'd ever owned but she loved its flowery fabric in blues and pinks and purples, its fitted top and flowing skirt. Worth having to do without a single other new stitch from now till Christmas at least.

She'd worn it to mass last Sunday, and Matt McCarthy, bumping into her on the way out of the church, had told her she was a vision of loveliness, and she'd laughed and said maybe he needed to get his eyes tested, but it was nice to hear all the same. She always looked forward to meeting him when she was home at the weekends: he had the knack of making her feel better, whatever mood she was in.

But now she was in the company of Jason O'Donnell, who was close enough for her to smell his aftershave. Spice with a hint of lemon, she thought. Tangy. Taller than her five foot two by inches only, but wide-shouldered and broad-chested. Worked out, maybe. 'Let me guess,' he said. 'Annie O'Reilly is a Pisces.'

'No, she's not a Pisces.'

'Capricorn then.'

'Nearly. Sagittarius, just before it.'

'You're joking – me too.' He emptied the last of the wine into his own cup and deposited the bottle on the windowsill, where it joined half a dozen more. 'What date?'

'December the twenty-first. The shortest day.'

'Hey, so close. I'm the nineteenth.' He tapped his cup against hers. 'It's a sign, Annie. Drink up.'

She took another sip, knowing she'd be sorry in the morning but wanting the encounter to go on. The room was too warm and too noisy, and far too small for the crowd that currently inhabited it, with a fug of cigarette smoke in the air, but she had no desire to be anywhere else. While she was trying and failing to come up with some witty remark, Cora reappeared.

'Hello, you two!' Pressing close to Annie so she could deposit a furtive pinch at her waist. 'I don't think we've met,' she went on, eyeing the man whose name, Annie realised to her horror, she'd forgotten.

Thankfully, he didn't wait for her to make the introduction. 'Jason,' he said. 'Annie and I are old pals. We go back, oh, at least five minutes.'

He was funny. He smelt good and his teeth were very white. His eyes were really marvellous, and every so often he caught and held Annie's gaze, and she felt a pleasant rush within her. Cora wandered off in search of more wine, and still he lingered. What did he see in her? She was timid and self-conscious, and not nearly as chatty or as interesting as Cora, and not half as pretty as a lot of the other females in the room.

He seemed not to notice. She learnt that he was the youngest of seven, and staying with relatives in Limerick for the duration of his extra year in college. 'I didn't get a good enough Leaving Cert to go straight into primary teaching,' he admitted cheerfully, 'so I'm taking the back-door route. We're not all brainboxes like you, Annie.'

He told her he was twenty-three, and from Tipperary. 'About a mile outside the town, which makes me a total culchie. How about you?'

And every now and again he lurched in her direction, and she was forced to lift a palm and brace it against his chest, laughing, to prevent a collision. 'Oops, sorry,' he said each time it happened, but it was accompanied by a grin, which made her wonder if he was doing it on purpose. He felt wonderfully solid. She thought he might be a rugby player, but he looked scandalised when she suggested as much, and told her the only game worth playing was hurling.

'You can come to a game sometime,' he said, 'cheer me on,' and Annie, who had never in her life had the inclination to watch hurling, or any other sport, on television or in real life, said she'd love it. She mustn't have more alcohol: she could feel her own balance beginning to desert her – and just as this

thought crossed her mind he leant towards her, just his head this time, and kissed her emphatically on the mouth.

'There,' he said. 'Been wanting to do that for a while' – and she, dizzy from it, or from the wine, didn't know whether to protest or laugh it off.

And while she was still trying to decide, he did it again.

Julia

'*CHARLES DE GAULLE AÉROPORT, S'IL VOUS PLAÎT,*' SHE says, getting in and pulling the door closed, and the taxi driver takes off without comment. It is the middle of the afternoon, with harsh yellow sunshine that holds no warmth. She looks through the window at white-aproned waiters standing with folded arms in café doorways, and small dogs trotting on leashes, and two men manoeuvring a large container from a van, and little pinafored children skipping along pavements, and an older couple seated on a bench with a red straw basket set between them.

In four hours, around that, she'll be at Annie's. *I'll have dinner ready*, Annie wrote, and Julia remembers her dinners, her floury potatoes with butter melting into them, her thick slices of bacon, the fat cut off for Julia, her pies filled with juicy meaty chunks.

She remembers the Sunday chickens, the Friday fish fingers, the ice-cream wafers afterwards. The apple and gooseberry and rhubarb tarts, dolloped with cream. *Eat up*, Annie would say, *you're a growing girl*, filling Julia with more than food. Almost nine years Julia had enjoyed with her, from the age of three until Karen arrived to claim her. Other children came and went from the house in that time, some younger than Julia, some older, but Annie always gave her the job of showing the newcomer to his or her room, which made her feel very important.

Ella Fitzgerald is singing about a holy night on the taxi's radio. You have a voice like Ella's, Annie wrote, when Julia sent her the first CD. So rich and velvety – and I love the wonderful stories your songs tell. Well done, my darling, I'm so happy and proud for you, and I wish you every success. Julia's mixed style of indie folk, jazz and bossa nova has led to many comparisons – Diana Krall, Ellie Goulding, Lana del Rey. Thirty-four when the first CD was released; took her long enough to get there. Took her years of teaching music by day and playing in bars and restaurants by night, before Lucien walked into one of her venues and liked what he heard. And now, in her fortieth year, she's about to release her third CD. The world is waiting, Lucien declares. The world is holding its breath for more of Julia M's songs.

Julia M, not Julia Murphy. It's not sexy enough, Lucien said. Let's keep the initial, and lose the rest – and because he seemed to know what he was doing, she went along with it.

The taxi driver keeps glancing into his rear-view mirror, but Julia has the distinct feeling that it's her he's checking out rather than the traffic. After catching his eye by accident she directs her gaze downwards, not in the mood for a conversation.

In her pocket her phone vibrates. She takes it out and sees her manager's name. She sets it down and waits for the vibrations to stop. A few seconds afterwards, it gives another short buzz. She looks again at the screen and sees the voicemail icon.

Julia, Lucien says, *I thought I might catch you before you left, but you must be in transit.* A tiny pang of guilt, which she smothers. *I have the tour dates. I'll ring you on Monday to discuss.* Bon voyage, *enjoy your trip.*

The tour dates. Was it fourteen European countries he'd said, or more? Airports and train stations, and five or six weeks of hotel rooms in unfamiliar cities. Relentless rounds of interviews and red-carpet events, and every few nights another concert, another two hours of being Julia M in front of thousands of strangers.

She waits for her phone to ring again. She waits for her lover to call and wish her *bon voyage*, and tell her once more how sorry he is about last night, and how he can't wait to see her on her return from Ireland. All the way to the airport she waits, but the call doesn't come.

The departures area is busy, less than a week before Christmas. As soon as Julia takes her place in the queue at the

check-in desk she pulls a book from the front pocket of her bag and holds it open. Not reading – she needs silence to read properly – but a book gives a reason for a lowered head. A book is a buffer against intrusion.

Her turn arrives. She stows the book and offers her passport and boarding pass. The male official glances at her passport, where she is Julia Carmel Murphy – but she knows it's not enough of a disguise, not as long as her photograph is there to betray her. She sees his sudden alertness as he looks at it. She lowers her scarf and endures his quick scrutiny of her features.

'Julia M?' he enquires, and when she gives the small acknowledging tilt of her head that she must give, his face breaks into a grin. She wills him not to make a fuss, and to her relief he doesn't. '*Belles chansons*,' he murmurs only, before sliding her documents back across the desk. She thanks him with a brief smile and moves away.

Going through security, obliged to remove her scarf and dark glasses and send them separately along the conveyor belt, she is aware of more recognition from officials – an elbow nudge of a colleague's arm, hurried whispered words into an ear before the other looks up, searching for the famous singer. A small buzz in the queue behind her lets her know that she hasn't gone unrecognised there either. She pretends not to notice any of it as she gathers her things and again shields her face. She moves off briskly, making her way through the Duty Free area, stopping only to pick up a planned surprise for Annie.

At the departure gate she positions herself to the rear of the

banks of seating, as far away from her fellow passengers as she can find. She could always use the VIP lounge – Lucien, when they take a trip together, insists on it, as he does on travelling first class, or even chartering a flight – but following an instinct she can't explain, whenever she's on her way to see Annie Julia tends to do things the way she's always done them, even if it makes her slightly uneasy to be so visible, and unprotected, en route. Imagine what Annie would have to say about a VIP lounge, or a first-class ticket!

Anyway, chartering a plane always feels too extravagant to Julia, too wasteful. At least her apartment, expensive though it was, is a solid investment.

'Frosty the Snowman' is playing at a reasonable volume over the intercom. The desk, as yet unmanned, is rimmed with red tinsel, but with just twenty-five minutes to take-off, and no warnings of a delay, it can't be long till the flight is called. Julia pulls her book from her bag again – a collection of stories by Maupassant that she first read over twenty years ago in school – and opens it.

And then, in the corner of her vision, she sees them. Two figures, hovering to the left of her, looking in her direction. She hears whispered hisses, giggles. Females, at least. Not certain it's her, one egging on the other to approach. She knows the routine well: she's experienced it often enough.

She waits – and here they come.

'*Excusez-moi, Madame.*'

She raises her head and sees to her relief that they're young, mid-teens at most. She gives them the usual guarded smile.

The shorter one speaks. Blonde hair, bright smile, a flush in her cheeks. Hanging on to her friend's arm. 'You are Julia M, *non?*' she asks, the flush deepening.

Julia inclines her head. '*Oui*, but I am travelling incognito, so please don't give me away,' experience again having taught her the best approach to such situations.

Some more delighted giggling. 'Your secret is safe, Madame,' the other whispers. 'We adore your music. May we please have your autograph?'

'Of course,' Julia replies, and waits while they rummage in pockets and bags, and finally produce a book, from which the blonde rips the last page. Julia takes a pen from her own bag – more experience – and asks for their names.

'We are Claudette and Marie-Claire.'

'*Bon.*' She scribbles the usual message and hands it over, and they thank her with more blushes and smiles, retreating just as the flight is called.

Julia is the last to board, waiting until everyone else has gone through. Her seat is by the window in the second row, chosen to minimise her need for movement through the cabin. The two passengers already seated get to their feet to allow her to pass. She murmurs her thanks without making eye contact, and settles in.

It's warm in the cabin. She loosens her scarf, lets it fall to her lap. She watches the last of the luggage being loaded below her, sees a worker slap his gloved hands together. Was there some mention of snow on the radio, or did she imagine it?

She thinks of her last trip to Ireland, back in May. Has it

really been that long? Jean-Luc had booked them into a hotel in Nice for a few days, but had been forced to cancel at the last minute because his father-in-law had died. Julia, bag already packed, had gone online and found a flight later that day to Ireland, and to Annie, needing the comforting surroundings of her foster home, even if Annie wasn't told the true reason for the last-minute visit. How can Julia tell her she's been having an affair with a married man for years?

'Oh – sorry!'

A magazine slithers from the adjoining seat to the floor of the plane, landing somewhere around Julia's feet.

'Sorry,' the woman repeats, unbuckling her seatbelt to lean forward. Julia presses against the window, but the woman comes up empty-handed. 'Would you mind?' she asks Julia. 'I can't reach it – it's gone under the seat in front of you.'

Irish accent. Young. Blonde hair with heavy fringe, blue eyes with dark circles under them. Julia undoes her seatbelt and retrieves the magazine, and returns it silently.

'Thank you,' her neighbour says. 'I'd go mad if I didn't have something to read on a flight.' Eyeing the book on Julia's lap. 'Is that any good?'

She might have something to read, but clearly she'd prefer to talk. She gives no indication that she's recognised Julia, which is a blessing, but even the most casual of conversations would risk revealing her identity, and eliciting the inevitable barrage of questions that would follow – and right now, upset about Jean-Luc and anxious about the upcoming tour, it's the last thing Julia wants.

'It's very good,' she replies, clipping her seatbelt closed again. 'And if you don't mind, I'd like to get back to it.'

She angles her body towards the window and opens the book – and hears, all the way to Shannon, the woman's offended silence.

Steph

BITCH.

Irish accent, and reading a book in French: talk about pretentious. She has money too: that bag doesn't look like the knock-offs Steph has seen being sold on stalls at Piraeus, that bag is the real thing – and the coat she hasn't taken off, that didn't come cheap either. And get the scarf up around her mouth, as if she might catch something from the common people. Probably raging the plane has no first-class cabin.

Gareth despises people with money. They feel such entitlement, he says – and this woman certainly feels entitled

to be rude. It would be nice if Steph and Gareth had a bit more money though. It would be lovely if she could buy a new dress, or a pair of shoes, without worrying about the cost. The writing retreats bring in a nice bit – Steph is secretly amazed that people are willing to pay the fee that Gareth has set. The trouble is, the week-long courses only take place off-season – two a month, from September to February – and the rest of the time they must manage on what Stavros pays Steph in the pottery shop, which isn't much.

Oh, she knows Gareth needs to concentrate on his writing, she understands that. It's just … since she met him he's been working on his next book, but he refuses to show her anything, refuses even to discuss it, so she can't help wondering – furtively, guiltily – how much he's actually producing. Then again, what does she know about writing?

His first book apparently was a hit – he's shown it to her, and she's tried to read it – well, she *has* read it, but she found it full of words she didn't understand, and really, she felt it was aimed at someone very different to her. It was published eight years ago, while he was in the process of divorcing his wife in England and putting as much distance between them as he could. The proceeds of the book paid for the olive mill he eventually found – which couldn't, Steph imagined, have cost very much, not that she'd dream of saying so, but it's pretty … basic.

His second book, a follow-up to the first, wasn't as successful – again Steph struggled through it, and found it as impenetrable as the other – but it gave him, as a twice-published author, the authority to open the retreat. Hopefully his third book,

whenever it gets finished, will go down well with readers. His kind of readers.

But really she can't complain. She loves the island, and she enjoys the work in the pottery shop. Stavros is a lovely boss, and his wife Elena regularly drops by with *baklava* or *kataifi* for the coffee break. And Steph has Gareth, even if she's in his black books at the moment.

She's tried calling him three times. On the bus that brought her to Athens airport, knowing he'd be up by then; in the airport café, where she'd bought a seriously overpriced *spanakopita*, and in the departure lounge at Charles de Gaulle, just before boarding the plane. Each time her call went unanswered, and each time she disconnected without leaving a message, her nerve failing her. Clearly, he's angry. She'll try again tomorrow, if he hasn't called in the meantime.

She smothers a yawn. Feels like an eternity since she got up. Two hours on the ferry, three and a half more in the air to Paris, the waiting and the queuing and the bus trip in between. She's tired now, so tired, but she's never been able to sleep sitting up. And the travel won't be over when she lands, with thirty miles or so still to cover before she gets to Annie's house. Hopefully people will take pity on her, this close to Christmas.

She feels a small dart of unease at the thought of going back to Annie's, which she knows is ridiculous – but the truth, the unvarnished, ugly fact of the matter, is that she was never really happy there. Nothing to do with Annie, everything to do with Steph herself.

She thinks back to the half-dozen Christmases she spent

at the house, from when she arrived as a twelve-year-old to when she left, a week after her eighteenth birthday. She remembers the carols in the sitting room with Annie plonking at the piano, and Steph pretending to join in with the rest of them. The tree in the big hall that they all helped to decorate – well, all apart from Steph, who refused every year to have anything to do with it. The presents on Christmas morning, the vouchers and selection boxes and scarves and fancy notebooks that they had to pretend came from Santa, for the sake of the younger ones in the house, but that Steph guessed were charitable donations from the villagers. She hated that, hated the idea that they were dependent on, and pitied by, the people who lived in the area.

And there was always another present that came for her, the one she never opened, despite Annie's coaxing. Would you not give him a chance? Annie would plead, and Steph would retort that he didn't deserve a chance, not after running out on her and her mother.

Poor Annie. She'd certainly earned her money with Steph.

What'll it be like being back there? What changes will Steph see in the village after six years? Will Annie have changed? She sounds the same in her letters, but letters only tell so much. How will they be together now, after their fractured history? The closer they get to Ireland, the more Steph wonders about the wisdom of this trip. Will she have annoyed Gareth for nothing, will she feel awkward all weekend?

No, of course she won't.

I'd so love if you could come to the wedding, Annie had written.

It would be wonderful to see you again. She'd never once lost faith in Steph, had always been ready to forgive her, to give her the benefit of the doubt, even when Steph had done her best not to deserve it. God, she'd been a horror.

She thinks of the eighteen-year-old who took the boat to Wales with Annie's hundred-euro gift and a list of London hostels in her pocket, but no real idea of where she was going, or what she wanted to do once she got there. She'd been so clueless. No wonder Annie had done her best to get her to stay in Ireland.

And then, pulling out pyjamas on her first night in a London hostel she'd found the envelopes, six of them, at the bottom of her rucksack. Annie's name and address written on the front of each one in her sloped writing, the small stack held together with a shoelace. No note with them; no need for it. Keep in touch, they said, all by themselves. Don't lose contact.

Steph's first impulse was to chuck them out – what was the point of keeping stuff she was never going to use? – but when it came to it, she couldn't bin them. It was the thought of Annie writing her own name and address six times, and searching for something to keep them together, and sneaking the bundle into Steph's bag. It was everything she'd done, and everything she'd tried to do, for Steph. It was all the times that Steph had shouted at her to leave her alone, mind her own business, and worse. It was all that – so the envelopes stayed put.

Didn't go near them again for about eight months though. Left them where they were through all the weeks of waitressing and bartending, and cleaning toilets and emptying bins and shoving leaflets through letterboxes, and doing whatever she

could to earn enough money to get her through the next week – until one night in Düsseldorf, after too much beer made her sentimental, she scrounged a sheet of paper from a barman and found enough words to fill it.

It's me. I'm OK. I've been travelling around, and getting jobs here and there. I've been in England and France and Spain, and I'm in Germany now, but I'm thinking of moving on because it's expensive. Hope all is well with you, hope you've got nobody as bad as me, ha ha! Say hello to the others.

The first letter she'd ever written, apart from the ones she'd sent to Santa in school as a kid, and they didn't count. Putting the words down felt strange, like a conversation but not really. She imagined Matt the postman bringing the letter to Annie in a few days, and Annie opening the envelope and reading the words. The image brought unexpected tears to her eyes: she swiped them away and finished her beer.

When she returned to her hostel she slipped the page into the first envelope, and bought a stamp for it the next day. Over the following months, through Italy and Croatia and Bulgaria, she filled the rest of the envelopes, and bought more when they ran out, never giving a return address because she never stayed long enough anywhere. Not until she found her way to Greece, and to the island, and to Gareth. Not until she moved into the olive mill, the first place she planned to spend more than a couple of weeks in, the first place she didn't have to pay for since leaving Ireland.

The captain announces the beginning of the plane's descent. She checks her watch and sees five forty-five. The cabin crew is moving swiftly through the aisle, collecting litter and checking table tops and seatbelts. Their green uniform is somehow reassuring, which makes no sense. It's a gut thing, it must be, an affinity with the colour green, along with a fondness for harps and shamrocks, sewn into every Irish person's DNA.

The plane continues its downward path, bouncing and rocking through the clouds. The stewards and stewardesses are summoned to their seats. Steph turns to glance past the neighbouring seat to the window, but sees only blackness beyond. She left Greece in darkness, and is arriving in Ireland in more darkness. She hates this part of a flight, hates waiting for the thump that connects them to the earth again, and the terrifying headlong gallop down the runway that follows before the plane drops its speed.

She closes her eyes and grips the armrests, and tries to distract herself by imagining what they're doing in the olive mill now. Two hours ahead, so it's almost dinnertime. In the kitchen, Gareth will be pouring wine into carafes for the table, and taking the lamb stew, or whatever he's made, from the oven. In Steph's absence he'll have to get one of the guests to give him a hand, someone to make the salad, set the table, ferry dishes from kitchen to dining room. Barbara will probably offer: she's made no secret of her interest in Gareth, taking every opportunity since their arrival on Monday to spend time with him outside the group sessions. Steph pictures her heavyset figure, her puff of dyed black hair, the paleness of her sturdy calves beneath

startlingly colourful cropped trousers. She has nothing to fear, she thinks, from Barbara.

She wonders how Gareth will explain her absence to the group. A family emergency, he'll probably say. Called back to Ireland, had to leave immediately. She's fairly certain he won't lose face by admitting the truth to them.

The wheels touch down with a bump, taking her by surprise and causing her to let out an involuntary gasp. She keeps her eyes tightly closed through the roar of the forward rush, relaxing only when she feels the reverse thrust kicking in, causing the gradual reduction of the aircraft's speed. She exhales slowly.

'You OK?'

She opens her eyes to find her neighbour studying her. 'Nervous flier?'

Now she decides to be friendly. 'Not in the least,' Steph replies shortly, reaching down to scoop her bag from the floor, making a show of rummaging in it to avoid further conversation. She moves into the aisle as soon as the plane comes to a halt and retrieves her backpack from the overhead bin, never once looking in the other's direction. The sooner she gets out the sooner she can be on the road, and on her way to Annie's.

The sting of the air at the top of the steps takes her by surprise. She'd been expecting cold – Ireland in December was never going to be balmy – but this is savage in its intensity. She scurries into the terminal building and pulls her spare sweater from her bag again, shivering as she removes her jacket to put it on. No scarf, no gloves, no woolly hat – she'll perish unless someone picks her up quickly.

She bypasses the baggage reclaim area and makes her way rapidly past the customs posts and into the arrivals hall, which is warm and noisy and full. She edges past the embraces and the laughter – is everyone being met apart from her? – and skirts the giant Christmas tree and makes her way outside. As soon as she's clear of the buildings she sticks out her thumb and smiles hopefully at the oncoming vehicles – but it's several frozen minutes before someone takes pity on her and pulls in.

'Ennis any good for you?' An older male driver, peering across the passenger seat at her. She assures him that Ennis is perfect, and gets in. Over the course of the next twenty minutes, in response to his many questions, she tells him all about the French vineyard where she works – drawing on one of her previous jobs – and the parents in Galway she's going to surprise by coming home early for Christmas. Who wants the truth, when fantasy is so much more interesting?

By the time he drops her outside a hotel on the outskirts of Ennis – a cousin, she tells him, is on standby to pick her up from there and ferry her home – it's getting on for seven o'clock. She thanks him and waves him off, and when he's out of sight she crosses the road and takes the turn, a hundred yards back, for Annie's village. Ten or twelve miles to her destination: nearly there.

Something soft and cold lands on her cheek, another directly afterwards on her nose. She looks up and sees snowflakes, large and pale, floating down in the glow of the streetlight she's positioned herself under. She tugs down the sleeves of her jacket

and prays for someone to pick her up quickly, before she has a chance to freeze again.

Someone does. A small boxy vehicle, high off the ground, some kind of Jeep, she thinks, stops just a few minutes later. As she approaches it the passenger window is cranked down, and she hears Chris Rea on the radio before it's snapped off.

He's a bit older than her. Lean face, woolly hat hiding his hair. Clean-shaven. Looks fairly harmless, not that you can go by looks, but what choice does she have? She'd put up a good fight though, if she had to.

'Hop in,' he says when she names the village. 'Going there myself, actually.'

There is a God. She hops in.

Eddie

AT FIRST HE THOUGHT IT WAS A CHILD, SO SLIGHT she was. Drawing closer, he decided she was older, a teenager maybe – and now that she's in the car, he can see that she's older again, but not by much. Pretty face, even with that pink nose. Lots of hair.

'Thanks a million,' she says, blowing on her hands. 'That cold is savage.'

Irish. 'You want me to throw that in the back?' he asks, indicating the rucksack she's wedging into the narrow space in front of her seat, but she tells him it's grand and rests her feet on it, so he pulls away.

She cranks up the window, shoves her hands under her thighs. 'Forgot how freezing it gets in Ireland in the winter.'

'Sorry it's not warmer in here,' he says. 'I've the heat up full, but it's on its last legs.'

'Jesus, don't apologise – you did your bit picking me up, and it's a hell of a lot warmer than out there.'

Hard to place her accent, nothing that would jump out at you. No gloves or hat in this weather, hair disappearing under the collar of her jacket. Her skin looks tanned, but it could be the light.

'I'm Eddie, by the way.'

'Stephanie. Steph.'

'Have you come far?'

'Greece.'

He darts another look at her. Her fringe is heavy, and long enough to hide her eyebrows. 'Funny time for a holiday, just before Christmas.'

'I live there. On one of the islands.'

'Wow. What's that like?'

She doesn't answer immediately. She slides her hands out; he hears the soft sound of them rubbing together again. 'It's good. Weather's better than here, and it's cheap to live there.'

He waits for more, but it doesn't come. 'Are you from the village?' he asks.

'No. Visiting a friend for a few days.'

He switches on the wipers to brush away the snow that's beginning to fall more heavily. Just as well he doesn't have far to go. He remembers the near miss on the motorway, and checks his speed.

'White Christmas,' she says. 'Maybe.'

'Yeah.'

A short silence falls, the only sound the squeak of the wipers. 'So where've you travelled from then?' she asks.

'London.'

'You drove all the way from London?'

'I did. Left this morning.'

'You're based there?'

'Yep.'

'Doing what?'

'Chef.'

'Cool. So do you work in a fancy restaurant?'

'Yep, very fancy.' She doesn't need the truth. He'll never see her again.

He pictures his workplace at this time of the evening, tables filling, buzz of conversation, clink of glasses, clatter of cutlery. The kitchen hot and frenetic, all steam and sizzle and shouts, swing doors flapping with entrances and exits.

'So do *you* come from the village?' she asks.

'Not really. Spent a few years there when I was young.' Not going to get into all that.

Silence. He darts a glance, catches her in the act of turning away. 'You can listen to the radio if you want,' she says. 'No need to turn it off on my account.'

A hint for him to shut up? She's asked as many questions as he has, if not more. 'Not worth it,' he says. 'Nearly there now.'

About a mile to go, and there is the familiar scatter of farmhouses and barns, the crossroads with the rusted petrol

pumps, the garden centre beyond it, closed now for the winter. Familiar not from his time with Annie but from all the visits to her afterwards, all the return trips he and Francey made to see her, and later when he came back on his own, when he was old enough not to need a driver anymore.

They reach the sign that announces the village. He sees the start of the orange streetlights up ahead. 'Where can I drop you?' he asks.

'Well, I'm going to the far end, but—'

'Me too. Say when.'

He drives slowly past the supermarket and the pubs that flank it, and the chemist and the hairdresser and the butcher, and a clothes shop he doesn't remember from his last trip, and clutches of joined-together houses between the shops. A string of coloured bulbs criss-crosses its way from lamppost to lamppost down the street, and there's a tree with flashing lights in the yard to the side of one of the pubs, and various Christmas touches – candles, cribs, trees – in most of the windows along the way.

They pass the church and the school and the chipper – and a hundred yards beyond them, set a little way in off the road, is the big old farmhouse he hasn't seen since September.

He stops the Jeep just before it. 'That's me,' he says, indicating.

She stares at him. 'You're going to Annie's?'

'Yeah, for the wedding. You?'

She nods. A beat passes. 'You were fostered too,' she says. It's not a question.

'I was.'

He doesn't know what else to say, and she volunteers no more either. Weird how he'd stopped for another of Annie's charges.

He manoeuvres the Jeep through the gates. There's Annie's ancient Fiesta outside the sitting-room window – he can't believe it's still going, even older than his jalopy – and a second car he doesn't recognise, a white hatchback, parked next to it. He pulls in behind them and switches off the engine.

Neither of them moves. It's still snowing, more heavily now. Snow is beginning to stay on the ground. A bush in the neighbouring garden – he can't remember the names of the people who live there – is lit up with coloured flashing lights.

There's a wreath of some kind, with tiny white lights threaded through it, hanging from Annie's front door knocker. He hasn't been here this close to Christmas since he left, aged five. Light spills from the hall through the glass panes above the door, throwing yellow splashes onto the ground. The sitting-room curtains are drawn – he fancies he hears faint music behind them.

'It's my first time back here.'

The change in her voice makes him turn. She's gazing at the house with no trace of a smile. 'How long since you left?' he asks.

'Six years.' She draws in a breath that has a shudder in it. 'It's … a bit weird, being back.'

'But you've stayed in contact,' he says. 'Obviously.'

She nods, her eyes still on the house. 'Just letters.'

'I left here when I was five,' he says. 'I went back to my home place, to live with my father and his – my stepmother – they're

just over the border in Limerick – but I'd been with Annie since birth … I don't really remember, but apparently I was upset when they took me away, so my stepmother would bring me back for a visit every now and again, and she helped me write letters to Annie in between. We never really lost contact. I still come to see Annie whenever I'm home.'

His passenger makes no response. The music in the house stops. In its aftermath the silence is absolute, the snow making no sound at all as it goes on falling.

'We should probably head in,' he says, opening his door – and as he steps out, the front door of the house opens too.

Annie

SHE FLIES ACROSS THE GRAVEL TO HIM, NEARLY losing one of her slippers on the way, hardly noticing the snow that has started since Julia's arrival. 'There you are!' she cries, pressing him close, rising on tiptoe to dot his cheek with kisses. 'It feels like an age since I've seen you – have you got taller? Oh, I'm just so glad you could come, I'm so glad!' and he laughs and hugs her back. 'Now we're just waiting for one more, and then you'll all be landed.'

'I'm here.'

What? She draws back, not sure if she imagined the words

– and then she sees a slight figure emerge from behind Eddie's car.

'Hi, Annie.' Quietly. Coming to a halt, lowering a rucksack to the ground.

For a second she doesn't react, doesn't move, and then she steps towards the girl. 'Steph,' she breathes, and takes her into her arms and rocks her gently. 'Oh, I'm delighted you made it, so delighted – but I thought you were to ring me from the station. I told you I'd get Billy Maher to collect you—' and then she feels the small rhythmic catches in Steph's breathing, and realises she's crying.

She draws back. She lifts a hand and thumbs the tears gently away. 'Hush,' she murmurs, 'ssh, love,' falling effortlessly into her role of temporary mother, not that the old Steph would ever in a million years have cried in her arms. No tears, not a drop had she shed – or not in public anyway – in the six years they'd muddled along together.

But it's cold, so bitterly cold out here, and snow falling thickly down on them. 'Come on,' she says, turning towards the house with Steph's arm entwined in hers. 'You can both tell me everything inside, we have so much to catch up on! Eddie, grab her bag, would you? Lord, such a night!'

She shepherds them both through to the warm kitchen, where she sits them at the table and puts on the kettle while Steph blots her face and blows her nose. It must be a shock for her, being back here. It must be causing a lot of memories to collide with each other in her head.

Oh, but she's too thin, she really is, not eating properly half

the time by the look of it. And that tumble of hair could do with a good cut, so long it's got, and lighter in colour – and see how the Greek sun has darkened her skin. Her nails are longer, and white-tipped. A tiny stud in her nostril – that's new, and so is the wide silver band on her thumb. Same freckles dancing across the bridge of her nose, eyes the same brilliant blue. Shadows under them now, poor thing, in need of a good night's sleep after such a long journey.

Will she sleep though? Annie remembers the sullen girl who came to her with a single worn brown suitcase, twelve years old and distrustful of everyone. Couldn't blame the creature, badly damaged by a childhood spent with a woman who by all accounts couldn't look after herself, let alone a daughter.

She thinks of the nightmares the girl had at the start, waking Annie in the next room with her cries, then refusing to speak about it, refusing any comfort Annie offered. She thinks of the anxiety that Steph caused her throughout her six-year stay, the disappearances and the truancies, the moodiness and the defiance. All in the past, all behind them now.

'So – first explain to me how you two arrived together,' she says.

'I picked her up, just outside Ennis,' Eddie says.

'You picked her up?' Turning to Steph. 'You weren't hitching?'

Steph nods.

'Oh, but why would you do that? I told you to ring me from the bus station!'

'I didn't get a bus … I hitched from the airport. Sorry.'

'You hitched all the way from *Shannon*? Steph, anyone could have picked you up!'

An apologetic shrug is all she gets to that. It shouldn't surprise her: Steph never was one to follow the rules. But she's here, all three are here, safe under her roof now – and Steph is an adult, and able to make her own rules, so she must let it go.

She changes tack. 'Did Eddie tell you he's a chef in a big fancy London restaurant?'

'He did.'

She makes no other comment, still not ready to chat. Leave her alone, let her settle in. 'We'll have dinner in a bit,' she tells them. 'It's all ready and keeping warm; Julia has just gone up to take a quick shower. I'll make a cuppa to keep you going – or would anyone rather a hot punch?'

'I would,' they chorus, and Steph manages a small damp laugh.

'Punch it is,' Annie says, taking the bottle of Jameson from under the sink. 'Much better idea. This will warm the cockles.'

Eddie gets up. 'Let me help. Who's Julia?'

'She's another of my foster children – my very first, actually. She came as a little three-year-old, and I had her till she was twelve. She was still here when you arrived, Eddie. She left when you were about two, so you won't remember her.'

No need to go into the whole Julia M business: they'll find out soon enough when they clap eyes on her. Such a haunted look she wears now though, worn out from being everyone's property.

When the drinks are made they sit at the table. Annie watches the whiskey sending a slow bloom into Steph's cheeks as Eddie

tells them of the Christmas windows on Oxford Street, and the carol-singing flash mob on his tube to work the day before, and the busker in a Santa hat on Watford's high street who sounds exactly like Harry Styles.

Oh, she loves having them back with her, even if it's only for a couple of nights. But Eddie looks weary too; his job must be hectic. He'll sleep well here, where he was always so happy.

He drains his glass and gets to his feet. 'I should bring in the cake.'

The cake! She'd forgotten! 'Oh – I can't wait to see it!'

'It's not quite ready for viewing,' he tells her. 'I have to do the finishing touches.'

'Eddie Hanafin, I told you not to go to any trouble.'

'No trouble,' he says, and disappears, leaving Annie and Steph alone.

'It hasn't changed,' Steph says, looking about. 'This kitchen. It's exactly the same as I remember.'

'It could do with a bit of freshening up, I suppose.'

'No, it's good like this – and something smells good too.'

'That would be spicy chicken casserole. You used to love it.'

'Oh, yummy.' She rises and retrieves the rucksack that Eddie left by the door. 'I have something,' she says, opening the straps, fumbling inside. 'Just a small wedding gift.'

'Oh Steph, I didn't expect a thing – it's enough that you came.'

But she pulls out a large bowl, painted in bands of sea blue and grass green and vivid orange. 'It was made by the man I work for,' she says. 'He's a potter, he has a shop. I hope you like it.'

Annie takes the bowl, turns it carefully. 'It's beautiful. I love it, and I love that you know who made it.'

'I was terrified it would break on the way.'

Annie sets it on the worktop and embraces Steph. 'I love it,' she repeats softly. 'Thank you so much.'

They draw apart, and sit again at the table. Annie searches the girl's face. 'How are you, Steph? Really how are you?'

'Well, apart from being so tired I could sleep standing up, I'm fine. I'm all grown-up and sensible.'

'You're happier now?'

'Yes, I am.' Drawing a finger through a drop on the table, stretching it out.

'I'm delighted to hear it – and I want to hear all about your young man too.'

Something flashes across Steph's face, gone before Annie can make sense of it. 'He's not that young. He'll be forty next birthday.'

'Oh …' No mention was made of that in her letters. Still, what does age matter if they're happy together? 'And you told me he's a writer.'

'Well, yes – he's written two books that did quite well, I think, before he met me.' Still playing with the water, pulling it into a circle with her finger. 'I read them, but I don't think I was intelligent enough for them.' Giving a half-laugh. 'And he wants to write another. He *is* writing it, he writes all the time when we're not hosting a retreat – but it's just … well, it's taking quite a while. He doesn't really like to talk about it much.'

And before Annie can probe deeper – because it sounds like there's more to probe – the kitchen door opens again.

'Julia, there you are, love.'

She turns to make introductions and sees Steph taking in the new arrival with something approaching shock on her face.

Star-struck, just like Annie knew she'd be.

Annie, then

CORA TIPPED CORN FLAKES INTO HER BOWL. SHE spooned up a dry mouthful, the only person Annie knew who ate them without milk. Cora added milk to nothing, declaring that the thought of drinking something that came out of what was basically a cow's breast made her want to throw up.

'What's on for you today?' Cora asked.

The first years had been split into three groups for lectures, Annie and Cora ending up in separate ones. Some days they might only encounter one another at lunchtime, other days not even then, if one of them had something better to do in the

middle of the day than file into the canteen to eat the largely unexciting fare on offer.

'Two lectures and one tutorial this morning,' Annie replied, brushing toast crumbs from the table into her palm. 'Another lecture at two.'

'That's it?'

'That's it.'

'You going out tonight with Jason?'

His name, even just his name, never failed to send a surge of excitement through her. 'No, he's got an assignment to finish for tomorrow.'

A month they'd been seeing each other, that was all. A month of listening to Janis Ian and Supertramp and Horslips in the lounge between lectures, and walks by the river if they both had the same free hour in a day, and watching Monday-evening offerings of the Film Club in one of the lecture theatres, and slow dancing on Thursday nights at the student disco in a downtown hotel, and Friday lunchtime sandwiches in Punch's bar, just up from the college.

A month of soft, wicked whispers when nobody was near, and slow, deep kisses that brought waves of longing, and furtive, exciting touches. A month of coming to the gradual, thrilling realisation that she was falling in love for the first time.

Will you? he asked two evenings ago. I want to, he said, and Annie said maybe, because although she wanted it too, it would be her first time, and crossing that line felt momentous. We'll be safe, he said. There's a family planning clinic in town and

someone said they're selling condoms. I could call in and get some.

Maybe, she said again.

When she was younger she'd assumed that she'd wait until she was married to have sex, because that was always the line they'd been fed – only cheap girls let boys have their way before that – but more and more she was wondering if it would be so wrong to sleep with someone if you really loved them, and if they professed to feel the same. Who would they be hurting – especially if they were sensible and took precautions?

But they were together for just a month. This time five weeks ago they hadn't exchanged a word. Annie hadn't known his name – they hadn't even sat at the same table in the canteen. Was it too soon? Should they wait a little longer?

Cora crunched Corn Flakes and hummed along to the radio. Had she already taken that step, crossed that line? She'd told Annie about a boy she'd been going out with for two years who'd left her in February for someone else and broken her heart, but she hadn't mentioned sex, and Annie hadn't asked.

'I'm wondering,' Cora said, 'about asking Cathal if we could paint a few rooms in the house. We could buy paint out of our rent, something bright. What do you think?'

Their landlord, who had become Cathal, called to collect the rent and sign their book every Tuesday around teatime. Never said much, never came further than the hall. Annie thought he looked older than Cora's guess of early thirties, with a

moustache like Hitler's except Cathal's was red, and a missing tooth on his right side, and a wedding ring. 'I've never painted a room,' she said, 'but I wouldn't mind trying it.'

'Nothing to it – just load up a roller and off you go. I'll ask him next week.'

They'd already – well, Cora had – borrowed a lawnmower from a neighbour across the road and cut the grass in front. They'd soaked the awful net curtains in bleach, which had caused them to fall apart, so they'd cleaned the windows and left them bare. Annie's mother had donated a plaid blanket that was better than the one on the couch, and they'd invested in a cheap string of battery lights for the courtyard. The house still had a long way to go, but they were doing what they could.

'You want to come out with me and Sean this evening?' Cora enquired. Sean had replaced Noel in her affections, because she'd sat next to Noel once in the canteen and got a distinct smell of feet, which she said had put her instantly off him. Sean was perfectly nice, another final-year student, but Annie suspected he was a little too placid for Cora. 'We're going to meet a few in South's around nine for a drink, nothing mad.'

'Thanks, but I need to do a bit of studying myself. Better skip it.'

'Fair enough.'

It wouldn't be Jason's first time. He told Annie he'd lost his virginity the summer he was eighteen to a barmaid at the pub where he and his friends used to go. She was older, he said, late twenties I think, and she had a bit of a reputation. She

propositioned me one night, and of course I took her up on it, and we did the deed in the back of her car. Next time I saw her it was as if nothing had happened. I was put out for about an hour, and then I got over it.

'You going home on Friday?' Cora asked. Cora had spent only one weekend at home since college had started.

'I suppose so.'

Jason went back to Tipperary every weekend. His family owned a small supermarket in the town, and since Jason was the only member of his family not married or working away, it fell to him to do his duty behind the counter on Saturdays. Annie was happy to go on taking the five o'clock bus to Ennis each Friday – what was the point of staying in Limerick without him? – and she enjoyed the weekends at home anyway, dropping into Morrissey's pub on Saturday night, where she was always sure to find some of the old gang. Last Saturday, Matt told her that his application to become a postal worker had been successful. I'm coming to Limerick soon, he said. I have to do a three-week training course in the GPO, so Annie promised to show him the sights while he was in the city.

Today was Wednesday, and tomorrow night she and Jason were going to the disco. And Jason said he could tell his relatives that he'd been offered a couch in a pal's house, to save him bicycling back across the city late at night. I went ahead and got condoms, he told her. I'm not putting pressure on you, just letting you know.

And maybe, after all, it was time. Maybe she was ready.

'Cora,' she said as they walked to the college, 'there's

something I want to say.' The November wind had a bite in it. Her fingertips, even in gloves, were numb. Jason would rub heat into them when they were out together in the cold – and once he'd sucked each finger in turn till she'd felt the life coming back into them. 'Something I want to ask you really.'

'Ask away.' Cora's voice was muffled behind a thick wool scarf in stripes of bottle green and tan that an aunt had knitted for her last Christmas. The colour combination was vile; Annie and Cora were agreed on that – but the warmth of it, Cora said, made up.

'Could I – would it be OK if Jason came back tomorrow night, after Hanratty's?'

Cora regarded her with slitted eyes. Her eyes were all Annie could see, with the scarf hiding the lower half of her face, and her blue hat pulled right down.

They rounded a corner and passed a garage where the elderly man in navy overalls, who must own the place, was that morning poking under the bonnet of a red car. He raised a mittened hand that held a wrench and smiled at them, and Cora gave him a cheery hello from behind her scarf.

'Annie,' she said, when he was out of earshot, 'you can bring home whoever you like. I'm not your mother. I can't tell you what to do.' A gust of wind whipped at the end of her scarf. She caught it and tucked it into her collar. 'But just be careful, OK?'

'We will.'

'I mean, you haven't known one another for long.' She gave a bark of laughter. 'God, that *does* make me sound like your

mother.' The scarf escaped again: with a soft oath she recaptured it. 'Have you some kind of protection?'

'Jason has. He went to a clinic in town.'

'That's good.'

You're so sweet, he said. You're so pure and innocent. I've never met anyone like you. I can't believe you feel the way I feel. We were destined to be together, Annie. We were made for one another. And it was all she wanted to hear, all she yearned to hear from him.

That morning she looked for him in the common areas, in the space between her first and second lectures. There was no sign of him – but heading to the canteen at lunchtime with Cora and a couple of others she spotted him coming out of a lecture hall.

'I'll catch up with you,' she told her companions, and waited for him to approach.

'About tomorrow tonight,' she said, and stopped.

'Tomorrow night,' he repeated, finding her hand, twining his fingers in hers.

She looked at him, at the way his hair lifted in a little kick above his left temple. At the eyes that could seem green or brown, depending on how the light hit them. At the mouth he liked her to open with her tongue. She imagined him coming back with her after the disco, spending the night in her single bed, and the thought made her squeeze his hand.

'Yes,' she said simply.

His eyebrows lifted. 'Yes?'

'Yes.'

'Did you say it to Cora?'

'I did. She's OK.'

'And you?' he asked. 'Are you OK?'

'... Yes.'

'Sure?'

'I am.'

That evening, Cora handed her a slip of paper. Annie saw a woman's name, and a phone number.

'She's a doctor,' Cora said. 'Just if you wanted to go on the Pill.'

'I thought you had to be married to get the Pill.'

Cora shook her head. 'This doctor will prescribe it if you tell her your periods are painful. I heard a few talking about her in the lounge the other day, so I asked for her number. Don't worry, I didn't say who it was for.'

'Thanks, Cora.'

'Don't want you getting into trouble. Better safe than sorry.'

'Yes. Thanks.'

The following day she slipped out of the college at lunchtime and rang the number from a phone box in town, and was given an appointment a week from then. She shrank from the thought of having to lie to a stranger, but Cora was right. Better to err on the side of caution.

And later that night, after the disco, she led Jason quietly to her room, and he undressed her in the dark, and she undid the buttons on his shirt with trembling fingers, and for the first time she learnt the smell of a man's body, and the heft of it, and the

curves and hollows and wonders of it as she explored it all with eager hands.

And she wasn't ready for the sharp pain he caused, and he whispered sorry when she gasped with it, and he murmured her name and told her he loved her, and she gritted her teeth and pressed her fingers hard into his back and waited for it to be over. And he held her afterwards as she lay in his arms, her face tight with salt from the tears she hadn't expected, her body damp with her sweat and his. She hoped Cora hadn't heard the sounds they'd made.

'It will be better,' he told her, 'next time. It will be better for you,' and she hoped fervently he was right. And next time, which was a stolen hour the following Monday between dinner and the Film Club, it *was* better. It still hurt, but not so much, and she loved the nearness of him and the heat of him, and his face when he lost himself, and was content with that.

She told him about the doctor, and he laughed and asked if she didn't trust the condoms, and she said she'd prefer to be as safe as they could be. On the day of the appointment he skipped a lecture to go with her to the surgery, but she asked him to wait outside the shop across the road, because she thought walking in with a man would make it abundantly clear why the Pill was really being requested.

The doctor, who was older and friendly, wrote a six-month prescription when Annie, blushing and stammering and clearly lying, said she was looking for something to help with her monthly pain. And when she slid the prescription across a

chemist's counter the following day, sick with embarrassment, she was given a cardboard box of pills, which she brought home and stored in the drawer of her bedside locker, ready to start on the first day of her next period, as instructed.

And she never imagined or suspected that the damage was already done.

Julia

'STEPH,' ANNIE SAYS, 'I'D LIKE YOU TO MEET JULIA Murphy, my very first foster child.' She pauses – clearly waiting, Julia can see, for the other to show some sign of recognition – but no such sign comes. On the contrary, the young woman looks a bit put out.

'You don't know her?' Annie asks, smile dimming. 'You don't recognise her?'

'I do recognise her,' the other replies coolly. Still wearing an expression that almost verges on the hostile: what on earth can Julia have done to deserve it? 'We were on the same flight from Paris. We sat beside one another, actually.'

Ah. Julia recalls the dropped magazine, the attempt at conversation that she rebuffed, the offended silence afterwards. Her neighbour gathering her things as soon as they landed, leaving her seat, and the plane, without another glance in Julia's direction. Headed also for Annie's house, of all places, and clearly still annoyed now. Awkward, with the two of them thrown together for the weekend.

'On the same flight from *Paris*?' Annie repeats, the last of her smile dropping away. 'But you flew from Greece, Steph.'

'I went via Paris. It was the cheapest route I could get.'

'Oh, if only I'd known! I can't believe you were on the same flight – and even sitting together! You could have got a lift from Julia – I could have organised it. Julia, would you believe she hitched here, all the way from the airport!'

'Oh dear.' For Annie's sake, Julia must try to make amends. 'I'm sorry about that,' she says to the girl. 'I would have been happy to take you if I'd known. You're welcome to come back with me on Sunday, if you're on my flight again.' She puts out her hand. 'I didn't catch your name.'

The other's handshake is unenthusiastic, her smile stiff. 'Steph.'

'Steph was one of my last children,' Annie tells Julia, seemingly unaware of the undercurrent. 'She only left me six years ago.'

'Really?'

She looks in her mid-twenties now, so six years ago she would have been eighteen or so, the age fostering finishes, and children, young adults, whatever, are expected to make their way in the

world. By the look of her, she's been in Greece, or somewhere equally sunny, for some time. Hair bleached, skin tanned.

It occurs to Julia to wonder why their paths never crossed while the girl was living here. She met lots of Annie's charges over the years on her return visits to the house, but she's pretty sure she never came across this one. Strange.

'Steph,' Annie goes on, 'Julia is a singer-songwriter, a really famous one. She calls herself Julia M.'

Again she waits, head cocked, but Steph simply shakes her head – and just then, to Julia's relief, they're interrupted by the arrival of a tall man, dark-haired, lean-faced, his arms occupied with a tower of timber boxes, the top one anchored under his chin.

'Eddie!' Annie exclaims. 'What's all this? You didn't make *three* cakes, did you?'

He deposits his load at the end of the worktop. 'No, I made one with three tiers.'

'Oh, what'll I do with you? I told you I didn't want any fuss!'

'But I wanted a fuss,' he tells her, with a grin. 'You're my first wedding cake; I had to make it a good one.'

Listening to their exchange, Julia recalls the chubby-cheeked toddler who would sit on her knee while she read him a story. 'Eddie,' she says, wanting to see him properly.

He turns – and stops dead. 'You look like—' He breaks off, colouring. Embarrassed, fearful that he's got it wrong.

'I'm Julia,' she says, putting out her hand.

'You're ... Julia M.'

'I am.' Conscious, from the corner of her eye, of Steph's stare.

'Wow.' He steps forward and shakes her hand. 'Annie mentioned a Julia, but I never knew – I mean, I didn't know you were Julia M. I love your songs, honestly. Wow, I can't believe you're here.'

'Thank you.' His bashful reaction is sweet. 'Annie told me she'd invited you. I remember you coming here as a baby. We overlapped by a bit.'

'Yeah, she said that. But you left when I was …'

'Two. You were just two. We were all mad about you – we fought over who got to give you your bottle.'

He cried when she was leaving. He didn't want her to go, and neither did she. She recalls, out of nowhere, little yellow pyjamas he had, with elephants on them – or was it zebras? The scent of him after his bath, his hair damp against her shoulder as she read *The Cat in the Hat*, and *Goodnight Moon*, and *Guess How Much I Love You*.

'I was just telling Steph,' Annie says, putting her hands into oven mitts, 'about Julia. She hasn't heard of her – imagine!'

Eddie looks at Steph in astonishment. 'You haven't?' and Steph shrugs and says no. Probably wishing just as fervently as Julia that they'd drop it and talk about something else.

Annie bends to take a casserole dish from the oven. 'Eddie, would you fill that glass jug with water, love? Julia, sit there, across from Steph.' Setting the dish on the table, returning to the oven for a tray of baked potatoes. 'Julia has made two CDs, Steph, and there's another on the way, isn't there, Julia?'

'There is.'

Annie bustles back with the butter dish. She ladles casserole

onto each of their plates before taking her seat. 'I have them here, Steph, the CDs. You can have a listen to them later on.'

'Thanks.' Steph turns to Eddie. 'So you brought a three-tier cake all the way from London' – and Julia is relieved, and amused, at the abrupt change of subject. She's not exactly subtle.

'Oh, Eddie's cakes,' Annie is saying. 'He's a wizard in the kitchen.'

'I can make a fairly decent cake,' Julia puts in, 'but my pastry is a disaster.'

'Could be a few things there,' he tells her. 'If you handle it too much, or if your hands are too hot. Pastry can be tricky. Shortcrust is the most straightforward.'

'Could you send me a foolproof recipe?'

'Sure – or I could make you a demo video.'

'Oh, would you? Thanks awfully, that would be great.'

She likes him. Younger than her by a decade, so he's thirty now. There's something attractive about his lean features; she imagines he doesn't have trouble finding female company in London. She notes how Annie looks at him as they converse, the fondness in her face that's so lovely to see. The only one she raised from a baby, as far as Julia knows.

'So what's it like then?'

The question, from across the table, takes her by surprise. 'What's what like?'

There's still no sign of a smile on the other's face, but at least she's making an effort. 'Fame. And I presume fortune.'

None of your business, a voice in Julia's head says clearly. She ignores it. 'Well, the fortune part is good, I suppose. I

mean, money is a safeguard in case everything goes belly up, right?'

'And the fame?'

'I'm not sure fame is all it's cracked up to be. I'm not really at ease in the spotlight. I've had people … being too familiar, so now I get uncomfortable when strangers approach me – as you found out on the plane.' She smiles, but it isn't returned.

'What did you think I was going to do? I was just making conversation, trying to be friendly.'

Thankfully, she keeps her voice below the level of the other conversation. At least she has the sense not to upset Annie. 'Look,' Julia says in the same lowered tone, 'I'm sorry about that. I was tired, I had things on my mind – and like I say, I've learnt to be wary of strangers. Maybe we could just move past it and enjoy the weekend, for Annie's sake.'

A shrug. 'Sure.'

She doesn't sound very sure. Julia presses on, determined to thaw her out. 'Annie said you travelled from Greece.'

'Yeah.' Poking at a piece of chicken.

'So do you live there?'

'I do.'

'Mainland?' This is painful.

'No, one of the smaller islands. You won't have heard of it.'

'Sounds nice. I've only ever been to Athens.'

Annie offers seconds just then, and after that the conversation broadens to include all four. And for the rest of the meal, through all the memories and laughter and looking

to tomorrow that flavour the chat, Julia is conscious of Steph holding back, responding to questions but contributing little otherwise. She resolves to keep her distance from the girl for the weekend: she's come here for a break, and to celebrate the wedding of the woman who has always felt like her mother, and she's damned if anyone's going to spoil a minute of it.

Steph

SO THE WOMAN WHO COULDN'T BE BOTHERED TO
talk to her on the plane is a famous singer. Can't be that famous
if she was slumming it with the common people on a regular
Aer Lingus flight, with no first-class cabin for her to hide in.
Annie must be exaggerating – except that Eddie recognised her,
and seems dead impressed.

But she can't be as young as she looks, not if she was Annie's
first foster child. She does look good though. Slim and well
groomed, soft pink sweater over wide-legged grey trousers,
cool haircut – swept to the right, falling to just above her

shoulders, clipped short on the left – that's probably all the rage in Paris, where presumably she lives. A flash when she turns her head from what's probably a diamond in the lobe of her left ear. Her perfume is nice too: every so often Steph catches a drift of it that reminds her of the lavender fields near the farm in France where she picked apples for a season.

She wonders what kind of songs the woman writes. Annie might have said it – Annie certainly sounds like her biggest fan – but Steph wasn't paying a whole lot of attention. She might have to listen to one of the CDs at some stage, just to see what the fuss is about.

They're not going to be exchanging numbers anytime soon – clearly, the only thing they have in common is Annie – but for Annie's sake Steph will try to get along with her for the weekend.

They're talking now about some recent wedding in Dublin, an Irish model marrying a Hollywood actor. Big news by the sound of it, but the names mean nothing to Steph. They're so cut off on the island, the outside world and all its happenings pretty much passing them by. No TV, no radio, no internet in the olive mill. An old record player only, for Gareth's collection of vinyl – jazz, classical, some early pop – to break the silence of their evenings there.

No Irish newspapers in any of the island's supermarkets either. Over the summer months she's spotted some of the English ones, the red tops that Gareth despises, but they're already out of date by the time they arrive. Annie's letters are her only solid link to the rest of the world, and those give local news but not much else.

She never envisaged living in such an isolated place, not in a million years. Took her a while to acclimatise, but you get used to anything. And of course Gareth is there, which makes all the difference.

The writing students are completely charmed by the absence of outside influences at the mill. Talk about getting away from it all, they say, laughing together about withdrawal symptoms from social media, from Netflix and Sky TV and whatever else they're into. Tapping on their laptops during the morning sessions on the patio, dreaming of agents and book deals as Gareth talks of motivation and suspense and character development and story arcs. Steph has seen the women, and some of the men too, looking at him like he's a Greek god.

The current bunch are flying home on Sunday, the day Steph will be making her way back to Greece. Not to the island, not till Monday, her flight getting in too late on Sunday to pick up the ferry, so she must spend a night in a hostel in Athens.

She wonders what kind of a welcome she'll get. No call from him yet, no acknowledgement of hers. It might be down to the not always reliable phone signal at the mill, but she doesn't think so. If he really wanted to be in touch he could walk the three hundred metres up the hill to Ari's *taverna*, where the signal is generally better.

She becomes aware that the other three are looking at her. Did she miss a question? 'Sorry,' she says, 'miles away.'

'I was just wondering if you ever get snow on your island,' Annie says. 'It's still falling away outside,' and Steph turns to

see the flakes, ghost-like in the darkness, tumbling and whirling past the uncurtained window.

'Not while I've been there,' she says. 'Winters are chilly at night, but I don't think it ever gets cold enough for snow. Nothing like as cold as here.'

'How did you end up in Greece anyway?' Eddie asks.

She's aware of the three of them looking at her, and feels suddenly self-conscious. 'It wasn't planned. I travelled around a bit, after I left here. I just … ended up there.' She stops. She can't leave him out, not when Annie knows about him. 'I met someone who was living there, and I stayed.' Gareth flashes into her head, accompanied by a twist of anxiety.

'Have you been to Greece?' Annie asks Eddie, and he says yes, once, in his early twenties. 'I went with a few other lads. We slept mostly on beaches, saved our money for beer. We were on Ios, and Santorini.'

'Mine is the other side,' Steph tells him. 'The other side of the mainland, I mean.' She mentions the island's name, and he shakes his head like most people do when they hear it.

'Been there long?'

'Nearly two years. It's small, and not very commercialised like some of the others.'

'Sounds good,' he says. 'Might get there sometime.' He has a warm smile. She likes smiles where eyes get involved.

'Hope the snow stops soon,' Julia remarks, 'or we could be in trouble tomorrow.'

'Ah, it won't last,' Annie says. 'We never get it heavy in December – I don't recall a single white Christmas in my lifetime.'

She's aged a small bit in the six years since Steph has seen her. The lines fanning out from the corners of her eyes have deepened a little. New creases have appeared in the skin of her neck – and was that cluster of small darker patches on her jawline there before? More grey in her hair too, to join the strands Steph caused.

Her birthday tomorrow, as well as her wedding day. She always baked a cake on her birthday – well, she baked one on everyone's birthday, but her cake always held just one candle, and if anyone asked her age she'd say twenty-two, and follow it with a big laugh. Steph reckons she must be close to sixty now. Imagine getting married at that age. She'd always liked Matt, not that she'd ever admit it. He'd appear at the birthday parties – Annie must have said it to him – and he'd always have something small for the birthday person, and sweets for everyone else. She remembers him bringing Annie a new sweeping brush for one of her birthdays, with a red ribbon tied to the handle, and Annie chasing him around the kitchen with it.

She did have some good times here.

But being back in the house feels just as strange as she thought it might. She can't believe she cried when she met Annie – must be from lack of sleep. She's still a bit emotional now, keeps remembering stuff that happened here, most of it involving her doing something she shouldn't. She'd forgotten quite what a horror she was – how had Annie not chucked her out? And why had she still wanted to keep in touch, after she was finally rid of Steph?

There was no way Steph could have turned down this invitation, if only to let Annie see that she'd left the badness behind her, and was OK now. Why couldn't Gareth see that?

She saved me, Steph told him, trying to explain, trying to make him see how important the visit was. I was completely messed up when I was sent to her. I remember trying to get out of the car when the social worker was driving me there. I didn't want to go and live with strangers, even though there was nobody else to take me. And when I moved in, I didn't talk for ages. I didn't eat either, or not with the rest of them. I'd sneak down when they were all in bed and find stuff in the fridge. Annie was so patient … she never got cross. And now she wants me there, and I really want to go, for her sake. I feel I owe it to her.

But Gareth couldn't, or wouldn't, understand: he just kept insisting that both of them should wait until January. What was the point of that, when the wedding would be over?

Her thoughts are interrupted by Annie tapping a fork against a glass, causing Julia and Eddie to break off their conversation. 'There's something I should tell you all,' Annie says, the meal having moved on, dinner plates cleared and replaced with bowls of apple crumble and custard. Annie's meals always had comfort cooked into them. 'It's something I think you should know.'

Her jollity gone, her smile fading. Whatever's coming is not good news. Sickness, Steph thinks. A bad diagnosis. Her grip tightens on her spoon.

'This house,' Annie goes on, looking from one to another. 'It's

for sale – well, it's practically sold, I think. There were people here today for a second viewing … I get the impression they're serious.' A sudden shine of tears in her eyes that she blinks away. 'There's a sign up by the gate. You probably missed it in the dark, so …'

Her dessert practically untouched, Steph sees. Her hands busy with her napkin, folding and folding.

'I didn't want you seeing it in the morning – not without a warning, I mean.'

The house, this house, up for sale. The news leaves Steph inexplicably stunned. Why should it bother her when she'd never intended coming back to it? But it does, it does bother her. She looks from Eddie to Julia, sees the reflection of her own dismay in their faces.

Eddie is the first to speak. 'That'll be the end of an era, Annie. I mean, we all probably knew it was on the cards, but still, it's a—'

'No, we didn't,' Steph breaks in, glaring at him. 'How could we possibly have known?' How can he be so blasé about it?

He looks taken aback at her reaction. 'Well, with tomorrow, I mean. Things were bound to change, right, with Annie getting married?'

Stupidly, Steph feels another wave of tears threatening. She recognises the truth of what he says – yes, yes, some change was going to be inevitable – but Annie leaving the house, Annie selling up had simply not occurred to her. And faced with that stark reality, she feels like someone has just yanked away her security blanket and left her defenceless, and abandoned.

'It makes sense, love,' Annie says gently, putting a hand on her arm. 'I hate the thought of letting it go. It's been my home for so long, and so much has happened here, so many memories, but I have to be practical. It's old and in need of work, lots of work – a new roof, for starters, and it's full of draughts, and, oh, all sorts of other things – and there just isn't the money.'

'Annie's moving in with Matt and his daughter,' Julia points out, 'so this place would be empty' – and Steph wants to tell her to shut up, shut up, but instead she presses her mouth into a hard line and pushes aside her half-eaten dessert and stares miserably at the table.

'Right,' Julia says, getting to her feet, 'if everyone's finished I'm going to make a start on the washing-up – who'll dry?'

'Me,' Eddie says immediately, and Steph and Annie are banished to the sitting room with promises of coffee that Steph doesn't want, and won't drink. And once they're installed by the fire, Annie sits quietly and looks into the reddened coals, and understands that Steph just needs not to talk for a bit.

Eddie

'MY MOTHER DIED HAVING ME,' HE SAYS, DRYING A dessert bowl. 'We lived in County Limerick, about twenty miles from here. I have three older siblings, and my father was trying to keep a farm going as well, so he arranged for me to be fostered – there was nobody from within the family to take me, his brothers had emigrated to Canada, and my mother was from Scotland, all her family were still there – so I ended up here with Annie.'

She's easy to talk to. She listens when you respond to her questions, and doesn't butt in until you finish. Every so often

he catches himself thinking, *I'm talking to Julia M! I'm drying dishes with Julia M!* like a star-struck teen – but there's nothing arrogant or intimidating about her at all, nothing in her manner to suggest that she feels in any way superior to him.

'And then when I was five, my father remarried, and he and my stepmother took me back.'

Julia spoons coffee into Annie's pot. 'That must have been tough. I remember not wanting to leave here, and I was twelve at the time. You were so much younger.'

'I don't remember it really.'

Not quite true. A residue of the trauma it caused remains within him, a faint memory of being eased, red-faced, bawling, from Annie's arms – or is that image a false one, his mind concocting it from what Francey told him later, much later? We felt terrible, she said, taking you away from her. You were inconsolable – and Annie felt every bit as bad as you did. So they'd brought him back to see her, every couple of weeks or so – or rather, Francey had.

Your dad thought I was pandering, she admitted, when Eddie probed. He didn't mean it in a bad way – he just thought it was making it harder for you to settle with us. Trying, like she always did, to put the kindest spin on things. Trying to mend things between father and son, when she could see, when anyone with half an eye could see the gulf that existed, and that persists to this day, between them.

His father blamed Eddie for his first wife's death. The realisation of this, the truth of it, took a long time to dawn on Eddie – but when it did, somewhere in his teens, it made sense

111

of a lot of things. His father held him accountable, and he does to this day. If it wasn't for Francey, Eddie would have cut ties with him a long time ago.

If it wasn't for Francey, his father would never have reclaimed him.

'And you kept in touch all the time?'

Julia's question pulls him back. 'With Annie? Yes.' He hesitates, not wanting to sound soft. 'She … felt like my mother. I mean, I knew she wasn't – she told me, when I was old enough to understand, that she was just looking after me for a while, and that my mother was in Heaven, but still.'

'She loved all of us,' Julia says. 'She felt like my mother too. She was the best foster mother a kid could hope for.'

'Sure was.'

The kettle boils. He pours water into the coffee pot, and the room fills instantly with the burnt-nut scent. He watches Julia arrange cups and sugar bowl on a tray. There's a kind of grace, a fluidity, to her movements. She could be a dancer rather than a singer.

'Am I allowed to see the cake?' she asks.

He pretends to consider.

'Oh go on, just show me one' – so he peels the tape from the largest box and lifts the flaps.

'That looks good. What is it?'

'A fruit cake, just a light one, for the ones who like a traditional wedding cake. The other two are different.'

'Fabulous.' She leans over to sniff it, and he catches a whiff of her perfume. 'You must love your job.'

'I do,' he replies carefully, looking down at the neat parting in her hair. 'It's not exactly—' He breaks off. 'Never mind,' he says. Best not to pursue it. He casts about for a change of topic as she straightens up. 'Can I ask how you came to be living here?'

Her lips part, but no words come.

'Sorry,' he says quickly. 'Forget I asked.' She's Julia M, you idiot, not your new best friend.

'No, I just didn't expect it, that's all. And I did ask *you*.'

'If you'd rather not—'

'My parents … were killed in a road accident when I was three.'

'Oh God – I'm sorry. Really.'

She gives a little shake to her head, and again he catches her scent. 'I don't remember them in the least. I lived here for nearly nine years, until I was twelve, and then an aunt, an older sister of my father's, adopted me. She lived in France – she'd gone there straight out of college, into a job in finance. She was very ambitious, still is. She's a partner in the same company now.'

He wonders why the aunt had waited until Julia was twelve before coming to claim her – and as if he'd voiced the question aloud, Julia supplies the answer.

'She never married. She wasn't really the marrying type, totally into her career. She wouldn't have been able to look after me when I was younger, not with her job. She came back when my parents died, she stayed about a week, until arrangements were made for me. And she did visit me while I was here – she'd come to Ireland now and again on business – so it wasn't as if

I was going off with a complete stranger. And she was good to me, she really was.'

Her hair is very shiny. The kitchen light brings out a dark red gleam in it. The long side swings when she moves. She might have her own private hairdresser. He wonders if she's involved with someone – and then thinks, of course she is. Not that she'd look twice at a nobody like him, even if she was free.

'She sent me to boarding school,' she continues, adding spoons and milk to the tray. 'I'd been living with her for a few weeks of the summer, and she'd got an au pair, a girl from Sweden, to look after me until school started.' Then, seeing Eddie's expression, she says, 'No, no, it was fine actually – I enjoyed the experience of boarding. I'm lucky enough to have a good ear for languages so it didn't take me long to learn French, and there was a wonderful music teacher who really encouraged me.'

So that was where it had started. Not that long, a few years, since she'd gone viral. He remembers hearing her on the radio, remembers how her first hit, 'Learning to Breathe', appealed instantly to him. He wonders why it took so long for her to be successful, but he can't very well ask her that.

She lifts the tray. 'Can you bring the pot, and get the door?'

In the sitting room they find only Annie. 'Steph is gone to bed,' she tells them. 'She was exhausted, poor thing.'

Exhausted maybe, and also seriously out of sorts from the minute she arrived. Even in the car, now he thinks about it, she was tense. There's something brittle about her, some edge that makes her interesting. He'd like to hear more about her travels

after she left here, and what she got up to. Plenty to tell, he suspects. He might find a chance to ask her before the weekend is out, see what he can discover.

They take seats around the fire, and Julia pours. 'Annie was my first piano teacher,' she tells Eddie.

'Oh stop – I can't play for toffee!'

'Don't listen to her. It all started there, at that very piano.'

'I remember you playing,' Eddie says to Annie, and again she protests, but a long-forgotten memory has come to him of sitting on her lap and plinking at the keys – and later there were the singsongs she would organise, on the afternoons he visited with Francey.

He wonders if he dares to ask – and then Annie beats him to it. 'Would you do one song for us before bed? Just one?' she asks Julia.

'Would I wake Steph though?'

'Not if you do it softly.'

So Julia gets up and sits at the piano and plays a gentle, keys-muffled version of 'Heartstrong', and Eddie has another pinch-me moment as he listens to what he has only heard on the radio, and his Spotify playlist, until now. Julia M, performing just for him and Annie. Wait till he tells them at work.

She comes to the end and laughs, and tells them it's the most intimate venue she's played in yet. They finish their coffee and Annie puts up the fireguard.

'Eddie, have you brought in your things?'

He hasn't. He goes out to the Jeep, shivering in the cold of the night, tramping through snow which has by now completely

covered the ground, and is still falling steadily. Whatever about a white Christmas, it looks like Annie will have a white wedding.

He retrieves his bag and slams the boot door. Despite the frosty air he pauses for a moment on his way back to the house to take in the absolute darkness of the night, now that the lights on next door's bush have been switched off. Unheard of for the sky to be so dark in London, or even in Watford. He tilts his head and closes his eyes, and snow tumbles lightly onto his face, like the probing, curious fingers of a blind person.

In the hall Annie waits, a hot-water bottle tucked under an arm. She leads him up the stairs to a little room at the back of the house, right next to hers.

'This is where I slept,' he says, remembering. For all his visits back to her, this will be the first time he's spent the night since he left her care.

'It is indeed,' she says, 'once you graduated from your cot.' She slips the hot-water bottle between the sheets. 'I hope you'll be warm enough.'

He takes in the single bed, the narrow wardrobe, the miniature chest of drawers, the mirror hanging on the back of the door, the floorboards worn to a shine. The yellow paper on the walls with its kites of blue and red floating diagonally upwards, yes, familiar, and the navy curtains, yes, he thinks so. He's not so sure about the mobile of aeroplanes cut out of thin wood hanging from the ceiling above the dressing table, or the rusty orange bedside rug.

He thinks of all the nights he spent here, going from babyhood

to toddler and a little older, happy as Larry with Annie right next door. Annie, whom he loved, and whom nobody had told him wasn't his to keep.

'I was five,' he says. 'I was just five.' Feeling, to his great astonishment, a sudden prickling behind his eyes. Years, decades since he cried. He blinks hard to stop it happening now.

'You were going back to your family, which was only right,' Annie replies, giving no sign that she's seen his wobble. 'But it was hard, for both of us. I didn't want it either. I missed my little boy.' She crosses to the window. 'I meant to do this earlier,' she says, catching the curtains to draw them closed, pausing first to peer into the darkness. 'Can't still be snowing, surely?'

'It is. There's a fair bit on the ground now.'

She tuts. 'We'll get our shoes wet going to the church.'

'You'll have to wear wellies,' he says, and she laughs and tells him she might, they all might, as she draws the curtains together, shutting out the snow and the night.

She returns to where he stands. She reaches up to run a finger along his cheek. Always so tactile, finding a place to caress, stealing a hug whenever the opportunity presented itself. 'It's so good to have you back. I'll let you sleep now. You must be tired.'

She looks tired too. 'What time is the wedding? You probably said, but I've forgotten.'

'Oh, not till noon. You can have a lie-in.'

When she's gone he empties his bag and readies himself for bed. As he's turning down the blankets he suddenly remembers the cake. Best to assemble it now, save having to do it in the morning.

He pulls socks on again and tiptoes downstairs. The kitchen is warm, and still smells of coffee. He finds a big wooden chopping board and sets it on the worktop. He dismantles the largest box and slides the fruit cake onto the board. He follows with the chocolate cake, setting it carefully on top. So far, so good.

He opens the third box.

'Shit,' he says quietly.

Saturday,
21 December

Annie

THE LIGHT RIMMING THE CURTAINS IS TOO BRIGHT for an early December morning. Has she overslept? She reaches out to turn the clock towards her – can't have it facing her during the night, taunting her if she tosses and turns in the small hours – and sees twenty to eight. Shouldn't be bright now, not on the shortest day of the year. Shouldn't be even a small bit bright. What's going on?

She leaves the bed, gathering her quilt about her, and walks barefoot across the cold wooden floor to the window. She pulls apart the curtains and looks out at the back garden.

Oh Lord.

Oh God.

It's white. The world outside her window is blindingly white, dazzlingly white. A blanket of snow, a thick carpet of it covering the grass and the flowerbeds, lodged in the angles of the shrubs, sitting on the branches of the pines. A generous topping of it on the cast-iron table, on the seats of the chairs ranged around it, on the top of the coal bunker and the roof of the shed. The bird table covered with snow, the arms of the clothesline similarly hidden, her wheelbarrow full of it. The rockery vanished under a mound of it. Nothing but white as far as her gaze can go.

It's not snowing now but it must have fallen all night, softly, soundlessly changing the landscape while they slept unawares. And at some stage there must have been wind: she sees drifts of snow by the side of the shed, more piled against the coal bunker, more climbing up the back wall.

She replaces the quilt on the bed and takes her dressing gown from the chair. She puts feet into slippers and leaves the room. She stands silently on the landing, as she has stood on many other mornings over the years, checking for sounds from the other rooms. This morning she hears nothing. Everyone still asleep, weary from their travels. She slips downstairs and opens the front door. Maybe, the stupid part of her brain says, it won't be so bad out the front.

It's every bit as bad out the front. It's worse, with the driveway covered – half the car tyres disappeared – and the road beyond the gate completely under snow as far as she can make out.

She takes a cautious step outside. Her slipper and lower leg vanish. She pulls back hastily and retreats into the house, and finds her wellingtons under the stairs. Pulling them on, she's reminded of Eddie joking with her the night before about having to wear wellies going to the church. Not so funny now.

She crunches through the snow to the gate, shivering as the cold nips at her hands and face. She scans left and right, and sees everything covered with white, and white, and more white. The big snow, which could have waited just one more day. Was it forecasted? She didn't think so – but with so much on her mind lately she hadn't been paying a lot of attention to weather bulletins.

She recalls Matt saying something yesterday on the phone, something about the forecast not being great for today. Did he mention snow? He might have … but he was hardly imagining a complete deluge either, a burial of anything not moving. This snowfall, she suspects, has taken everyone by surprise.

And what are they to do now? What of the ceremony they've planned in the church at noon, and the festivities that are to follow in the community hall? What of the people who are to travel here, who are to be part of it all? What of Maurice and Brian, Matt's two middle boys, who flew into Dublin with their wives and children from Canada yesterday, and were to get an early train west? What are they to do about them? What can they possibly do?

Cora. She must ring her, even before she rings Matt. She returns to the house, placing her feet into the shapes she made

on her way out. Snow manages to find its way into her boots, to trickle unpleasantly between her toes.

Inside she takes a towel from the downstairs toilet and dries her feet and pushes them back into slippers. In the kitchen she rakes through the still-reddened coals in the range, and adds kindling to coax them back to life. When there's a flickering, she shovels on more fuel and returns upstairs for her phone.

Missed call, she reads. Cora, having seen the snow? But it's not Cora, it's Stella, the Ennis-based caterer who was bringing the food for today, and who has left a message on Annie's voicemail.

Good morning, Annie. Stella here – can you ring me when you get this please?

No need to ring, when she knows what she'll be told – but she can't ignore it so she dials the caterer's number and listens to repeated apologies, and a promise to reimburse monies already paid, and to cater at a reduced rate for any future gatherings. 'No,' she says, 'it's fine. No, Stella, we'll manage. Thanks, Stella.'

She hangs up and presses Cora's name. Her call is answered on the second ring.

'Happy birthday to you,' Cora says brightly. 'Welcome to the golden age.'

She'd totally forgotten about her birthday. 'Are you up?'

'Just about. Is everything OK?'

'Get up and look out.'

'What?'

'Just do it.'

She waits. It doesn't take long.

'Oh, good God. Oh no. Bloody hell, Annie – what'll we do?'

'I was hoping you'd tell me. Stella has just cancelled.'

'*What?* Oh Lord, no food – calamity. Have you spoken to Matt?'

'Not yet' – but suddenly she very much wants to. 'Look, I know you can't get here for breakfast, but hopefully —'

'What? What are you talking about? Of *course* I'll get there for breakfast – and I'm expecting something seriously gourmet, with a professional chef on the premises.'

'But Cora, the snow —'

'Snow, my foot. If I have to charter a helicopter I'll be there. Give Matt a ring – and maybe Father Dennis too, see what he thinks. I'll get dressed, and I'll put on my thinking cap. See you within the hour.' And with a click, the call is ended.

Annie stares at her screen. If anyone can overcome a problem, Cora can. When her husband Dan was laid up a few years ago with a back injury that put him out of action for several months, she took unpaid leave from her teaching job to keep the farm going with Dan's right-hand man. She got stuck in, he told Annie afterwards, did everything I asked of her, and more.

After their daughter Gilly left an expensive jacket behind in a hotel room last year that was nowhere to be found when she returned half an hour later to recover it, Cora called the manager and told him she would drive to the hotel and sit in the lobby until it was located, however long it took.

I said I'd bring my sleeping bag and camp out if I had to, she told Annie. Thank God he didn't call my bluff, because the last thing I wanted was to look for more unpaid leave. He said he'd

make enquiries, and the jacket was magically found. I didn't ask questions: I wasn't interested in having anyone sacked.

Cora believes in confronting problems head-on – but how can she solve this one? Short of waving a wand and making the snow disappear, there's no way they can go ahead as planned. Nothing for it but to postpone the whole thing, after Matt's family and Annie's three visitors making special trips, after Steph coming from so far to be here.

She calls Matt. Two rings, three.

'Morning, birthday girl.'

He must still be in bed too. 'Look out the window,' she says.

A beat passes. 'That might be tricky, since I'm not in the house.'

'What – where are you?'

'I'm out the back. I just refilled the bird nut holder.'

'So you've seen it. The snow.'

'Seen it, walked in it. Thought about making a snowman with Ruthie. Maybe after breakfast.'

'Matt – be serious! What are we going to do?'

Another tiny pause. 'Well, I thought we had that all sorted months ago.'

She wants to slap him. 'How can we possibly go ahead? Stella has just cancelled, so we have no food. People won't be able to travel – your gang must be stuck in Dublin. We'll have virtually no guests, only the ones who can walk to the church – and even then, anyone older won't be able to head out in this. How can you act as if nothing's wrong? How are *you* planning to get here?'

'Hang on,' he says, and she hears Ruthie's voice, too muffled

to make out the words but there's no mistaking his daughter's distinctive deep tone. The seconds pass by while Annie waits, drumming her fingers on the edge of the sink and looking out at the pale winter sun that has begun its climb into a sky that's moving from dark grey into pale blue, with no cloud in sight. Any other morning she'd be rapt at the sight of such a promising day.

'I'm back in the kitchen. Ruthie was looking for ketchup for her sausages. You'll be pleased to hear I've just found it.'

She takes in a deep, steadying breath. She bows her head as she lets it out. 'Matt,' she says, 'please. I love how laid-back you are normally, and how you can always calm me down when I get into a tizzy, but right now I need you to be serious. I honestly do.'

'OK,' he says. 'I'll be serious. Listen to me.' Pause. 'Today won't be quite what we had in mind. We'll certainly have fewer guests by the look of it – my gang in Dublin have already phoned to say there are no trains running until mid-afternoon at the earliest – and it sounds like we'll have nothing to eat unless the food fairy godmother shows up, but all we really need is Father Dennis and a couple of witnesses. I was planning to marry you today, Annie O'Reilly, and I'll be most put out if anyone tries to stop me from doing that.'

And despite everything, she finds a smile spreading across her face, and every fluttery frantic thing inside her settling down. 'How will you get here though?' He's four miles away as the crow flies, more by road. His house is down a rutted lane that he'll surely have to dig his way out of.

'You let me worry about that,' he says. 'I'm aiming to be at the church in plenty of time to admire you coming in. And now I'd like to eat my sausages before Ruthie gets her hands on them.'

She sends a kiss to Ruthie and tells him goodbye and hangs up – and sees that a text came in from Joe Dineen while they were talking.

A text, the day after a second viewing. A text, on the day he knows she's getting married. She stares at the screen. Maybe he's just wishing her all the best, but she doubts it. She counts to ten and opens it.

Annie, wonderful news, the Johnsons have bid just five thousand below the asking price! I know you're busy today but I thought you'd want to hear. I'll give you a ring on Monday, or you can get back to me before that if you want. Congratulations! Joe

A bid, just five thousand below the asking price. I thought you'd want to hear, he says. He hasn't a clue. She deletes the text and calls Father Dennis, who lives next door to the church.

'Annie,' he says. 'I was just about to ring you.'

No. 'Don't tell me you're cancelling too.'

'Not at all. I'm all set, as long as *you* still want to go ahead.'

'Yes,' she says. 'Yes, I definitely do. We definitely do.'

'That's good, that's good … It's just that we have a small problem. Audrey's been in touch to say she won't make it, so we'll need to find someone more local.'

Audrey, who plays the church organ every Sunday, and on any other occasion she's needed. Eighty-four-year-old Audrey, who lives a good ten miles beyond Matt, and who has no problem puttering to the village on a normal day in her

little Fiat, but who would have no hope at all of getting here today.

Thankfully, her absence shouldn't be a problem. 'I have someone who can do the music,' Annie replies. Julia won't mind stepping in – will she?

'Great – in that case, I'll see you there. The church will be open by half ten, and I told Matt I'd put the heating on in good time, so we'll be nice and toasty.'

'… When were you talking to Matt?'

'About half an hour ago, I'd say.'

So he'd already spoken to Father Dennis when she rang him. He'd already taken steps to ensure that today would go ahead. She can't decide whether to laugh or cry, so she does neither. She thanks the priest and hangs up – and as she reaches for the kettle, she finally notices the cake.

'Oh,' she breathes.

It sits on her big chopping board, tucked into a corner of the worktop. Two square tiers, the bottom iced in ivory, the top, positioned slightly off-kilter, in a glossy brown covering so dark it's almost black. The contrast between the colours is wonderful. Seven pale pink fondant flowers travel in a graceful curve from the lower half of the bottom cake to the centre of the top, diminishing in size as they go. The whole thing is a marvel, a feat. She thought there were three tiers, but she must have got that wrong. Two will be enough, more than enough for whatever small number can make the wedding out of the seventy-four they invited.

And then she spots the bowl sitting next to the cake, the lovely

striped one Steph brought. She'd put that away last night, hadn't she? She peers in – and sees what has to be the third tier. Heaped chunks of a white sponge mixture, iced in a deeper pink than the flowers, with what looks like a buttercream filling. Somehow damaged, broken in bits between London and here. Poor Eddie – but it's a cake. It's only a cake.

She leans against the worktop, the joy of what's to come rising and dancing inside her. It's going to happen today, on her sixtieth birthday. She's going to walk up the aisle on her brother's arm, or on someone else's arm if Ivan can't make it. He hasn't rung yet to cancel, but he possibly will, five miles away on the Ennis road.

Doesn't matter. However it happens, she's going to be a bride on her birthday. They may have nothing to offer whatever guests will show, apart from a cake that's missing a top tier, but in a few hours she will be a wife, and she will have a husband, and he will be Matt McCarthy, who is the best of men, and whom she has loved in one way or another pretty much all her life.

And what else could possibly matter?

She makes tea, alone in the kitchen, listening to the joyous trill of a robin outside the window. She eats a chunk of cake, humming.

Annie, then

IT STARTED AS A NIGGLING WORRY, ONLY THAT. SHE'D never counted days before, never noticed how regular or otherwise her cycle was, so she wasn't sure when exactly her period was due. But as the days went by with no sign, she became aware of a creeping anxiety. She tried not to let it bother her – worry probably held it up more, her body reacting to the signals coming from her brain – but the longer it went on, the more her fears increased.

'Have you started on the Pill?' Jason asked, and she told him no, not yet, and didn't make a big thing of it. By now they'd

been together half a dozen times, using condoms each time. She couldn't be pregnant, not when they'd been careful. She'd probably always been irregular. Any day now it would come.

But when the days went by and it didn't, when the niggle got too big to go on pretending that nothing was wrong, she told Cora she had a tummy bug and would skip college. 'If you meet Jason, tell him I'll see him tomorrow,' she said. 'I'm sure it'll be gone by then.'

'You want me to bring you anything? Alka-Seltzer? I could nip back at lunchtime.'

'Thanks, I think I just need a day off food.' If only that was all she needed.

After Cora left she showered and got dressed, trying to make herself feel better. She made tea and didn't drink it, made coffee and poured that down the sink too. She sat on the couch and tried to study, but for all the sense she made of them, her lecture notes might as well have been written in Russian.

Around lunchtime, when she was trying to summon the enthusiasm to go for a walk, the doorbell that their landlord had finally repaired rang. She started at the harsh buzz, and decided to ignore it. By rights she'd have been in college, and it would have gone unanswered.

A few minutes later, she heard the small flap of the letterbox. She rose to her feet and peered into the hall, and saw a white slip on the floor. A meter reader maybe, leaving a note to say he'd called.

It wasn't a meter reader.

Thought you probably wouldn't be here, but I'm on my lunch break so I took a chance. Pity you have no phone. I'll try dropping by later – could take you out to dinner this evening if you have no other plans? Matt

Matt McCarthy, who'd begun his training in Limerick this week. She'd completely forgotten him, and her promise to meet him after her lectures to give him the walk around the city she'd offered. Tuesday, she'd said, and they'd arranged to meet outside the GPO at five.

And today was Thursday.

She opened the door and hurried to the gate. No sign of him on the road. She went back and grabbed her key, and jogged to the main road – and there he was half a block away, his familiar stride easily identified.

'Matt!' she called. He turned and she waved, and he headed back. She walked to meet him. What a sight she must look, her face hardly washed this morning, not a trace of lipstick. Had she even combed her hair?

'There you are,' he said, looking pleased.

'Matt, I can't believe I forgot about Tuesday – I'm so sorry. Come back to the house and I'll make you a sandwich. It's the least I can do.'

He tipped his head to the side. 'Would that be to make up for Tuesday, I wonder, or for ignoring me just now when I rang the bell?' And then a grin – but still she was mortified.

'I – I didn't think it would be anyone I knew. Sorry.'

'Would you stop apologising, woman – I'm only teasing you.'

He draped an arm easily across her shoulders as they walked back to the house. He was tactile with everyone – and Annie had never appreciated it more. She wanted so much to tell him her fears, to blurt them out and wait for him to reassure her somehow – but of course she couldn't. She couldn't burden him with this, couldn't expect him to fix it.

'We'll do it next week,' she said. 'The tour.' It would be something to take her mind off whatever might be ahead. 'Say Tuesday again, and I promise to turn up this time.'

'Sounds good to me. How come you're not in college now?'

She told him, hating the lie, that she had a couple of hours free and had decided to come home. The excuse she'd given Cora would make him back off and go, not wanting to put her out if she was poorly, and she wanted the comfort of his company at least.

'Tomatoes,' she said, looking into the fridge. 'All I can offer, I'm afraid.'

'Tomatoes are grand.'

'And tea? Or coffee?'

'Tea. I'll make it.'

He filled the kettle while she sliced tomatoes and buttered bread. He was slightly taller than her, his hair cut shorter than usual, a small hole in the elbow of his blue sweater that stupidly brought her to the edge of tears when she noticed it. She coughed, and called it a tickle in her throat.

'So,' she said, when they were settled on kitchen chairs in the courtyard, the rain holding off, 'how's the training?'

134

'Fine so far. Well, a bit boring – I was never one for sitting listening to someone mouthing off – but easy enough.'

'Many doing it?'

'About twenty. It's for the whole of Munster.'

'Right.'

'And you?' he asked. 'Still having fun in college?'

Still having fun. She forced a smile. 'Busy enough at the moment. Teaching practice coming up soon.'

'You'll be grand.' He blew on his tea and sipped. 'I never thought to say it to you at the weekend,' he said, 'but you could catch a lift home with me tomorrow. We finish at four on Fridays. Just if you wanted to skip the bus.'

'That'd be great. I'm off at half three.'

He ate his sandwich, in between making her laugh with his descriptions of his fellow trainees, an ex-nun from Cork, identical twins from Kerry, a man from Waterford whose eight brothers were all postmen. Embellishing as he went, no doubt – he could never tell a story without making it his own – but she was grateful for the wonderful normality of him.

'Isn't this the life?' he said, stretching his legs. 'Me and Annie O'Reilly, having lunch in Limerick. Tomato sandwiches and tea in the courtyard.'

She smiled. He could always make her smile.

'I think,' he went on, 'that we should make a regular thing of it.'

'What – have lunch in the courtyard regularly?'

'Or dinner,' he said, scratching at something on the thigh of his trousers before lifting his gaze to find hers. 'Or a drink, or

whatever you fancy, really. And it wouldn't have to be here, it could be anywhere.'

She smiled. 'All of the above would be lovely. And you could meet Jason.' Something, some instinct, telling her to mention him.

He set his cup on the rickety little table she and Cora had picked up in a secondhand shop. 'Jason,' he repeated, brushing breadcrumbs from his lap onto the flagstones. 'Who would that be now?'

'Just someone I've been seeing. He's in the college.'

'Very good,' he said. 'Very good.' Pushing up his sleeves, drawing a hand over the top of his head.

'Will you have more tea?' Annie asked. 'I'm afraid we're out of tomatoes, but I could make toast for a second round.'

'I won't,' he said, getting to his feet. 'I'd better make tracks, or they'll be sending out the guards to find me.' Picking up his cup and plate, going ahead of her into the kitchen. 'So I'll see you tomorrow for the lift, yeah? Just after four at the GPO.'

'Are you OK?' she asked, because it suddenly felt different, and he gave her a grin and a hug and told her everything was just fine.

'Thanks for the lunch,' he said, and off he went, and for the rest of the afternoon she had a new anxiety on top of the other one.

Me and Annie O'Reilly, having lunch in Limerick.

Dinner or a drink, or whatever you fancy.

They were great pals, they'd been great pals for as long as she could remember – and maybe if Jason hadn't come along,

they might have become something more. Because she'd been aware for some time, hadn't she, of his interest? The way he would catch and hold her gaze sometimes when they were out in a crowd. The way he'd compliment her on an outfit, or a new haircut. The way he'd fall in beside her if a few of them were walking to the lake.

It had registered with her, and she'd been flattered, and curious – and then Jason had come along, sweeping Matt, and everyone else, to one side. Was today Matt's attempt to sound her out, see if she'd be interested in moving their friendship on?

He was a joker. He was the clown of the gang, always in good form, always able to cheer you up if you were feeling down. He was also kind and thoughtful, and would make the best boyfriend for someone – but not her. Not now that she had Jason.

Maybe she was mistaken, maybe he'd just been fooling around today. Maybe, after all, she'd imagined an interest up to this. But it was the mention of Jason's name, wasn't it, that had put a different colour on their conversation? It was directly afterwards that Matt had got to his feet and almost run out of the place.

She'd see how things were when she met him for the lift home: she'd know if there was a strain between them. She hoped there wasn't – she couldn't bear the thought of losing him as a friend.

She went to bed before Cora got home, unable to face a conversation. The lunchtime sandwich was the only thing she'd eaten, but she didn't feel like anything else, even when the smell of sausages drifted up the stairs.

Later, there was a soft tap on her door. 'Come in.'

'I didn't want to wake you.' Cora left the light off, perched on the edge of the bed. 'How are you feeling?'

'Not too bad.' Terrible. Eaten up with worry.

'Jason says get well soon. He won't see you tomorrow. His mother's having a hysterectomy so he's getting an early bus home to help in the shop.'

Yes, he'd said something to that effect the other day, and Annie had forgotten it like she'd forgotten about Matt, this awful foreboding pushing everything else aside.

That night, sleep didn't come. She lay in bed and counted days, telling herself it was her arithmetic that was at fault, nothing more, but whatever way she counted, the numbers told an ominous story.

Twenty days since their first night. Thirty-eight, around that, since the start of her last period. Nine months from their first time would take her to the middle of July. For the past three summers she'd worked in a café in Ennis that took on extra waitresses for their busy season, and she'd assumed that next summer would be no different. The money came in handy, took the pressure off her parents – her father a painter and decorator, her mother a part-time secretary – to keep her in funds.

What if her growing suspicion was right, and she and Jason had been unlucky, what then? What did the future hold for them? What would he say when she told him, as she'd have to if it were true?

Maybe she was mistaken.

She didn't think she was mistaken.

She got up at seven, unable to lie there any longer. She went downstairs and took a shower, and cried under it. She got dressed and filled the teapot and drank two cups and poured a third, eyes smarting with tiredness, stomach churning, heart heavy.

At eight she heard Cora stirring. She waited through the eternity it took for her friend to appear in the kitchen.

'You look rough,' Cora said. 'You should take another day off. I'll give you lecture notes.'

'I think I might be pregnant.'

Out it tumbled into the room. In the short silence that followed, her hands tightened on the cup that had cold tea in it.

Cora's expression didn't change. She dropped into the chair across from Annie. 'I thought you were a bit off. How late are you?'

No judgement. No 'why weren't you more careful?' Annie shook her head. 'I don't know, I never keep track, but it should be here by now.'

'Roughly how late?'

'Maybe … ten days. Maybe more.'

'Have you said it to Jason?'

'No. I've told nobody. You're the only one.'

'Right.' Cora tapped fingers on the table. 'You could wait another while. You still might just be late.'

'I might …' But the thought of more uncertainty, more agonising, made Annie want to burst into tears. 'I don't think I can wait any longer to find out, Cora. I feel sick with worry.'

'In that case, make another appointment with that doctor. And tell Jason, and bring him with you. Or I'll go, if you like.'

Annie let out a shuddering breath. 'What'll I do if – it's true?'

'You'll go to England and have it sorted, or you'll stay here and see it through, and then give it up for adoption.' Her voice was calm. She coaxed one of Annie's hands from the cup and squeezed it. 'They're your choices.'

Both sounded horrifying. 'What if – we had it, and kept it?'

Cora stared at her. 'Annie, you're eighteen. You told me you'd never had a proper boyfriend until Jason, and you met him – what? A month ago?

'Nearly two months.' She hears how ludicrous it sounds. But they love one another – doesn't that count? Doesn't that make all the difference?

'Look, one step at a time. Ring the doctor and make an appointment. I think you should say it to Jason – why should you be the only one worrying? – but if you want to wait till you're sure, that's up to you.'

'And you'll come with me?'

'Of course I will. That's what friends are for.'

Later that day, having made an appointment with the doctor for Monday evening, she left the college after her final lecture and collected her bag in the house. She walked to the GPO and found Matt waiting outside.

'Sorry – am I late?'

'Nope.' He took the bag and slung it over his shoulder. 'I'm parked just a bit away, near the station.' He set off, and Annie fell into step. 'So, are you looking forward to the weekend?'

She nodded the lie. 'I always do.' She always had, up to now. On impulse, she slipped her hand through his arm and held on.

He glanced at it but made no comment. Were they alright? She had no idea.

She had to ask. 'Matt, are we alright?'

He gave her a quizzical look without breaking his stride. 'Alright? Course we are. Why wouldn't we be?'

'It's just – you left in a bit of a hurry yesterday.'

'We're fine,' he said.

'So you're still on to meet on Tuesday.'

'Tuesday?'

'To give you a tour of the city.'

'Ah ...' He shook his head. 'Don't worry about it, Annie. You're busy with your studies. I can find my own way around.'

'But I'd like to.'

'We'll see.'

They reached his car, which was old and rusted, donated by an uncle a few months back. Their conversation on the journey home was easy – how could it be otherwise between them? – but something was different, something had changed. When he was dropping her at the house he said, 'I'll see you in the pub tomorrow night, I'd say.'

'You will.'

'I'll be going back to Limerick on Monday morning, around eight,' he went on, 'but I think you head back Sunday night, don't you?' and she told him she did, and Tuesday wasn't mentioned again, and something told her it wasn't going to happen, and she felt unaccountably sad.

'You're pale,' her mother said, when she walked in. 'Are you sleeping? Are you eating?'

'I'm a bit tired,' Annie told her. 'We're under pressure with assignments, and teaching practice coming.'

Please let it not be true. Please let it not be true.

The weekend passed. She skipped the pub on Saturday night, unable to face the friends, and the inevitable questions about college. 'Get enough sleep,' her mother ordered on Sunday night. 'Your health is more important than your exams. Mind yourself.'

'Any change?' Cora asked when Annie arrived back in Limerick, and Annie told her no, and yearned for Jason to put his arms around her and tell her that everything was going to be alright.

She'd still said nothing to him, clinging on to the hope that it was a false alarm. 'How's your mother?' she asked him the following morning, sitting in their usual corner in the lounge.

'She's grand, not a bother.' He took her hand. 'Can I come around before the Film Club?'

'We might skip it tonight,' she said. 'I'm behind in my assignments. Maybe later in the week.' Hating the lie, but unable to tell him the truth. Not yet.

That evening, while Cora sat in the waiting room, the doctor sent Annie into an adjoining toilet with a small plastic cup, and pulled blood into a syringe from a vein in Annie's arm. 'Phone me in three days,' she said. 'I should have a result by then.' But at that stage, Annie knew. She knew from the continuing absence of her period, and the queasiness she'd begun to feel on waking in the morning – and when the doctor confirmed her suspicions

on the Thursday, her initial feeling was one of relief that the uncertainty was finally over.

But what now? What was to be done?

'It's OK,' Cora said. 'Whatever you decide, I'll support you – but you must tell Jason. He needs to know.'

She was right. He had to be told. So that evening, Cora having gone out with Tim, who'd taken the place of Sean, Annie waited until Jason arrived to take her to the disco. She brought him into the sitting room where she'd lit the fire, and she sat him down on the couch.

And then she told him.

'You can't be,' he said. 'We've been using condoms. You can't be pregnant.'

'I am,' she said. 'They didn't work – or one of them didn't.' Waiting for him to tell her that it would be alright, that they'd sort it out together.

He got to his feet. He paced the floor, which didn't take long. Four steps one way, four the other. He sat again, took her hands. 'So what do we do now, Annie?'

We get married. You ask me to marry you and we get married and then we become parents, and we work it out. We make it work.

'I … don't know what we do.' She searched his face. 'What are you thinking? Tell me. Please tell me.'

He took a deep breath, holding her gaze. 'You're certain? There's no mistake?'

'Yes, I'm certain. I told you.'

'Would you – consider having a termination?'

She made to pull away her hands but he held on to them. 'Annie, I'm just asking. I need to know how you feel about this. What do *you* want to do?'

'I want to have it.'

He nodded slowly. 'You want to go through with it.'

'Don't you?'

Another breath. 'I— Look, I need some time to let this sink in.'

'You want me to get rid of it,' she said, the words shaking as they came out. 'It's your baby, Jason. It's our baby. Doesn't that mean anything to you?'

'Of course it does, Annie. It's just – it's a big thing to take in, you know? You must understand that. I mean, it's— This is a huge thing. This would change the rest of our lives. We need to take some time, and think about it.'

She didn't need to think about it. Terrifying as this new road ahead was, she knew she couldn't take the boat to England: everything in her rebelled at the thought.

He released her hands, rubbed his face hard. 'So you're saying you want to have it, and then what? Give it up for adoption?'

'No.'

'No? You'd … keep it?'

Why was it 'you' and not 'we'? Why had it suddenly become her situation, not theirs?

'I don't think I could give it up,' she said slowly. 'I don't think I could do that. Would you really want a stranger raising your child?'

A spark flew from the fire and landed on the carpet. He got up and stamped it out, and didn't sit down again. He put his hands into his pockets and looked into the fire. 'Does Cora know? Have you told her?'

'Yes.'

'Anyone else?'

'No.'

He chewed his bottom lip. 'Look, it's all— There's so much to consider right now. I'll drop around tomorrow after lectures, or I'll see you in college. We'll talk about this some more, OK? Let's sleep on it and talk again.' And when she made no response, 'Alright, Annie? Can we do that?'

'Yes. We can do that.'

He kissed her at the door, a soft touching of lips, no more. 'Sleep well,' he said, which showed how little he knew. She closed the door before he'd got as far as the gate – and the note he posted through the letterbox, sometime between Cora getting home from her date and both of them rising in the morning, came as no surprise.

Annie,

I've taken the decision to leave college. If you go ahead with this, I'll support you financially. I'll put my address at the bottom. Let me know where you want me to send money.

I'm sorry. It's just too soon. I'm not ready for this.

All my love

Jason

Julia

'OF COURSE I WILL,' SHE SAYS. 'LET ME HAVE YOUR LIST
of songs after breakfast, and I'll have a quick practice on the
piano here.'

'Thank you, my darling. You don't mind?'

'Not at all. I'm thrilled to be part of it.'

This kind of performance she can handle, this she loves. Like
when she sang for Annie and Eddie last night, with no bright
lights, no stage, no big crowd full of expectations. She was just
Julia Murphy at the piano – and in the church it will be even
better, with the attention focused on bride and groom, and Julia
merely providing the musical backdrop.

A fire glows in the kitchen stove. They sit at the table, the two of them, with slices of buttered toast topped with Annie's homemade lemon curd, and mugs of strong tea. Outside, the snow dazzles and gleams in the sharp winter sunshine. Waking up to find the world blanketed was a surprise, but Annie seems unfazed by it.

We're going ahead, she told Julia. It'll be different, but it'll happen.

You've spoken with Matt?

I have. He says he'll get here. I have no idea how – I don't think he has himself, but he seems confident that he can.

Julia can't say she knows Matt well, although he's always been part of the background of this place. When she lived here she would hear him whistling his way in from the gate with the post in the mornings; if she spotted him out and about in his green van she'd get a cheery wave. His wife was still alive then, waiting with a buggy outside the school each weekday afternoon, sitting at the opposite end of a pew to Matt in church on Sundays, their little growing family slotted between them.

And later, when adult Julia would fly back from France for a visit, she remembers Annie collecting his motherless children from the school and taking them back to her house for a few hours to play with whoever she was fostering then. Helping him out in his time of need, doing what she could for him.

He's still the local postman, still driving the lanes and roads of his area, still delivering the postcards and the letters and the packets – but now he's a lot more than that.

Matt McCarthy, Annie wrote in a letter at the beginning of the summer. The postman. You'll remember him, I'm sure. We've reached what I suppose you'd call an understanding. In fact, we're getting married! We're thinking we might do it on my birthday in December – and Julia had to put down the letter and try to recall him with Annie, try to pick out any hints that might have been there, and marvel that she'd noticed nothing. It must have been slow, she decided. A slow blossoming, a gradual dawning on both of them.

'How did he propose?' she asks now. 'You never said. Tell me to mind my own business if you like.'

Annie shakes her head, laughing. 'He didn't propose – I did! He's the most laid-back person I know – if I'd waited for him to do it, I'd have been drawing the pension.'

'Really? So how did you know? I mean, you've always been friends with him – when did it change?'

Annie takes her time with this. The smile is still on her face, and in her voice, when she eventually responds. 'I think I knew for a long time, actually. I mean, nothing was ever said, but I loved being in his company, and I knew he felt the same … and then one day, I don't know why, I imagined what it would be like if he wasn't around anymore, and the thought of that was so awful, so sad and lonely, that I realised where we'd got to. So I rang him and asked if he wanted to go for a walk, and he did. And somewhere along the way' – she lifts a shoulder, lets it fall – 'I suggested that we get married.'

'Just like that.'

'Just like that.'

'And how did he take it?'

Another laugh. 'He stopped walking. He frowned at me for the longest time, as if he was trying to figure me out, and I became convinced that I'd got it wrong, and that I'd just made a giant fool of myself – and I was about to tell him I was only joking, and try to save the situation if I could, when he smiled and said it sounded like a good idea. And then I asked him why *he* hadn't thought of it, and he said because he wasn't half as smart as me. And I said, "Is that a yes?" and he said it was, and that was it. We went shopping for a ring the next day.'

Her face as she tells it – Julia can hardly bear the soft, gentle, lovely happiness in it, and the cruel contrast with her own situation.

'What about you?' Annie asks then, following her into her thoughts. 'How are things with your relationship?'

She knows about Jean-Luc. She knows because Julia told her, unable to pretend, not to Annie, that there was nobody. She knows he exists, and that he's the music producer behind Julia's CD, and that he and Julia have been involved for years. She doesn't know about his wife, and his two children, and his promises to Julia that increasingly ring hollow.

'Things are …' She stops, tempted to tell the truth. Annie would listen, and understand, and only offer advice if it was looked for. Telling her, letting out all her frustration and disappointment and hurt, would be such a relief – but she can't do it. Not today, not on the day that belongs to Annie, and to Matt. 'Things are fine. He's fine.'

'Any sign of him putting a ring on your finger?'

The words sting. She must raise her cup and drink, she must hide how much they sting – and Annie reacts instantly. 'Oh, pet, I'm sorry. It's absolutely none of my business. It's between both of you. Forget I opened my big mouth.'

'No, I don't mind you asking.' She pauses, searching for a response that will straddle truth and fiction. 'No plans for the moment,' she says, as brightly as she can. 'You'll be the first to know.'

But she won't – because it will never happen.

The thought is there, suddenly there, bringing with it a swoop of despair. She pushes it away swiftly and takes an envelope from her shirt pocket – as good a time as any to produce it, and turn the conversation in a new direction.

'I'm not sure,' she says, 'if this is a birthday or a wedding present – probably a bit of both.'

Annie shies away from it. 'Oh, what? I told you I didn't need a thing!'

'It's not something you need, it's something I wanted to give you – and as you'll probably share it with Matt, I suppose it's more of a wedding gift.'

Annie accepts it, still tutting. She opens it, and exclaims at the voucher and booklet she finds within. 'Oh Julia, it's far too much, you shouldn't have spent that on me!'

'You're worth every cent. You can find a nice hotel in the booklet when you feel like a break. I fancy the one in Wicklow, with the spa.'

Annie reaches out and touches Julia's cheek with the back of her hand. 'You're too good, you know that? You're full of

kindness. Thank you so much, my darling – that man in France doesn't know how lucky he is.'

And before Julia can think of a response, the front door knocker is thumped repeatedly, and when they investigate they find a triumphant Cora on the doorstep, swaddled in a padded coat that meets the top of her wellingtons, and cradling a black bin bag.

'Told you I'd make it!' she cries, passing the bag to Annie so she can embrace Julia. 'Our superstar is here!' Over her shoulder, Julia sees Cora's husband Dan leaning against the gatepost, smiling and waving and calling out happy birthday to Annie, and wearing what looks like fishing waders under his coat.

'He's a bit wrecked,' Cora tells them. 'He had to piggy-back me here. I thought we could come on the tractor, but it kept getting stuck so we had to think again.'

'Oh, no – poor Dan. Won't he come in for a cuppa?'

So he does, shedding the waders at the door – and while they're waiting for the kettle to boil again, Eddie and then Steph appear. Annie goes on a hunt and locates a battered packet of birthday candles left over from her fostering days, and they stick one in each chunk of the cake that didn't survive the journey from London, and after they've sung 'Happy Birthday', Annie blows them all out.

And before the tea is drunk, the cake is gone.

Steph

'IT'S ME AGAIN,' SHE SAYS, HATING THE FALSE brightness in her voice, knowing he'll hear it too. 'It's just after eleven, and we've had breakfast – which was actually mostly birthday cake that started out as the top tier of the wedding cake, but the guy who brought it had a motorway skid, and it got damaged, long story! – and we're all getting ready for the wedding now. You should see the snow that fell here last night – it's unreal! The roads are all out of commission, so lots of people won't make it, but it's going ahead anyway – which is a good job, considering I came such a long way for it!'

No. She shouldn't have mentioned that.

'Annie's so happy I'm here,' she says. 'She really is. She's so excited for today, even though it's going to be nothing like the day she planned. She's just happy to be getting married.' What else? 'I hope you're OK, Gar. Please don't be mad, please get in touch. Try to understand that this wasn't—'

A beep sounds, so she stops talking. Did he hear his phone ringing? Did he see her name and ignore it? Is he about to delete her message now, without even listening to it?

It's lunchtime in Greece. She pictures him assembling a salad in the kitchen, washing leaves in water from their well, cutting feta into rough cubes, slicing cucumbers and tomatoes and onions, tossing in olives. She sees him in the space behind her eyes, shirtsleeves rolled to his elbows, black linen shorts, feet bare. Hair still damp from the shower he would have had after the morning session.

If she was there instead of here they'd have showered together, and she'd be helping him now. Slicing bread, mixing oil and vinegar, putting out bowls and cutlery and napkins. Leaning in for a kiss each time she passed him.

They'll be OK. He'll ring later, or tomorrow. He might be waiting till after the wedding, just to make a point. He won't keep this up.

She tosses her phone onto the unmade bed and stoops to see her head and shoulders in the mirror on the wall that's still hung at a child's height. She gathers her hair into a bunch at the nape of her neck. It's too long and too heavy, especially in summer, but Gareth likes it this way. Likes her nails long too, and drop

earrings rather than the studs she prefers. But they're only small things, easy ways to keep him happy.

She'll get him a bottle of Glenfiddich in Duty Free. He likes Glenfiddich, and it's nowhere on the island. She'll have to wait till Paris, since she's not checking in a bag. She'd bring him aftershave too, but Tom Ford costs a bomb, even in Duty Free, and coming here cleaned her out, pretty much, even with the cheapest flights she could find.

That'll be another thing. He'll want to know where she got the money to travel. She'll have to lie and say Annie paid, rather than admit to the cash she sets aside each week from her salary at the pottery shop, and lodges quietly to the bank account she had before she met him. She calls it her emergency money, her just-in-case money – and hasn't it come in handy now?

She opens the little wardrobe and lifts out the dress she packed for the wedding. Will it do? It'll have to. Not warm enough, she knew it wouldn't be, but it's her only dress with sleeves. She picked it up in a flea market in Berlin, partly because she loved its caramel colour and crossover top, and partly because she knew its jersey fabric would travel well.

Because she was still a nomad then, still searching for something she couldn't name. Putting down no roots, taking whatever job she could find to pay for room and food while she figured out if she liked the place well enough to stay longer, and if not, moving on. Making few friends, and keeping none. If she'd known she was going to wind up living on an island where jersey was too warm most of the year, she'd probably have ditched the dress somewhere.

Wouldn't wear it much anyway, even if it wasn't too warm. Gareth doesn't like the colour on her.

She strips off jeans and jumper, and pulls the dress over her head. She'd forgotten how comfy it is, how soft and swirly. She goes to her rucksack and takes out the black sandals Gareth bought her when they went on a trip to Athens last year. Higher in the heel than she'd normally go for; she'd never have picked them up if he hadn't drawn her attention to them.

Try them on, he said, and she did, more for the laugh than anything, but he liked them on her – Sexy, he whispered, just loud enough for the salesperson to overhear – so she didn't demur when he took them to the cash desk. She wears them when they go out to dinner, usually the night after a group has left. They're not terribly comfortable, and negotiating the rutted path around their neighbourhood is a real challenge, but she wants to show him she appreciates his gift. And they're coming in handy now, aren't they? Although how she's going to walk through the snow in them is a whole other question.

There's a tap at her door. 'Come in,' she says, dropping the sandals onto the bedside rug. Time enough to put them on.

Annie appears, wearing a trouser suit in the fresh green of an apple. 'Look at you!' she says. 'Beautiful dress.'

'It's only from a flea market.'

'Oh stop that, it doesn't matter. It's perfect on you.'

'… You look gorgeous, Annie.'

She does. Her short hair shines, her face glows. Happy, Steph thinks. She looks truly happy.

Matt would never tell her what to wear, or what not to. The

thought flies through Steph's head – she feels disloyal, and banishes it. Every man is different. 'Happy birthday,' she says. 'I don't have a present for you.'

'What – didn't you bring me a beautiful bowl? I don't need separate presents.' Annie crosses to the bed and sits. 'One thing,' she says, 'I want to ask you,' and Steph immediately feels everything clench up in her.

'Don't ask,' she says, because she knows what's coming.

'Just for me. On my wedding day. On my birthday wedding day. Just read it.'

'Annie, that's not fair. Don't. Please don't.'

Silence. Annie sighs, runs her hands along the thighs of her green trousers.

'I can't, Annie. Really I can't. Not even for you.'

'OK.' She gets to her feet. 'I'll leave it so. But if you change your mind –'

'I won't. I'm sorry.'

Annie smiles. 'I'm sorry too, but we won't fall out over it. I just have to keep trying, you know that.'

'You don't. You *have* tried, you've done your best. You should just throw it out and forget about it.'

Annie gives a small sad shake of her head. 'I'm a stubborn old thing though – and an awful busybody. And sometimes things aren't what they seem. I learnt that a long time ago when I was young and foolish, more foolish than you.'

Steph makes no response.

'OK,' Annie says. 'OK.' Resting a hand briefly on Steph's shoulder before moving to the door. 'Julia has gone to the church

with Cora – she wants to try out the organ. I told you the usual lady had to cancel, did I?'

'You said it downstairs.'

'Aren't we lucky we have Julia?'

Steph pulls her hair back into a bunch. 'Should I put it up? I have a clip.'

A beat passes. 'Try it up,' Annie says, and Steph gathers it into the clip as best she can, and Annie pronounces it perfect. 'I'd better go: poor Eddie is tackling the washing-up on his own. Follow me down when you're ready.'

'I will.'

Left alone, she paints on eyeliner and mascara, and pats shimmering powder onto her cheeks. She blots lipstick with a tissue and dots perfume onto wrists and behind ears.

And all the way through, she tells herself she's got nothing to feel guilty about. He deserted her, and now he wants forgiveness, and a chance to explain himself, or whatever is in the letter. Well, he won't get it, no matter how many times Annie urges her in that direction. She'll never forgive him, never. He doesn't deserve forgiveness. Whatever Annie says, sometimes things are exactly what they seem.

She sits on the side of the bed, trying to banish her bleak mood. It's Annie's day: she must try to be happy for her. She won't bring her phone to the church, or she'll be checking for a message every few minutes. She'll leave it here, set Gareth aside for a few hours, and maybe when she looks again there'll be something to see.

She should go down and help with the washing-up – Annie

shouldn't have to work today. But still she sits, in the dress that's too light, with the unsuitable sandals waiting to be put on. Still she sits, looking out at the patch of pale blue sky that is all she can see from the side of the bed.

Still she sits, wishing with all her heart that she could feel happier.

Eddie

WHEN THE TOP TIER OF CAKE HAD BEEN EATEN HE scrambled eggs, and Annie made more toast. Cora's husband went home directly after that to see to his cattle, and Steph wandered back upstairs. Preoccupied, subdued. He wondered again what circumstances had led to her ending up in this house, with a mother who wasn't her birth one.

Now he and Annie are alone, Cora and Julia having left for the church, Julia in wellingtons Annie found for her in the shed. My stash, she said, any size you like. She's scrubbing the egg saucepan in her wedding clothes. Eddie said he could do it, but

she shushed him and took off her green jacket and rolled up the sleeves of her blouse.

He senses a different feel to things today. He senses something – is it recklessness? – in the air, as if the usual rules have been suspended, and they're free to do whatever they want. Maybe it's the unexpected heavy snowfall, or the wedding, or Annie's birthday. Or maybe it's all three, mischievously conspiring to stir them all to bad behaviour. He's never turned down the chance to behave badly.

He loves snow, always did. He loves the way it muffles sound, scattering silence as well as whiteness over everything. Snow in London isn't the same, millions of tramping feet robbing it quickly of its softness, car tyres turning it to brown slush almost before it has a chance to settle – but here in the village it has full rein, nothing to disturb it in the garden outside the kitchen window but the tiny tracks of bird feet, nothing to ruin it.

He might make a snowman before the day is out. Julia might help him.

'Did we ever have snow like this when I was with you?' he asks Annie now, and she pauses to recollect.

'Not this heavy, I'd say – but I think maybe one year there was enough for a bit of fun.'

She couldn't be expected to remember. So many years in this house, so many different kids to look after. 'You fostered for a long time, Annie.'

A soft smile as she resumes her scrubbing. 'I did. Thirty-six years.'

'And did you always want to do it?'

'No.' Turning the pot under the running tap. 'I wanted to be a teacher, but … it wasn't to be.'

He thinks she would have made a good teacher. She'd have been patient with kids who gave cheek, or kids who struggled to learn. She'd have been the kind of teacher who preferred to reward good stuff than punish bad.

She sets the saucepan on the draining board and turns to look at him. 'I started in college but it didn't work out, so I came home.'

Failed her exams, maybe failed the repeats too. He won't ask.

'And while I was trying to figure out what to do with the rest of my life I got talking with an old teacher – she'd taught me in sixth class.' She pauses, looking somewhere beyond him now. Hands braced on the edge of the sink, reddened from the hot water.

'Brenda, her name was, Brenda Galvin. She was lovely. She'd grown up in this house. She never married, never moved out. She lived with her parents till they died, and then was on her own after that. I'd see her around the village after I moved on to secondary, and she'd always stop and ask me how I was doing, like she was really interested, you know? And after I gave up college I met her by chance one day. We had a chat, and she told me how sorry she was that I wasn't going ahead with the course.' Pulling the plug from the sink, watching the water draining out. 'And then she offered me a job.'

'What kind of job?'

'She said she wanted to open a playschool, here in this house, but she needed someone to help her.' She breaks off,

wiping her hands on the little kitchen towel. 'She was sick, you see. She'd given up her teaching job because of it, but she still wanted some contact with children. She wasn't able to do a lot – she tired easily, but she told them stories, and they loved her. When she got too sick to keep going we had to close the playschool, and then I looked after her here in the house for as long as I could.'

She falls silent, gazing out the window. He dries the remainder of the dishes silently, wanting more of the story he's never heard, a part of Annie's life before he knew her.

'And when she died, she left me the house in her will.' Half to herself, so quietly he barely heard.

He'd never thought to question her ownership of the place. It was always just Annie's, a rambling old farmhouse with room enough for up to four kids at a time. Shabby now certainly, money needing to be spent on it, like she said. Doors that stuck in cold weather, taps too. Uncertain plumbing, creaking floorboards, draughty windows, uneven walls, but always, and still, a place you loved coming to.

'I remember the first time I opened the door again, after the will had been read and I'd been given the keys. Brenda had spent her last few weeks in a hospice, and I'd been calling in here every few days to water her plants, and open the windows for an hour to air the place. But it was still her house then, and now it was mine. I remember how empty it felt – I suppose it was the knowledge that she'd never be back to it … I remember thinking that I wanted to use it in some way that would honour her memory, and her kindness to me.'

She pulls down the sleeves of her blouse and fastens their buttons. She reaches for her jacket and slowly puts it on.

'I could have opened the playschool again, but a woman at the other end of the village had started one when we closed ours, and I didn't think there'd be demand in the area for two. I liked children, though. I'd always liked them. It's why I wanted to be a teacher. So I thought about it for a while, and wondered if I could be a foster parent. I felt it was something Brenda would have approved of. I thought she'd like if I filled her house with children.'

She turns to look at him again. 'I was … upset, after leaving college. My future was all up in a heap, I felt … lost. But I made the right choice, Eddie. You and all the others were a blessing. You helped me to find my way again. And you were so sweet, such a good little boy – but honestly I loved all the children who passed through my hands, even the ones who were a bit … harder to manage.'

A beat passes. In the face of her disclosures he's tongue-tied, but he feels some comment is called for. 'I was lucky,' he says, conscious of the heat rising in his neck, spreading to cover his cheeks. 'To get you as a foster mother, I mean.'

'No, you deserved it, pet.'

'My father—' He breaks off. He can't. He can't say it.

'It's still not easy with him?'

He gives a shrug. It's her wedding day. 'It's OK, really,' he says. 'It's better when I'm living away, and we only meet up the odd time.'

Annie's smile is full of sympathy. 'Families,' she says.

'Families,' he agrees. 'Francey is brilliant though.'

'She certainly is.' She glances then at the clock above the window. 'Look at that – time is moving on. Julia and Cora shouldn't be long.'

Almost eleven o'clock. An hour, a little more, to the ceremony. 'What about the cake?' he asks. 'Should I bring it across to the community hall before the church?' He'd been going to drive the short distance with someone carrying it in the passenger seat, but that's out of the question now. He'll have to walk with it, which could be tricky.

'Leave it where it is,' Annie replies. 'I don't have the keys of the hall – we'll have to get them from Father Dennis. We'll sort it out after the church, plenty of time.'

She's very calm for a bride-to-be. Maybe older brides don't stress so much. A thought occurs to him, making him grin.

'What?'

'I'm just thinking – at the rate I'm going, I'll be your age when I get married.'

'Oh you will not – I bet you have lots of girlfriends!'

'That's just it – I have lots.'

'Nobody special?'

'Nope.'

'I'll have to find you someone,' she says, and he laughs and tells her to go ahead.

Just then they hear the front door opening, and Julia appears. Cheeks and nose rosy from the cold, hair swaddled in a big orange scarf. 'I'm back,' she announces.

'How's the organ?'

'Fine, it's got a lovely tone. It's actually a beautiful day out there – and I have a surprise.' She advances into the room to reveal two green bottles. 'I left them in the car last night, so they're nice and chilled.'

At the sight of them, Annie's face lights up. 'Champagne!'

'Duty Free's best.'

'Oh Julia, you shouldn't have! I love it, but it makes me terribly tiddly!'

'In that case, you'll be severely rationed – we don't want you disgracing yourself going up the aisle.' She opens the fridge and finds room for the bottles. 'Right, give me ten minutes to get myself ready – and you too, Eddie. Has Cora gone upstairs?'

'Cora? Wasn't she with you?'

'She left the church before me. She said she had to drop in somewhere on her way back here—' and just then Cora shows up, turning the key that's been left in the front door, exclaiming at the mention of champagne, tut-tutting at Annie's rolled-up sleeves, ushering Julia and Eddie up the stairs – and fifteen minutes later they've all reassembled, and Steph has shown up too.

Eddie wears his only decent suit – well, his only suit, full stop. Serviceable navy, cheap and cheerful, as Francey would say. His interview suit, for all the good it's done him. Dry-cleaned, all jacket buttons present and correct, clean white shirt. As good as it gets.

'You look smart,' Steph tells him, as Julia uncorks the champagne.

'So do you.'

He loves how she's caught up her hair, and how some of it has already escaped. Sexy-messy. The dress suits her. A shade darker than the pale colour of her hair, the fabric crossing over itself on top to sculpt her shape. She's less curvy than the women he usually goes for, but there's something very cute about her. Look at her sandals though, high strappy things – how will she walk to the church without ruining them, or getting frostbite?

She spots his downward glance, makes a face. 'I think I'll have to borrow some wellies from Annie's collection – or find a pair of stilts. I'm never going to make it to the wedding in these silly things.'

'I'll carry you,' he says, half joking – but when it comes to it, when he, Julia and Steph are about to set off at a quarter to noon, and feeling the bubbles of a glass and a half of what's probably very decent champagne dancing inside him, he scoops her up – she's light as a feather – and drapes her over his left shoulder, ignoring her giggling protests, and transports her in that fashion all the way down the snowy street to the church.

Annie

'ANNIE – COME OUT HERE, QUICK!'

Cora, on the landing. What new calamity now? Annie lowers her blusher brush and pokes her head out of the bathroom, and Cora beckons her to the front window. 'Quick – you'll miss them!'

She hurries across the landing and looks out, and sees her husband-to-be and his best man ambling along the street – or rather, travelling eight feet or so above the street. They're sitting astride a giant farm horse, plenty of room for both of them on its broad back, the animal clopping easily and steadily through the snow.

A horse. One of Peadar's working horses. Of course.

Both men wear dark suits, and wellingtons. She thinks of them steering the animal along the rutted lane that leads to both their houses, with every chance of a stumble that could have had disastrous consequences for all three of them. And even after they got onto the main road they could still have hit a pothole, and gone tumbling. He could have been killed, both of them could. She could have been burying him instead of marrying him.

'Well, if that isn't romantic,' Cora says. 'Your knight in shining armour.'

He doesn't look remotely like a knight, in armour or out of it. He's nowhere near tall enough, or toned enough, to merit that title. He sits bolt upright and hangs on tightly to Peadar's waist. Probably terrified: heights were never his thing.

But he's doing it for her, which is about as romantic as it gets. And as she looks out he turns his head and finds her, and gives her a broad, triumphant smile that causes her sixty-year-old insides to melt.

They follow the progress of the two as they make their way along the street. They watch people coming out of houses to cheer them on with waves and shouts and clapping. They'll remember this, she thinks, when the wedding is done and they've settled into their Mr and Mrs routine. When they wake some morning, or sit side by side on the patio to enjoy a summer evening, or walk the quiet roads together. One of them will say, 'Remember the horse' – and that will be enough to set the two of them off.

'Ruthie,' she says. Ruthie, who was so looking forward to it, will miss all this. Ruthie, who was to have walked ahead of Annie up the aisle, in the blue dress she picked out herself when Annie took her shopping a month ago. Not flattering in the least, shiny and fitted and making her look far bulkier than she is, but the one she wanted, the one she'd feel beautiful in.

'Ruthie is already landed,' Cora says. 'Peadar brought her to Father Dennis's house earlier.'

'On the horse?'

'Yes. I had to keep you in the kitchen so you wouldn't see.'

'How did you know?'

'Matt rang me.'

Annie tries to imagine thirty-seven-year-old Ruthie sitting up behind her brother on the big animal, and can't. Then again, she might well have delighted in it.

'And what else,' Annie demands of her friend, 'are you not telling me? What else has everyone been plotting and planning?'

'Well, I'm hardly going to answer that, am I?'

'But you can't keep a secret. You never could.'

'Maybe I'm learning.' Cora takes Annie's arm and steers her back to the room where she spent her last night as a single woman. 'Now, have you got everything sorted?'

'Nearly. Will you fasten my necklace?'

The necklace is her mother's eternity ring on the fine gold chain that Annie found for it after her mother died. When it's around her neck she takes up the ridiculous little bag she borrowed from Cora that barely has room for her lipstick, and the card she wrote her vows on, and the shard of sea glass

she found on a long-ago beach that she's bringing along as her something blue. Her something new is the trouser suit that amazed her when she put it on – she'd never have thought of green but Cora had insisted she try it, and Cora had been right.

Downstairs they pull on the wellingtons that sit waiting – thank goodness she hadn't thrown out the collection she'd amassed over the years – and deposit their shoes in the little satchel that Cora hitches onto a shoulder. 'You want to delay a while?' she asks. 'Be fashionably late?'

'No, I'd rather get going' – but just for a moment, she remains where she is.

'Cora.'

'What?'

'Thank you.'

'For what?'

'For everything.'

'Would you stop that' – but Cora's hug is tight, and in her embrace Annie thinks of the friendship that was born on a sunny Limerick day over forty years ago, and the sorrows and the laughter they have shared since then. She remembers her own great loss, and Cora and Dan's wedding day when the rain never stopped, and Cora's devastation when she miscarried two babies within a year of each other, and her joy when the third baby stayed safe, and became Annie's goddaughter.

She thinks of the day, full of trepidation, that she opened the door of this house to her first ever foster child, with Cora by her side to make sure everything went alright.

She remembers how she and Cora helped one another through their parents' final illnesses, and how they went off for a weekend to Killarney, just the two of them, halfway between their fiftieth birthdays. She recalls wanting Cora to be the first person she told when she and Matt got engaged, and how Cora burst into delighted tears at the news.

When they draw apart her eyes are shining. Cora produces tissues from her satchel, 'Stop – you can't cry till after the ceremony!' and blots carefully beneath Annie's eyes.

They emerge from the house and pick their way arm-in-arm along the street, past the neighbours who appear again to applaud the bride and wish her well, a village custom that's been around for as long as Annie can remember. They reach the church and enter the vestibule, and exchange wellingtons for shoes. Annie hangs back as Cora advances to the inner door and pushes it open just far enough to catch the eye of her husband Dan, waiting in the wings with Matt's daughter Ruthie, and summon them out. Dan has been drafted in to substitute for Annie's brother Ivan, who was unable after all to make it to the church and walk her up the aisle.

'Annie!' Ruthie rushes out and wraps her in a clumsy, excited embrace. 'I was on the horse with Peadar!'

'I heard, darling. Cora told me – and don't you look gorgeous in your new dress. Dan, thanks so much for stepping in.'

'No bother at all. You all set?'

'… I am.'

'I'm going to head up,' Cora whispers. 'Wait till I'm sitting before you start. I'm so happy for you, my friend.'

She gives Annie's hand a quick squeeze and opens the door fully. Annie watches her give a signal to Julia, seated behind the organ, before scurrying up the side aisle and settling into the second pew beside Eddie and Steph. Dan extends his bent arm and Annie threads hers through it, aware of a fluttering within her.

'Ready, Ruthie?' she asks, and Ruthie steps out in front of them, like they practised so many times.

Annie takes a breath, and then another. This is it. This is where one part of her life ends and another begins. This is what she's been looking forward to since the summer, what she wants more than anything. At the organ, Julia's hands are poised over the keys.

Wait, though.

Wait.

'Hang on,' she says. 'Just …'

She thinks of her beloved house, where memories are tucked into every nook, where she often fancies she hears in the hall the ghost-patter of quick, light footsteps, where door frames are marked with the nicks and scrapes of a hundred bumping suitcases, where the piano keys are yellowed from the prints of so many little fingers, where she can't look at a bed without remembering everyone, everyone who slept in it.

She thinks of Brenda who paved the way, and who didn't live long enough to realise how she rescued Annie, how she made it possible for her to piece together her fragmented heart and begin again.

Tonight she'll spend her last night under the ramshackle roof of the house that was Brenda's, when she and Matt will share the bed she's had to herself for over thirty-six years.

Time to let go, Annie. Time to let it all go now.

'OK,' she says. 'I'm ready.'

She squeezes Dan's arm as the music starts, as Ruthie starts her walk up the aisle in her shiny blue dress, as heads begin to swing around and people rise to their feet, as Matt McCarthy breaks off his conversation with his son to look down the church, to travel past the rows of pews and beyond his daughter, to find Annie O'Reilly.

Annie, then

SHE BROKE THE NEWS TO HER PARENTS IN THE LAST week of February, while she was home on midterm break. She waited until Ivan had left for work one morning, and before her father had begun to pack up his van.

'I need to tell you something,' she said. The three of them were still in the kitchen, her mother filling the twin tub as she sorted laundry, her father tamping tobacco into his pipe for the brief smoke he enjoyed after breakfast.

They both looked at her. Her heart was pounding so hard it hurt her throat. Now she had to say it, and face their reaction. Now she had to change everything that came afterwards.

'I'm going to have a baby,' she said.

In the immediate aftermath nobody spoke, nobody moved. The only sound was water rushing through the hose that ran from the kitchen tap into the drum of the washing machine.

And then her mother said, 'What?' Faintly, still holding one of Ivan's shirts, white with a thin blue stripe.

Annie didn't repeat it. There was no need.

'When?' Her mother again.

'July. The middle of July.'

More silence. They were counting, of course. She didn't dare look directly at her father.

'I'm sorry,' she said. Not directing it at either of them, just putting it into the room.

Her mother turned off the tap. She draped the shirt over the edge of the sink and dropped into a chair. 'How could you do this to us?' she demanded, and Annie remained silent because there was no answer to that question.

Her mother turned to her father. 'Have you nothing to say?'

He looked from her to Annie, his pipe unlit, his face unreadable. 'You'll give it up,' he said. 'Won't you?'

His voice full of defeat, of disappointment.

She had disappointed him. She forced herself to look at him. 'I don't want to give it up. I want to keep it.'

Her mother snorted. 'Well, you needn't think you're going to keep it here.'

'I wasn't. I'll have it in Limerick. You won't have to have anything to do with it if you don't want to.'

They'd worked it out, she and Cora. Between now and

175

June they were going to find someone, preferably in their neighbourhood, who would look after the baby when Annie returned to college in September. Her brother Ivan would lend her money, she was fairly sure. She'd pay him back when she could.

A few of the Limerick neighbours looked friendly – and a few did not, like the older woman who lived directly across the road, and who darted a fierce look at Annie whenever they encountered one another. Didn't approve of students maybe. They'd thrown just a single party since they'd moved in, for Cora's birthday – by the time Annie's had come around she was no longer in the mood for celebrating – but maybe one was all it took.

'What does the father have to say?' Her mother again.

The thought of Jason brought a fleeting image of his face that sliced like a blade through her. 'He's not involved.'

'What do you mean he's not involved? Of *course* he's involved!'

She curled her toes inside her shoes. 'He's not ... He doesn't want to be part of it. I don't have contact with him anymore.'

Better to say that, better not to give them a way to get in touch with him. Better not to mention the letter, the note, which was tucked into the pocket at the back of her diary that was meant to hold reminders of happy things, like photographs and cinema stubs and concert tickets. Better to make no mention at all of his note, with his address at the bottom of it.

'Were you forced?' her mother asked. 'Did he force himself on you, Annie? You can tell us.'

'... No.'

No forcing. How willingly she'd agreed to it, how ready she'd been to believe him when he'd told her he loved her. How trusting, how innocent. How stupid.

'Is he in the college? Is he a student?'

'No.'

It was no lie. He wasn't a student, not anymore. He'd left, just like that. She hadn't seen him again, although for a week, longer, after his note had dropped through the letterbox she'd looked for him, searched among faces in the college for his. She'd seen, or imagined she'd seen, his friends glancing at her, and she wondered what he'd told them, what slant he'd put on things.

'So what about your degree?' her mother asked. 'Are you just going to give all that up?'

'No, I still want to be a teacher. I'll sort something out.'

If she could find someone to look after the baby she'd stay in college, returning in September as normal. She'd already cut her spending down to the absolute minimum: from now on she'd have to set aside every penny she could.

'You'll still pay, won't you?' she asked. 'For college, I mean, and for my accommodation.'

Her mother sniffed. 'We'll have to see about that,' she said, and Annie had to hope it was just an initial reaction. She had to qualify, had to get a teaching job if she wanted to be able to raise a child with a degree of financial security.

Not a penny was she going to ask Jason for. Not a single penny.

I can help, Cora had said. I can chip in – but Annie didn't

want that. In standing by her, and promising to stick with her, Cora was already doing more than Annie could ever repay. Cora was all for asking Jason to help – it's the least he can do, and he *has* offered – but Annie would rather starve than ask him for a single thing.

'I can't believe it,' her mother said. 'Your whole future ahead of you, and now this.'

'It's still ahead of me. Nothing needs to change.'

'Nothing needs to change?' Her mother rose abruptly to her feet. She gave a rough, angry twist to the tap, sending water gushing once more into the twin tub. 'You haven't a clue, Annie! A baby changes everything! *Everything!*'

Annie took in the hard pursed set of her mouth, the clench of her shoulders. She saw her father's quieter dismay, his hands folded over the stem of his unlit pipe. She'd caused that: she'd taken away their contentment.

'I'm sorry,' she said again. 'I'm really sorry. I won't come home at Easter, or afterwards. I wouldn't want to … embarrass you.'

By Easter, which was late that year, she'd be five and a half months gone, and according to the book she'd bought, probably starting to show. She could hide it with baggy shirts and jumpers, but someone might realise, and it would take only one for the entire village to hear.

'I won't come home again until …'

Until what? Until when? Would they ever want her back, now that she'd presented this bombshell to them? Would they ever accept their first grandchild?

Since her pregnancy had been confirmed she'd taken to spending her free periods in the college library, siting herself away from other students, surrounding herself with books so nobody would bother her. She'd always enjoyed studying; thankfully, she still found herself able to get lost in an assignment. She would work hard, and get through the rest of her first year. After that, she'd figure it out.

She'd welcomed the two weeks of teaching practice just before Christmas, forcing her to push Jason's abandonment of her from her head. She'd thrown herself into lesson planning, and had done her best to engage her class of twenty-seven eight-year-old boys, and she felt it had gone mostly well. Thankfully, her supervisor had agreed. You've got a lovely rapport with them, Annie, she told her. I'll be giving you a special commendation in my report.

It helped, a little – but once it was over, once her charts and lesson plans had been put away, her fears and doubts and uncertainties had come rushing back. It was tough: it had been nearly impossible to try to pretend to her family over Christmas that nothing was wrong. It didn't make things easier that she felt queasy most mornings, the nausea lasting sometimes until lunchtime. Are you alright? her mother would ask, frowning, and Annie would paint on a bright smile and say, yes, yes, fine, and make a renewed effort to appear as if everything really was fine.

By the time she was back in college the morning sickness was abating, but there was still the great unknown hanging heavy over her, still so many unanswered, and unanswerable,

questions – and of course, still the appalling prospect of having to break the news to her parents.

At least that was behind her now. 'I'll let you take it in,' she said to them. 'We can talk about it later if you want.' She left the room. She took her coat and scarf from the hall and walked to the lake that was situated half a mile of country lanes from the village, and sat on a bench by water that ruffled in the stiff breeze, and tried to still the fears that had taken up residence in her head.

Word would get out, of course. Even if she never brought the baby back here, the news would eventually find its way from Limerick.

At some stage, Matt would hear it.

The thought of her being diminished in his eyes killed her, despite him having pulled away from her since their lunchtime conversation, and the mention of Jason. They never did the walk around the city that Annie had promised him: she'd had no further contact with him during the remaining two weeks of his training, no repeat offer of a lift home at the weekends. As cheery as ever when they met up in the pub on Saturday nights, but she knew something had been lost, and mourned it.

And just after Christmas he started working in the post office in Ennis, and he wasn't around as much when Annie met up with the gang, and she missed seeing him.

And now he had a new girlfriend.

I believe she's from Kilkenny, her mother told her at the end of January. She works with him. I'm glad he's found someone; I always liked Matt. And her friends, when Annie questioned

them that evening, confirmed it. She was lovely, they told her. Mary, her name was. He'd brought her out to meet them during the week.

And what of her old teacher Miss Galvin, who stopped to chat anytime they met on the street, who'd presented Annie with a pen on hearing that she'd got her college place, and told her how proud of her she was? Call me Brenda, she'd said. I think you're old enough by now – and Miss Galvin makes me feel ancient. What would she think when she heard Annie's news?

A baby changes everything, her mother had said, but Annie already knew this. Before it was even born a baby had taken Jason away, and caused Annie to cry a river of after-dark tears, and destroyed her parents' trust in her. You haven't a clue, her mother had said, and she was right about that.

But …

She was going to be a mother. She was going to give birth to a brand new person, and she would cherish it because it was innocent of any wrongdoing, and because it had come from love, if only her love. If people turned their backs on her when they found out, so be it. She would care for her child to the very best of her ability, and when the day came when it asked about its father, she would tell the truth. She would always tell the truth.

By the time she qualified, her child would be two. Maybe by then her parents would have become reconciled: maybe they'd have accepted their grandchild. Maybe Annie could apply for a position in the local school – Brenda had suggested it, the last

time they'd spoken. Rory Dunphy will be retiring that summer, she'd said. I know they'd love to have you, Annie.

It might just work out, if the school was willing to consider a teacher with a baby and no husband.

She hadn't a clue though. She had no idea what was ahead of her. But she was a good student, and she would learn what she needed to know. She'd cope.

Julia

HOW MANY WEDDING GUESTS? THEY'D ASKED ANNIE
last evening, and Annie had said seventy-four. From her seat
at the organ, located just inside the back door, Julia counts just
eighteen, including Eddie and Steph, and herself. There's Dan
and Cora, and Cora's daughter Gilly, whom Julia has met a
few times, with what must be her husband and their little girl.
A group – two men, three women, two young boys – whom
she takes to be family members of Matt's. More expected – he
has seven children and a few in-laws and more grandkids –
but clearly the rest have been unable to make it. Three other

183

women sit together whom she can't identify, maybe friends of Annie's.

Being in the little church again has brought Julia back to her childhood Sundays, when she and Annie's other children would sit with her in their good clothes, waiting for the part of the mass when Father Dennis, who was a young curate then, brought all the village children up to stand around the altar for the Our Father.

The guests hardly glanced Julia's way as they entered the church, more preoccupied, by the look of it, with discovering who else had managed to get here, and who was missing. She felt blissfully anonymous as she ran softly through the snatches of Bach and Mendelssohn and Chopin she had picked out to provide the backdrop before Annie's arrival.

Now, with the ceremony underway, she plays 'Here Comes the Bride' as Annie processes up the aisle on Dan's arm – specially requested, Annie told her, by her bridesmaid Ruthie. She watches as Matt accepts his bride, and as his daughter Ruthie and Cora's Dan take their seats in the front pew. She sits through the priest's welcome and opening prayers, and the readings by two of Matt's daughters, whom Julia correctly identified.

And as Annie and Matt get to their feet for the main event, Father Dennis directs the bride and groom to face one another, and to join hands. 'Dearly beloved,' he begins – and the familiar words, just those two words, make Julia's eyes swim with tears. She wipes them away as she listens to the age-old questions and responses. She watches rings being produced and exchanged,

and hears bride and groom promise to love one another for the rest of their days.

Directly after the burst of applause that follows the proceedings Julia begins 'Amazing Grace', chosen because it was the favourite hymn of Annie's mother, who died two summers earlier. At communion time she plays 'All Things Bright and Beautiful' as the few assembled souls file to the altar.

And then, in the immediate aftermath, in the small hiatus before Father Dennis starts the concluding prayers, when Julia should fold her arms and wait for her final piece as the happy couple make their way down the aisle, some instinct brings her hands again to the keys, and she finds herself playing the opening bars of 'Safe In Love', because it was inspired by Annie, in whose house she always felt safe, and loved.

Aware but not caring that she's blowing her cover, she begins to sing the song that's been played thousands of times on radio stations across the world, the song that she always ends a concert with because it strikes her as a good one to finish on. It sounds a little different now with the organ rather than the piano accompanying it, but before she gets to the end of the first line she sees heads swivel, and she hears the sibilance of puzzled whispers above the music. Is it her? she can almost hear them asking. Could it be her?

Clearly, Annie didn't tell the guests that Julia was going to be here today. Julia loves this, loves how protective Annie is of her privacy – but in this familiar safe place, among these friends of Annie's, she feels almost an eagerness to reveal her identity. It's

me, she's saying with her song. I'm Julia Murphy, I'm Julia M, and this is my tribute to Annie.

She catches Eddie grinning at her from his pew, and she sends him a return grin. And now Annie and Matt have turned too, and Annie mouths, 'Thank you', and Julia smiles as she sings.

The song ends, the closing prayers are said. The newlyweds disappear with Father Dennis to sign the register, and the murmur of soft conversations acts as an accompaniment to Julia's undertone riffs, her hands finding chords effortlessly as she keeps watch on the door to the sacristy, ready at the first sight of the couple to slide into the opening notes of 'What A Wonderful World', their choice to accompany them on their first walk as husband and wife.

She doesn't have long to wait. The couple's reappearance prompts a second enthusiastic burst of applause from the assemblage. They cross together to the podium and Matt approaches the mike, waiting until the clapping fades.

'On behalf of my wife and me,' he says – whoops, cheers – 'we'd like to thank you all for braving the elements and making it here. Sadly, we can't say the same for our caterer' – a collective disappointed groan – 'but the good news is that the drinks order was already sorted' – cheers, mostly male – 'and we do have a wedding cake, thanks to Eddie' – gesturing to the second pew, where Eddie rises to his feet and bows, to more applause – 'and since it seems to us that we might be too small a crowd to do justice to the community hall, we thought you might all join us in Annie's house instead for a glass or a cuppa and a slice of cake, and maybe a bit of a singsong. What do ye say?'

More cheering and clapping – and as they leave the altar and approach the aisle, Ruthie rushes from her seat to embrace both, to everyone's approval and merriment. Down the church they come, the three of them, halting every few steps to pose, smiling happily, in front of someone's raised phone as Julia's music, and soft singing, conjures up skies of blue and red roses too.

At the door of the church Annie blows a kiss to her. See you at home, she mouths, and Julia nods, and continues to play as bags and gloves and scarves are gathered up, as people follow the couple outside, some stealing stealthy glances in Julia's direction. Still wondering maybe, still not wholly certain that she is who she is.

And who is she, exactly? She's a singer and a songwriter with music running through her veins as surely as blood, but she's more than that. She's a fairly decent cook, and an avid reader, and a good listener, and a mediocre solver of crosswords, and a faithful friend.

She's also a mistress, in love with someone who will always put her second. She is richer than she ever imagined she would be, but achingly lonely. And does she not deserve to be happy?

Last night she slept more soundly than in months. Here in the village, in the house of the woman who took her in and loved and nurtured her, she feels protected from everything that makes her sad, and afraid. Oh, if she could only stay here. If she could only live here, and be Julia Murphy who likes to sing and play the piano.

'I think you're allowed to leave now.'

She turns to see Steph standing alone by the door, a coat of

Annie's draped across her shoulders, over the pretty dress she wears. She would look very good, Julia thinks, with a short blunt fringe to open up her small pretty face, and layers to rid the rest of her hair of its weight.

'Was that song one of yours? The one you played in the middle, I mean.'

'Yes. I wrote it for Annie – well, with her in mind.'

'I liked it. It was very sweet.'

Julia's been forgiven. Steph is trying to make amends for the sharpness of last night. 'Thank you. I'd be happy to send you a CD from Paris. I didn't bring any here.'

'Thanks, but we haven't got a player,' Steph replies. 'No mod cons in our house – we're lucky we have electricity.'

'I have a tour coming up,' Julia tells her. 'I'm going to be playing in Athens. I'm not sure of dates yet, but it'll be sometime near the end of January.'

'We might make it,' Steph says, 'if you let me know when.'

'I sure will – and I can sort a couple of tickets if you're coming. Give me your phone number, or email or whatever, back at the house.'

'Will do. Thanks.'

Eddie appears at the door, in the navy suit that somehow makes him seem younger. 'Piggyback?' he enquires, looking at Steph.

She laughs. 'If you don't mind.'

'Sandals,' he says to Julia, pointing at Steph's footwear, 'in the middle of December. She's been living in Greece too long.'

'They're my only dressy pair,' Steph protests. 'I thought I'd get away with it. I didn't reckon on the snow.'

'Come on then. Julia, good job on the music.'

'Thank you.'

'You coming back?'

'I'll follow you,' she says. She watches them exit the church together, and wonders if this weekend will herald a new romance. And then she remembers Steph mentioning someone in Greece – and for all she knows there's a girl back in London waiting for Eddie too.

She exchanges her shoes for the woolly socks and wellingtons that got her to the church. Nice to be going back to Annie's now, instead of the rather characterless community hall. She's gathering her bits and pieces when Father Dennis approaches from the top of the church, carrying his folded vestments over an arm and rattling keys. 'Well played, Julia,' he says. 'Not every church can boast a private recital by an international star.'

'No indeed – in fact, you're my first church.'

'Well, I think that might merit a plaque in due course. You can come back for the unveiling.'

She laughs. 'I'd be delighted.'

'Now let's go to Annie's and drink tea, or maybe something a little stronger to keep the cold out.'

They leave the building together. 'I'm going to drop these home,' the priest tells her at the bottom of the steps. 'You go ahead, I'll catch up with you.' He turns onto the little path that leads to his house in the adjacent grounds, and Julia makes her way through the snow towards the street.

And just inside the church gate, she stops dead.

For a second she wonders if she might be hallucinating – but she's not: she can hear the low, rough snort of its breath, she can smell the musk of it in the air. It's there, it's right there, standing by the wooden fence that separates Father Dennis's garden from the church. A big, shaggy, magnificent beast, very different from the horses of her teenage years – this one is built for work, not play – but she's just as mesmerised by its chestnut-coated beauty, its shaggy mane, its enormous legs.

She steps closer – and only then does she realise that someone is standing by the horse's head, largely hidden from her view by the bulk of the animal.

'Hello?'

At the sound of her voice the person, the man, pokes his head out and lifts a hand to shield his eyes from the harsh light of the winter sun. 'Hello there.'

She approaches, skirting the animal's hindquarters. 'You're the best man. You're Matt's son.'

'I am.' Crinkles about his eyes, but he's not old. Her own age, she thinks, or around that. Weatherbeaten from working outside. Wearing a grey suit that she suspects he's not often found in. Oats, she thinks, in the cupped palm he's holding beneath the animal's mouth. Well used to handling them, perfectly at ease as this one snuffles into the food.

'He's been busy this morning,' the man goes on. 'Brought the groom and the bridesmaid to the church. Needs his grub.'

Julia steps closer. 'Has he got a name?'

'Henry.'

'Hi, Henry.' She places a palm to the horse's neck, feels the ripple of muscle.

'You did the music in there,' the man says. 'Very nice,' and she realises that like Steph, and maybe quite a few others in this small rural community, he's never heard of Julia M.

'Thank you. You're a farmer?'

'I am, along with a few other things.' He brushes the last of the grains from his hands. 'Peadar is my name.'

She feels the calluses on his palm. 'I'm Julia.'

'Good to meet you. Friend of Annie's?'

'One of her foster children. Her very first.'

'Ah,' he says. 'The first of many. We might have met,' he goes on. 'Annie used to collect us from school after Mam died, and bring us back to hers. She always gave us biscuits and milk.'

'How old were you when your mother died?'

'Ten,' he says, and she thinks they must have met, if he's around her own age. She dimly remembers others in the house after school, even when Annie had a full complement of foster children. Some in the back garden kicking a ball around, others playing cards or draughts at the kitchen table.

'Henry is beautiful.'

He grins. 'My father tells me I collect horses like other folk collect cars.'

'How many do you have?'

'Only three so far. They work, they earn their keep. I'm old school – I have more faith in a horse than a tractor to plough a field.'

'I had a friend,' she says slowly, 'in boarding school.' Running

191

a hand over the rough mane. 'Her family owned a riding stables. I used to spend holidays there.'

He squints at her. 'You've ridden them then.'

'Yes, lots of times.'

He undoes the looped rope that anchors the horse to the fence. 'Fancy getting up on Henry, just as far as Annie's?'

'Oh! Well, I would fancy it, but I'm not exactly —'

And then she stops. Why not? Why not just do it?

'But he's so big, it's so high,' she says – and in answer he laces his fingers together and presents them to her. 'Grab onto his mane when you get up,' he says, 'Henry will take good care of you' – and she lifts a foot and places it in the cup of his hands, and he raises her effortlessly. With a small delighted cry she sails up high, high enough that she can swing her free leg over the folded blanket on the horse's back, gripping tightly to the mane to anchor her.

And just like that, she's on a horse again. Her dress hoicked well above her knees, a fair bit of thigh on show, what a sight she must look in the wellingtons – but she's there, and it's wonderful.

'You found a taxi!'

Father Dennis, emerging from his house. 'I did!' she laughs, as Matt's son steers the big animal away from the fence and turns him towards the gate. The little group makes its leisurely way back up the village street, the snow already starting to soften and melt in the sun. As they clop past houses and shops, as Julia instinctively adapts to the shifting movements beneath her, the beautiful rhythmical sway of the horse, she's

brought back to Eloise's house, and the stables behind it, and the animals they brushed and fed and loved, and rode at every opportunity.

And in the two minutes or so it takes them to reach Annie's house – too quickly, far too quickly – she feels truly and perfectly and wonderfully happy.

Eddie

THEY RESURRECT THE STOVE IN THE KITCHEN. IT'S NOT
a difficult task: over the winter months its fire is seldom allowed
to go completely out. They scurry about, collecting chairs from
the dining room that's rarely used, and the four cast-iron chairs
from the patio that Cora wipes dry and finds cushions for, and
more chairs, canvas but sturdy, from the shed.

Younger wives sit on husbands' knees. Small tables are
found and unfolded to service chairs lined up against the wall.
Somehow or other, everyone is accommodated.

Julia is formally introduced to the gathering by Annie,

and receives an enthusiastic cheer – 'I knew it!' one of Matt's daughters exclaims – and an immediate request for a song. 'Oh, leave her alone,' Annie tells them. 'She's on a weekend off, and I've already pressed her into service once today. Now, what are you all having to drink?'

'I wouldn't mind doing a song,' Julia puts in, prompting a fresh hurrah. She came back from the church on the back of the horse that had ferried Matt and his daughter there earlier. Eddie, on his way downstairs after shedding his suit jacket, happened to glance through the landing window and there she was, turning in at the gate, sitting tall and looking perfectly at ease on the huge animal's back. He rapped on the glass; she looked up and gave him a wave, clearly delighted with herself.

'I wrote this song three or four months ago,' she tells her audience. 'It's called "Broken Things", and this will be its first public performance.'

Silence falls, and she begins. The kitchen fills with her voice as she sings unaccompanied. The song is gently sad, telling of missed opportunities and lost dreams: listening to it, Eddie is reminded of his own ambitions, all the plans he had at twenty, and of how far he still is, now in his thirty-first year, from making them happen.

And then she sings the closing lines –

But nothing's over till it's over,
The fat lady has yet to sing,
Broken things can still be mended,
Who knows what tomorrow might bring?

– and listening to them, he feels a surge of – what? Fragile hope, maybe. Optimism, maybe. All not over yet, his dream still there. Maybe he's just going about it the wrong way. Maybe there's another road to be taken to make it come true.

The applause is loud. During it he steals a glance at Steph, standing with Annie by the worktop, both of them waiting to serve drinks. She's shed the ridiculous sandals, swapped them for a pair of chunky woolly socks that he guesses she didn't bring from Greece.

She weighs nothing at all. He could have carried her further than the church and back, much further.

Up close, he was able to inhale the interesting gingery scent of her hair, or maybe it was her perfume.

Drinks are doled out. Hot whiskey and hot port, wine and sherry. Tea and coffee, and hot water for a woman whose name Eddie has already forgotten, but who he thinks is a daughter-in-law of Matt's. Cidona for the only two of Matt's grandchildren who made it to the wedding, and for Cora's little granddaughter, and also for Matt's daughter Ruthie, who's served it with a slice of orange into which a cocktail umbrella has been stuck.

The heat begins to rise in the crowded room. Suit jackets are shed, ties loosened. Shoes are kicked off, wraps draped on backs of chairs. Conversations are loud, and punctuated with laughter. Cora's husband Dan and another man go out the back for a smoke. The sun shines on, turning more of the snow to water. Eddie wonders what the roads will be like for his trip back to England tomorrow, or if he'll even get going. Seems like

he's been here just five minutes, but already the weekend is half over. He's about to ask Annie if he should cut the cake when the front door knocker sounds, two sharp, loud thumps.

Conversations halt. Annie pauses in the act of refilling Ruthie's glass. 'Who could that be?'

Cora pushes back her chair. 'I'll go.'

They wait. Through the open kitchen door they hear the sound of her bright greeting, and a male's reply.

'That sounds like Ollie Barrett,' someone remarks.

'Ollie Barrett? What's he doing here?'

A small round man appears at the kitchen door, his head covered with a black woolly hat, a stainless-steel container cradled between his mittened hands. 'Hello, all. Congratulations to the newly-weds. I heard ye might be stuck for grub.'

Annie looks at him in astonishment. 'Ollie – what have you there?'

He crosses the room and deposits the container on the draining board. 'I have a rake of cod,' he announces. 'And there's sausages outside in a wheelbarrow, and chips to go with them – someone might help me bring them in while they're hot. I brought some plates as well, in case ye hadn't enough.'

Annie's face is a blend of delight and puzzlement as two of the men rise and head to the hall. 'But how did you know?'

'That one,' he says, pointing at Cora, who stands by the door. 'She came to me earlier and told me about your caterer letting you down. 'Tisn't exactly the gourmet fare you were expecting, but it'll fill the bellies.'

'I had to phone him from the church,' Cora adds, 'to give

him a head count, and let him know about the change of venue. Don't tell God.'

Annie envelops him in a hug. 'Ollie, thank you so much – we'll settle up later.'

'You will not – call it my wedding present.' He turns down an invitation to stay – 'That chipper won't run itself' – and disappears with an offer of dinner at Matt's house on his next night off. The food is distributed, cutlery and salt and vinegar and ketchup passed around.

All things considered, Eddie thinks, biting into a battered sausage, the cake now relegated from main course to dessert, this might just be the most original wedding he will ever attend.

Steph

'SO WHAT DO YOU DO WITH YOURSELF IN GREECE?'

She's lost track of the time. Champagne before the church was a mistake: it's left her with a dull, achy feeling in her head. The two glasses of red wine since then probably didn't help, or the fish and chips that seemed like a good idea when they arrived – her first chipper food in ages – but that now sits like a lump of concrete in her stomach, forcing her to turn down chocolate cake when it came around earlier.

She rubs her forehead. 'Sorry, what?' She's hemmed into a corner with someone's husband, whose breath smells like he

forgot to brush his teeth this morning. It's too hot in here, and too noisy. Other people have turned up, now that the snow is melting. Some of them, she could gather, were more of Matt's family. They spill now from the kitchen into the hall, with a few more sitting on the stairs when she went to the loo a while ago.

'I was wondering what you do in Greece. What job have you?'

'I work in a pottery shop, and I … help run a writer's retreat off-season.' Suddenly she's had enough. 'I think I need to get some fresh air.' Without giving him a chance to respond she turns and steps around people till she reaches the kitchen door. No sign of Annie, but her new husband is standing by the wall and chatting to Julia, who's flavour of the month with everyone today.

In the hall she finds Annie's long coat, buried beneath a load of others on the hallstand, and makes her way past knots of people to the rear of the house, not catching anyone's eye. There's a scatter of wellingtons by the back door: she pulls on a pair that are way too big, and slops outside.

The cold hits her like a physical thing, as it did when she stepped from the plane in Shannon. The sun has slipped away, taking much of the light with it and leaving a dark grey sky that's streaked with yellow and lavender. The snow is hanging around, still piled up at the sides of the garden and still sitting on the shed roof, but patchier in the middle of the lawn, grass beginning to show through.

She draws the coat around her shoulders and hunches into

it. She won't last long out here, but it's so good to feel the air on her hot cheeks. She turns to peer through the kitchen window, ready to duck if anyone sees her. She spots Eddie's head bobbing above the rest, and Matt's son who was best man and whose name she's forgotten, talking to Cora who is eating cake.

Hello, Cora had said to Steph this morning. You're back to us. Smiling, but not really, not properly. The hard kind of smile that let you know she didn't mean it. Probably thought Annie was mad to invite her to the wedding. Probably said as much to her. Cora believed in speaking her mind. Spoke it plenty when Steph lived here.

Don't talk to Annie like that, she'd snap, and Annie would shush her, trying to keep the peace like she always did. You shouldn't take it from her, Cora would insist, and Steph would laugh in her face and ask her what she was going to do about it.

She turns from the window and leans against the wall. God, she was such a brat when she was younger. Messed up and angry, and not about to let anyone love her, not even Annie, who never stopped trying. She remembers a birthday once – she might have been fourteen or fifteen. Come straight home from school, Annie said. We'll have a surprise – so of course Steph stayed in town till the last bus, and got back to find everyone in bed, apart from Annie in her dressing gown.

Didn't give out to Steph, didn't say a word, just told her there was cake in the fridge, which Steph said she didn't want even though she was starving. Upstairs a wrapped package sat on her bed, a new Pearl Jam sweatshirt – and the cake, when she

snuck down after Annie's bedroom door had closed, was a Black Forest gateau that Annie must have got someone to buy for her in Ennis, since she didn't bake those ones.

Steph wonders if the sight of the sweatshirt and the cake, the evidence of Annie's thoughtfulness, had made her feel guilty, and thinks probably not. God, she was a horror, a bitch of the highest order. She's better now though. She's put all the ugliness and misery behind her, and she has Gareth.

No word yet from him. It will take a while to be forgiven. She'll have to find a way to make it up to him.

She thinks of the words Annie spoke in the church, just before she and Matt were married. About how her life and Matt's had always been intertwined, but how today was the start of a new connection. Thanking him for the happiness he'd brought her, and for the happiness he was going to bring. Looking at him all the time, hardly needing to glance at the slip of paper she'd taken from her tiny bag.

Steph thinks of Matt's face as he listened to the words, clearly visible to her as she sat with Eddie in the second pew. His face as he looked at Annie, like he'd won the Lotto. Like he couldn't believe his luck. And when it was his turn to speak, he said he couldn't possibly put things as well as Annie could, but that he was hoping Father Dennis would marry them quickly, before Annie realised what a poor bargain she was getting. That got a laugh, of course, but when the laughter died away he told her he loved her. I love you, Annie O'Reilly, he said, right there in front of everyone, and that felt like all he really needed to say, and then the priest took over.

She blows on her hands, rubs them together as she tries to remember the last time Gareth told her he loved her.

Just then, the back door opens.

'There you are,' he says. His face is in darkness, the light coming from the hall behind him, but she knows the voice.

'I'm hiding,' she tells him, and he laughs.

'I know the feeling. Aren't you frozen though?'

'A bit. It was just so hot in there, and so noisy.'

'You missed the carol singers. They've just gone.' He steps out and pulls the door closed. He leans against it and takes a deep breath. 'Feels good. Wish I didn't live in a big city.'

'Why do you then?'

Silence. Maybe that came out a bit sharp.

'I mean, I know you have a job in London – but you don't have to stay there, do you?'

He makes a sort of hiss that might be a laugh, or might be something else. She wishes she could see his face properly. 'You make it sound so simple,' he says. No amusement in the words. He wasn't laughing.

'Well, isn't it? You're not married, are you? Or tied there in some way?'

'I'm tied with my job.'

She lets it go, not interested enough to pursue it. Another silence falls, in which she feels a new awkwardness. She thinks of him carrying her to and from the church, and feels bad. 'Take no notice of me,' she says. 'I'm not in great form.'

'Anything I can do?'

She's surprised, and touched. 'No, but thanks.' She wriggles

her toes inside the roomy wellingtons. 'It was nice today – in the church, I mean.'

'It was. They seem made for each other.'

'Yeah.' Another pause. She must go in, too cold. 'Well, I'm going to—'

'Can I tell you something?' he says, speaking over her, and she feels obliged to say yes, and hopes it won't take too long.

'I don't work in a fancy restaurant,' he says. 'I told Annie I did, because I didn't want her to know the truth. I'm working in a café that calls itself a restaurant, but the menu is a laminated page, and the glasses are cheap, and nobody gets dressed up when they come in to eat. It's about half a step up from a greasy spoon. And I'm not the head chef either, I'm the one he gives orders to.'

It comes out of nowhere, wholly unexpected. She has no idea how to respond. She balls her hands into fists and shoves them deep into Annie's coat pockets, and says precisely nothing.

He rubs his nose with the heel of his hand. 'I don't know why I told you that.'

He felt bad about lying is why he told her. She can't count the times she's lied over the years, with no qualms at all. She makes stuff up at the drop of a hat: clearly he has more qualms. 'Don't worry about it.'

'I want to be in charge of somewhere decent,' he says, as if she hasn't spoken. 'It's all I ever wanted. My stepmother taught me to cook, after I left here. I think it was her way of bonding with me, or something … I thought London was the place to go, but I've followed up every lead I could find since I moved there, answered every ad, and it's so competitive you wouldn't

believe. I've been working in the café for three years now, and I hate it. The head chef is a wanker. Sorry,' he adds, and she tells him she's heard a lot worse.

She wonders why he's telling her this, why he's blurting it all out. 'How long have you been in London?'

'Eight years, nearly.'

'What did you do before the café?'

'Worked in a self-service sandwich bar, and in a regular bar. Delivered pizzas, worked in a cinema. Walked dogs for a while. Worked on a building site – that didn't last long.'

'Sounds a bit like me,' she says. 'When I left here, I had no idea what I wanted. I just went wandering, stopping anywhere I could get a job, staying until I got bored, or fired.'

'What kind of stuff did you do?'

She laughs. 'God, just about everything. Delivering stuff, picking fruit. I walked dogs too; I liked it until one of them bit me, and the owner blamed me. I did waitressing, and bar work, and selling lottery tickets. You name it.'

'Did you work in London?'

'Yup. Cleaned offices by night. I hated that – it felt spooky. I stuck it for a few weeks and then I packed it in, got a ferry to France.'

'When was that?'

'Six years ago. I was there from October to December. Left right after Christmas.' They might have met.

'We could have met,' he says. 'Six years ago I was working in a bar in Clapham.'

'I don't remember what part I was in.'

'Where did you stay? Did you know anyone?'

'No. I stayed in the cheapest place I could find, bunks so close together you could reach out and touch the feet of the person in the next bed. Slept with my money under my pillow, didn't have anything else worth taking.'

'Sounds like an adventure.'

She gives a short laugh. 'You could call it that.' A shiver travels through her, catching her breath, and he steps away from the door. 'I'd better let you in before I'm responsible for you freezing to death. You'll say nothing, yeah? To Annie, or to anyone.'

'Of course I'll say nothing. Come on, let's have more wine' – because the fresh air has lifted her headache, and because she doesn't want him to feel she's deserting him.

They go back inside, shutting out the evening.

Annie

IT'S LATE. HOW LATE? SHE LIFTS A SLEEVE AND SEES twenty past ten. It feels later than that. It feels like a week, or more, since she pulled open her bedroom curtains to see a world painted white.

'You're quiet.'

She looks at Cora, sitting across the hearth from her. 'Just tired. Nicely tired.'

'I know. A lot packed into a day. My Annie is sixty, and she's married. She's a married woman.'

They're alone in the sitting room, the wedding guests all

departed. Steph is in bed, and Eddie and Julia are cleaning up in the kitchen, having forbidden Annie to help. Dan left earlier to feed his animals, and will return to walk Cora home in a while.

Matt is outside saying goodnight to Philip O'Malley, who was once in their gang, and who lives above the chemist he inherited from his father, five hundred yards up the street. Philip was Matt's best man at his first wedding; today he was just a guest. Annie can hear the low murmur of their voices in the hall, interrupted by the occasional bark of laughter from Philip. They never run out of conversation, those two.

Peadar and Ruthie left directly after the meal, travelling home the way they arrived, on Henry's back. They're spending the night under the same roof, because Ruthie can't be alone. The house Peadar built for himself a decade ago is only a field away from the one they both grew up in: Ruthie could have gone there with him but she doesn't take kindly to change, so instead he's gone back with his sister to his old home.

You had a good day? Annie asked her before she left, and she said yes, very good. When will you come to live in our house with me and my dad? she asked Annie, and Annie told her tomorrow.

Tomorrow.

'There's a bid put on the house,' she says now, looking into the fire. Watching the yellow flames lick at the edges of the briquettes she just added. 'Those people who came yesterday.'

'What? You never said. When did you hear?'

'Joe sent a text this morning. He's delighted.'

'For God's sake – imagine texting you with that on your wedding day! What did they bid?'

Annie twists the gold band that's new to her finger. 'Five thousand below the asking price.'

'Ah.' Cora gives a few slow nods. Knowing how Annie feels about letting go of the house, not wanting to say the wrong thing. 'That was quick, wasn't it? They must be keen.'

'Must be.'

'Will you take it?'

Annie shifts in her chair. 'I might wait and see – if there's any more interest, I mean. It's only been on the market a few weeks.'

'It's not a great time to be selling a house.'

'So I'm told.'

'And there hasn't been anyone else, has there?'

'No.'

'A few other enquiries, right?'

'Right.'

'But nobody else came to view it.'

'No.'

She knows what Cora is saying. She'd be mad to let the bid go, with no other sign of interest. The house certainly wouldn't be to everyone's taste: too old, too rambling, in need of too much restoration. If she wasn't moving out, it would fall down around her in a few years. They'd find her buried under a heap of cracked roof tiles and crumbling masonry.

'Steph was a bit the worse for wear tonight,' Cora remarks, her voice taking on the tone she always uses when she talks of Steph. Sharp, tight.

'Leave her alone, Cora – we were well able to drink too much when we were young, and I get the impression all isn't well with her. I hope she doesn't feel too rough in the morning.'

A sniff is all that gets. Cora never had much patience with her.

'I tried to talk to her about her father this morning,' Annie says, 'but she cut me off. She doesn't want to hear about him.'

'You can do no more.'

'I wish she'd just read his letter though. I really wish she would.'

'She might, some fine day. She knows you have it.'

Silence falls. A briquette slides sideways, towards the hearth. Annie reaches forward and pushes it back in with the poker. 'Thanks for organising the food today. I never even thought of asking Ollie.'

'You had enough to think about. Julia's songs are marvellous, aren't they? I loved that one she sang in the church.'

'She put that in as a surprise. Did I tell you I was the inspiration for it?'

Cora rolls her eyes. 'Loads of times. More times than I can remember.'

Annie laughs as the sitting-room door opens.

'Ladies, I'll say goodnight,' Julia says. 'See you in the morning.'

Annie gets to her feet. 'You won't have another drink, or a cuppa?'

'I won't, thanks. Ready for my bed now. Cora, you'll be around tomorrow?'

'I will, at some stage. See you, my love, sleep tight.'

Annie hugs her. 'Thanks for the music,' she whispers. 'Thank you, my darling.'

'Thank *you* for the wonderful day. I hope you enjoyed it.'

'I did.'

A few minutes afterwards Eddie appears, also on his way to bed. 'Cora, you might come for breakfast – Julia has requested pancakes.'

'I'll do my best,' Cora says. 'Goodnight, love.'

Annie walks out to the hall with him. The front door is slightly ajar; she can hear Matt outside, still talking with Philip. They'll be perished, both of them.

'Is Steph OK?' she asks Eddie. 'Do I need to check on her?'

'Not at all. She'll be grand.'

'See you tomorrow then, love. Sleep tight.'

She returns to the sitting room, where they're joined a few minutes later by Matt, and the newly returned Dan. The fire grows lower as the four old friends relive the day, laughing over its unexpected turns.

And then Cora stands and says they should be off, and coats and scarves and hats are retrieved. 'I won't have to carry you,' Dan tells his wife. 'It's clearing up.'

'You might want to, though. We could pretend it's still bad.'

He looks at Annie and Matt. 'See what I have to put up with – and you two are just starting out.'

'All ahead of us,' Matt agrees – and the words, lightly spoken as they are, cause a small burst of pure joy in Annie. They stand side by side at the front door, watching as the others walk down the path and through the gate and out of sight.

They step inside. Matt closes the door with a soft click. 'Do you lock it?' he asks, and she says she doesn't bother, feeling a sudden unexpected shyness. The first time he's been here at the tail end of the day. The first time for him to stay the night, although she wouldn't have said no if he'd asked. It would have been tricky for him with Ruthie – but maybe he wanted to wait. Maybe he wanted him and Annie to be as different from Jason and Annie as it could be.

And maybe that's no bad thing.

'We'll go up,' he says, 'will we?'

'We will' – but they stand there still. He finds her hands and holds them.

'Annie McCarthy,' he says. 'I've waited a long time for you.'

For an instant, she wonders what would have happened if there had been no Jason, if she'd responded to Matt's tentative offer in the courtyard that lunchtime, as they ate tomato sandwiches. If they'd gone out to dinner that night, and maybe tipped the balance of something that had been hovering between them.

Forty years more they might have had. A family together, a teaching career for Annie. A different life entirely.

'What are you thinking?' he asks, and because she never wants to be dishonest with him, she tells him.

He ponders it silently.

'I don't mean any disrespect to Mary,' she says.

'I know you don't,' he replies. 'It's hard to say though, isn't it? Hard to wipe out what happened, and think about what might have happened.'

'It is … Tell you what,' she says. 'Let's leave all the what-ifs, Matt. Let's make this our starting point, and take it from there.'

'Let's do that, Annie.'

They turn out the lights. They go upstairs and undress, and climb into the same bed. And then, not rushing anything, they discover one another for the first time.

Annie, then

EASTER CAME. ANNIE, AS SHE'D PROMISED, REMAINED in Limerick. Want me to stay here with you? Cora had asked. I could just go home for the weekend and be around for the rest – but Annie had told her no, suspecting she'd need her a lot more later on.

You sure you'll be OK on your own?

I will.

In fact, she hadn't been home since the midterm, when she'd broken the news to her parents. When it came to it, she felt unable to face them again. Instead, she wrote to them each

Thursday evening, struggling to find enough trivia to fill a page, and they wrote back dutifully, and separately – and in none of the letters, neither Annie's nor theirs, was any direct mention made of the pregnancy.

I hope you're eating well, her mother would say. I hope you're sleeping. How is college? she would ask. How was your second teaching practice? I hope you didn't find it too tiring.

The clematis is in full bloom, her father would write. I planted a climbing rose by the shed; your mother wants the wall covered. I had to water it every day this week; we got no rain at all. As if Annie was at the other side of the country, or the continent, rather than forty-five minutes away from them.

Each of his letters had a ten-pound note tucked into it, although he never once referred to them. They felt like forgiveness, or at least a softening. Annie put them away with the rest of her savings, and didn't thank him in her replies, in case her mother wasn't aware that they were being sent.

She wondered what they said to anyone who asked why she wasn't appearing back in the village. She imagined them saying she was too busy studying to come home. She wondered what her friends thought, and was glad that she wasn't contactable by phone. She didn't feel ready to tell them, hadn't found the right way to put it yet.

She missed them. She missed Matt. She wondered how he was getting on with his girlfriend. The thought of never going home again was awful, unthinkable, so she tried not to think of it. She would get through the next few months and hope for the best, on all fronts.

On Easter Monday her brother Ivan showed up at the house. Annie was still in her dressing gown, although it was the middle of the afternoon. Her pregnancy had begun to show, but in loose clothing she still got away with it.

'Took me ages to find you,' he said, and Annie remembered how she and her mother had had trouble too, the first time they came to the house. A lifetime ago it felt like, Annie full of excitement about leaving home and starting college.

'I brought you a few things,' Ivan said, and she opened the plastic bags he handed over, and found groceries and toiletries. 'I didn't know,' he said, 'what you'd need,' and she assured him it was all very welcome, although both she and Cora disliked Ovaltine intensely.

'It's good of you.'

She brought him in and made coffee, trying not to inhale the scent that had become nauseating to her. She put ginger nuts on a plate, the only biscuits she could stomach now.

'Will you need money?' he asked, and she said she might. He took out his wallet and handed her two fifty-pound notes. 'Let me know when you need more.'

She wanted to cry, but didn't. 'You'll be an uncle,' she said, and he grinned and told her he'd try to live up to the name. 'How are Mam and Dad?' she asked.

'They're OK. They'll come round.'

'Did you tell them you were coming here?'

He hesitated. 'I didn't. It'll take time, Annie. It'll just take a bit of time.'

It sure would.

'Don't be a stranger,' she said when he was going, 'now that you know where I am,' and he promised he'd call again, and she cried after he left at the thought of him having to see his sister in secret.

The day after his visit she invested in two pairs of cheap trousers with elasticated waists, and shirts three sizes larger than she'd normally have worn. They were laughably loose, and hid Annie's increasing girth perfectly. Making space for them in her little wardrobe, she pulled out the dress she'd paid far too much for in Todds, the one she'd worn to the party where she and Jason had spoken for the first time. The one she hadn't been able to look at since the doctor had broken the news.

She held it up against her at the mirror, and regarded the foolish person in the glass. No, not foolish anymore. Not trusting anymore. Sadder, and not necessarily wiser. Less innocent, more apprehensive.

After Easter she floated through her days, which never varied much. Lectures and tutorials, and the library in between. At lunchtime she avoided the canteen, not wanting to risk prolonged interaction with anyone, and instead took her sandwich to a nearby park if the weather was dry, or the back pew of the college chapel if it wasn't.

Reminders of Jason were all around her. The corner of the lounge they'd always sat in, listening to music or chatting with others. The table they liked by the window in the canteen. The statue at the front where they'd meet if they'd planned to go for a walk. Every day she thought of him, and hoped for a letter or a card telling her that he'd changed his mind and wanted to

marry her, but none came. Every time the doorbell sounded her heart skipped, but it was never him.

And then a letter did arrive, a couple of weeks after Easter, but it wasn't from him. And it wasn't so much a letter as a note.

Dear Annie

I hope this finds you well. We all miss you around, and look forward to seeing you again. Let me know if there's anything you need.

Love Matt

Was he aware of her situation? Had her parents let it slip – her mother was friendly with his – or had Ivan? Impossible to tell from the few sentences. She tucked it into a bedroom drawer, not wanting it to share diary space with Jason's parting, terrible message.

On Saturdays she went to the city library, where she studied and wrote assignments, and sometimes stared into space, and on Sundays, if the weather allowed, she and Cora would take the bus out to Castleconnell or Mungret or Cratloe, and walk for a bit, and find a spot to eat whatever snacks they'd brought along.

The day she felt the first kick, on an evening when she was watching television alone, she didn't know what it was. She waited, not sure if she'd imagined it – and there it was again, and she understood that her baby was making contact. She sat cradling the curve of her womb, trying not to move, waiting for another small nudge.

218

Billy, she thought, if it was a boy. Susie for a girl. Neither name was in her family, or not that she knew of, but since her family might never want to acknowledge the child, she might as well give it a name she liked.

There were times, of course there were, when the enormity of her situation overwhelmed her, and tears came that would not be stopped, so all she could do was let them out. And afterwards she would dry her eyes and wash her face, and tamp down her heartbreak and her regret, and move on.

Midway through the third term, she was returning home from college. They'd been enjoying a largely fine May. Annie wore one of the loose shirts that covered her to mid-thigh, and a long skirt she'd picked up the previous week at a church jumble sale. Two months to go, and her feet were swelling and her ankles thickening, and her breasts had gone up two cup sizes, but her face, so far, wasn't showing any sign of change.

'Stop!'

The command, coming out of nowhere, startled her. On the point of turning in at the gate, Annie stopped and glanced around – and saw, to her dismay, their across-the-road neighbour advancing towards her. The woman who never smiled, or certainly not at Annie or Cora. What had they done now?

'Your name,' she said, on reaching Annie. Standing with arms cupping elbows, large feet outspread in their flat black shoes, aggression written all over her face. 'Are you Annie?' she demanded when Annie hesitated.

'... Yes.'

'So you're the one in the family way.'

Annie was aware of a wave of heat sweeping into her face. 'I – yes.' Useless to deny it – but how had this woman heard? And then she remembered that Cora had mentioned it a week or so ago to Geraldine, who lived two doors up and dropped them in a few scones whenever she baked, and Geraldine had promised to keep an ear open for a possible baby-minder.

'You're not the first,' the woman went on grimly, 'and you won't be the last. What does the father say? Legged it, I bet.'

The nerve of her. Annie wished for Cora, who wouldn't be long telling her to mind her own business. 'I don't think—'

'They all leg it, unless they're forced to face up to their responsibilities. I hear you're looking for a babysitter.'

Oh Lord. Oh no. 'Well, I was going to—'

'When are you due?'

'July, but I wouldn't need—'

'I'll do it,' the woman said. 'I'm at home all day. I have more time than the younger ones around here. They all have jobs.'

'Oh, well—'

'Raised three children myself, in case you're wondering about my qualifications.'

Annie wouldn't dare. 'Um, that's very kind of you—'

'Kind my foot – you don't think I'm going to do it for nothing, do you?'

'No, of course—'

'I'm not looking for a fortune, but I expect to be paid for my work. I was thinking thirty pounds a week, Monday to Friday.'

About half what Annie had calculated, after checking the small ads in the paper. 'Right, thank you, that sounds ... fine. Er, what's your name?'

'O'Donnell. Patricia O'Donnell. You can let me know when you want me to start.' She nodded, and was gone as abruptly as she'd appeared.

Cora thought it was hilarious. 'Not that witch across the road – she'll have it potty-trained in a fortnight!'

'Cora, it's not funny. I'm terrified of her.'

'Look, if she's had children herself, she'll know what to do. An older woman is probably a better bet – and like she said, the younger ones are all working, or busy with their own kids.'

Annie hoped she was right. From then on, Patricia O'Donnell nodded at her when they encountered one another on the road, which, Annie supposed, was as friendly as she got. Would her baby ever get a cuddle from her, or a kind word? Still, she should be glad it was one thing sorted.

May gave way to June. Annie sat her exams with the rest of the first years – some of whom, she was sure, must have guessed. She was neat, nowhere near as big as some pregnant women she'd seen, but at eight months she was a lot larger than she'd been at the start of the academic year, and there was only so much her loose clothing could hide.

Nobody had asked her outright, but she thought she caught glances. She hadn't made close friends, partly because she'd gone home every weekend while people were forming friendships, and partly from a natural shyness. Cora was the

one with lots of friends – and Cora was the one who couldn't keep a secret. Maybe she hadn't kept this one – but did it really matter? In September it would be public knowledge: she didn't intend hiding her child.

'OK,' Cora said, bag packed, the afternoon of their final exam. 'I'll see you in two weeks.'

'Cora, I'm not due for another month. You really don't have to –'

'I know that, but I want to. Two weeks is more than enough with my family' – they'd rented a *gîte* in Normandy – 'and anyway, I'll have you know that I take my position of honorary aunt very seriously.'

'How will I ever thank you?' Annie asked. 'Really, how? I'll spend the rest of my life making it up to you.'

'Annie O'Reilly, you know you'd have done exactly the same if I was the one who'd got pregnant, right?'

'Of course I would, but –'

'Of course you would. Anyway,' hefting her bag into her arms, 'I'll see you July the third. You'd better not let anything happen before that.'

'I won't' – but she did. Two days before Cora was due to return, at a quarter to eleven in the morning of a sunny Monday, in the act of taking a tin of beans from a supermarket shelf, Annie felt a pain like she'd never felt knife through her, causing her to drop the tin with a loud clatter that alerted a woman further down the aisle.

Eleven hours later she gave birth to her son, with no friend or family member by her side.

And less than an hour after that, having been worked on in the delivery room by two doctors, and hurriedly baptised by one of the nurses, he was pronounced dead.

Sunday,
22 December

Julia

🌲🌲🌲

KEEPING HER EYES CLOSED, SHE LIES ON HER BACK
and listens to the birdsong that drifts in through the narrow slit
she cracked open last night in the sash window. She picks out
individual songs, identifies keys and pitches and beats, fingers
tapping out an accompaniment on an imaginary piano. What
music they create each dawn, even in the heart of winter, every
sweet chirrup and trill and peep swelling and merging into a
glorious symphony. What a treat to be able simply to lie here
and enjoy it.

The room she's been assigned for the weekend is at the front
of the house, the one she was moved to after spending her first

couple of years in the little room next to Annie's at the back. That room was earmarked for the youngest children, the ones who might need Annie during the night. Eddie had just moved in there, graduating from his cot in Annie's room, when Julia was moving out. Annie's put him in that room again for the weekend.

Steph is in the room next to Julia, and the last bedroom, currently empty, lies between Steph and the only bathroom, unless you count the loo under the stairs. Five bedrooms in all, four of which Annie filled over the years with children – and now she's called three of them back to her.

I've managed to keep in touch with most of my foster children, she told Julia in the letter that contained the wedding invitation, *and I'd love every one of them to come to the wedding, but I have to be practical, so I'm asking my first child (you!), my baby Eddie – I know you'll remember him – and one of my last girls, Steph. You'll meet her if she can make it.*

In addition to the bed, this room holds a wardrobe, a dressing table and a chest of drawers, all mahogany: Julia assumes they were in the house when Annie took possession of it. There's a rocking chair by the window with a grey throw slung over an arm, and a china basin and ewer on a tall narrow table, and a three-panelled mirror on top of the dressing table. While her recollection of the room has been blurred by the passage of time, it all feels comfortingly familiar.

She has no memory, none at all, of the people who brought her into being forty years ago. The father who worked in the civil service in Limerick, the mother who gave classes at a

secretarial college in the city, both killed instantly when their car skidded on ice and hit a wall as they were returning home from a December dinner party. Julia, their only child, had turned three the previous spring.

Shortly after she'd gone to live with her aunt Karen, Julia was shown her parents' wedding album. I thought you might like to see this, Karen said, and twelve-year-old Julia turned page after page, waiting to feel something, anything, but all she saw was two strangers getting married.

She must have been upset when it happened, when the two people at the centre of her world vanished without warning. She must have felt her own confusion and fear, but she remembers nothing of it. Her earliest memory is of sitting beside Annie on the long piano stool, and Annie's hands guiding hers across the keys to play – what? 'Three Blind Mice', she thinks, or maybe 'Frère Jacques'.

She hears a door opening, and footsteps creaking across the wooden floor of the landing. There's the click of a key being turned in a lock, followed by the rushing hiss of water through pipes. She turns her head towards the window – no curtains drawn, a habit picked up in Paris – and sees a rectangle of white sky, and the quick flash of a bird, and another.

When she hears the bathroom being vacated she pushes aside her blankets: better jump in before someone else does. She lifts her towel from the back of the chair, the floor cold on her bare feet, slippers left in France. She patters out to the landing and takes possession of the bathroom, warm and steamy after the previous occupant, and showers quickly.

Back in her room she pulls on the jeans she arrived in, and two pairs of socks and her pink sweater. Through the window she sees a morning that's dry and bright, with snow continuing to melt on the road: good. Her flight departs at five, which gives several hours of further thawing before she must drive.

Her phone beeps. She crosses the room and picks it up, and reads the text.

I miss you. I'll call you this evening.

No signature, none necessary. The message already deleted from his phone, more than likely, in case his wife sees it. She returns to the window and leans her forehead against the cold glass and closes her eyes to remember.

Julia, I would like you to meet Jean-Luc Martin, Lucien said, and his wife Claudia. Julia was aware of the producer, of course – he'd been behind all the significant French musical releases of the past decade, and he and Claudia often featured in the social columns – but this was her first time coming face to face with him. No mistake, no accident: Lucien had carefully orchestrated their meeting at an art-exhibition launch.

Julia M is my Irish *chanteuse*, Lucien declared, my latest discovery, as Jean-Luc took her hand and kissed it, as his wife nodded and smiled at her. I would like, Jean-Luc, to send you some of her songs. I think you won't be disappointed.

I shall look forward to it, he murmured, holding Julia's gaze. His voice was unexpectedly deep. She took in his beakish nose, his wide mouth, the pouches of skin beneath brown eyes, hooded lids. A charmer, she thought, already having met

her share of them in the weeks since Lucien had become her manager.

He was a charmer. He is a charmer. He charmed his way into her bed within weeks, and into her heart not long after that. Five years ago, when she was poised on the edge of the fame that was to follow. Five years of stolen nights and snatched afternoons and rare, precious weekends, and expensive gifts of jewellery and perfumes and paintings when all she wants is him.

She puts him to one side and thinks ahead to this time tomorrow, when she'll be getting up in Paris. No, she'll be already up, with France an hour ahead of Ireland. She'll have had her coffee and croissant, and Lucien will more than likely have rung and invited her to lunch at Le Cinq, where he likes to be seen. He'll wait until they've placed their orders, and then he'll tell her about the tour, and give her dates and venues. And at some stage he'll ask her about a new song, and she'll have to lie and say it's coming along.

And then what? Then she'll just have to find a song, have to pull one out of her somehow, and it will have to be soon, in the next few days. She simply has no choice.

She leaves the room and goes downstairs and discovers Eddie in the kitchen, standing by the worktop as he beats something in a bowl with a wooden spoon. She takes in the bag of flour, the eggshells, the milk jug.

'Pancakes?'

'Pancakes. Just what you ordered.'

'Aren't you nice?'

'Not really – I love an excuse to cook.' He sets down the bowl and folds the top of the flour bag. 'Anyone else up?'

'Not yet. How can I help?'

'You could make coffee if you want. This needs to rest for a bit.'

'Was Steph OK last night?' she asks, filling the kettle. 'I thought she looked a bit rough at one stage.'

'She was fine,' he says, his back to her as he sets the bowl in the fridge. 'Too much wine, nothing major. Oh,' he says, 'and you have a letter.'

'A letter?'

It's Sunday – and even if it wasn't, who would be writing to her here?

He nods towards the table. 'Stuck in the letterbox when I came down.'

She plugs in the kettle and goes to investigate. It's a white envelope with *Julia* written on it. Nothing else, and no stamp. Slipped through the letterbox, sometime between last night and now. Light enough when she picks it up to suspect that it holds nothing at all.

She makes a ragged opening with her finger. She parts the envelope and peers inside. She draws out the photo and studies it. She turns it over, and reads the words on the reverse, and smiles.

Dear Julia
It was nice to meet you yesterday. Peadar tells me you have
a lovely voice. Here's a picture of me so you can remember
what I look like.
Henry

Henry, the horse that carried her on his back from the church to Annie's house.

Henry has written to her.

She's got a letter from a horse.

It's foolish how happy it makes her feel.

Eddie

'JUST A JOKE,' SHE SAYS, SHOWING HIM THE PHOTO. 'Very silly,' she says, but he can see the pleasure she's taking from it.

'You obviously like horses.'

'Love them.' She tells of holidays spent at a friend's family stables as he squeezes juice from oranges. 'It's my dream to have my own pony,' she says, spooning coffee into Annie's cafetière, 'but considering I live in the centre of Paris, it's not a very practical dream, not right now anyway.'

'Do you have to live there?'

She looks at him.

'In the middle of the city, I mean. Could you not move to the countryside, and commute when you need to?'

She hesitates. 'Well, I could in theory, but I love my apartment, and it's very convenient really. The recording studio is nearby, and it's good for when I need to meet my manager, or whoever.'

He's not convinced. For all her success, he senses discontent within her. 'Is it what you wanted?' he asks. 'I often wonder. The fame, I mean.'

As soon as the words are out, he regrets them. It's like telling Steph yesterday that he wasn't a head chef in a fancy restaurant – he should just stop talking permanently. The three of them are strangers, or near strangers, to one another. Julia will tell him to mind his own business, or simply ignore it.

She does neither. She pours boiling water onto the coffee. 'That's pretty deep for a Sunday morning.'

'Sorry, I don't know why I asked. My gob runs away with me.'

She gives a half-laugh. 'No, no, I don't mind. I'm reasonably sure you won't go running to the papers with my response.'

'Well, you're perfectly safe there – but, honestly, you don't have to answer.'

'No, I want to.' She pauses, still holding the lid of the cafetière. 'You asked,' she says slowly, carefully, 'if it was what I wanted – which is another way of asking if I'm happy with my life now.'

He can't deny it.

'The thing is,' she says, 'I never wanted to be famous. I know it's easy to say that now, but it's true. I only ever wanted to

write songs and to sing them, and for people to hear them. I was teaching piano to private students, and playing my own songs at night in various bars, and I always wished there was a way I could reach a bigger audience – so when Lucien, who's now my manager, offered to represent me, I jumped at it. I didn't foresee the outcome – I don't think anyone did, even Lucien. It happened so fast, and it was … exciting, I suppose, at first, and exhilarating, and my songs were finding their way all over the world, pretty much, and suddenly I was earning money, real money, ridiculous money really, for the first time in my life.

'But,' she says, looking at the lid, but he thinks not really seeing it, 'sometimes it's like being on a runaway train, and not being able to get off, so I just have to hang on tight, and hope for the best.' She darts a look at him. 'It doesn't sound that great, does it?'

'Well …'

'No, it doesn't,' finally putting on the lid, 'but it's not all bad. I have financial security, which is good, and I've met some lovely people. And I still love writing songs, and recording them, that will never change, but as for the rest' – a twist of her mouth – 'the touring, the interviews, the publicity, the awards ceremonies, I'll never be at ease with any of those. Lucien says they're part and parcel, and of course they are, so I must play along, and act like I'm enjoying them.'

She pushes the plunger down slowly. 'I can't really be myself anymore, or not with very many people. I've been … coached in how to behave. I've been taught what to say, and what to keep to myself. I'm told how to answer questions from the press, and

how to steer a conversation, and how to behave with my fans. Sometimes … I feel like I've forgotten how to be me, how to be Julia Murphy, not Julia M. Except here, of course. I know I can always be myself with Annie, which is why I love coming back. And … with a few people in France too.'

'Do you often come back here?'

'Well, I did. We always stayed in touch after I left, we always wrote – I remember Annie telling me when *you* left, and how sad she was to see you go – and then when I was old enough, and earning a bit of money, I began flying back from France for the odd weekend. I couldn't stay in the house because it was always full, but I'd book into the bed-and-breakfast at the other end of the village.

'Up to when the music started taking off, I came three or four times a year for a weekend, or a few days midweek, and I loved it – but I can't come as often now, partly because I don't have time, and partly because I'm too exhausted from other travelling. I probably wouldn't be here now if Annie hadn't been getting married. I'm so glad I'm back, though. It's been lovely meeting you again, and hearing how your life has turned out.'

How his life has turned out. The successful head chef. Best say nothing about that.

'It's been great meeting you too. I still can't quite get my head around it. I'm making pancakes for Julia M – how mad is that?'

'Ha!'

Funny, he thinks, how both of them are living a lie. Vastly different circumstances, but the same bottom line: life not working out the way either of them had planned.

So maybe it's time for a change. Maybe he needs to think seriously about that. Easier for him, surely, than for a world-famous musician.

He claps his hands. 'Right, time to get these pancakes under way.'

'Great, I'm starving. Don't tell anyone how much I eat.'

He smiles. 'You don't exactly look like someone who needs to watch what she eats.'

'That's because I work out most days. I have a roomful of equipment, and a trainer who keeps me focused.'

Her own gym, and a personal trainer: money really can buy everything. He hunts among Annie's collection of battered cookware and selects the larger of her two frying pans. As he sets it on the cooker, footsteps sound on the stairs.

'Morning, you two.' Annie, in the grey jeans and blue sweater she was wearing on the night of his arrival. 'I thought I was first up.'

'Where's your husband?' Eddie enquires, just to see the reaction it gets, and she laughs and blushes a little, and says he'll be down shortly.

'Any sign of Steph?' Julia asks.

'No, not a peep.'

I think I need to go to bed now, she said last evening, the words slurring into one another, so Eddie pretended he was going up too, and climbed the stairs with her, an arm behind her in case she tilted back. Not long after nine, some of the guests having already departed, others still there. Donated apple tarts and packets of biscuits doing the rounds, the wedding cake long gone.

She stumbled a little on the second last step, would have fallen if he hadn't grabbed her arm. Sorry about that, she said, and leant into him, her head dropping onto his chest, her arm going around his waist. Again he inhaled her perfume. They made their way entwined like that to her bedroom door. He opened it, and waited for her to disengage.

She lifted her head and looked up at him, eyes unfocused. Come in, she whispered. Nobody will know. Still holding on to him, her breath smelling of wine, body pressed to his.

He was tempted, no point in saying he wasn't.

I'm so lonely, she said, tears welling. I need someone. I just want someone to be nice to me.

I can't, he said. Not here, not in Annie's house.

It wasn't because of that though. It was because she wasn't sober, and because she'd mentioned having someone in Greece, and he wasn't that kind of man. He eased out of her embrace. I'm sorry, he said. It wouldn't be right. He left her leaning against the door jamb, swiping at tears, and made his way back downstairs.

Will she remember? He'll just have to wait and see.

Matt appears. The coffee pot is topped up. Pancakes are made and distributed, lemons cut into wedges, maple syrup hunted for and found. The photo of Henry is produced, and shown to the older couple, and smiled at.

'I wonder how it got here,' Matt says. 'Peadar couldn't have delivered it himself, not with Ruthie to mind.'

'What about Jackie Walsh?' Annie asks. 'He'd have been passing your gate on his way to early mass.'

'Might have been Jackie, right enough.'

Look at them, Eddie thinks. See how natural they are with one another, how content in the other's company. See the way Matt's arm rests so easily along the back of Annie's chair, the way she leans into it. They might have been married for decades.

Eddie recalls the women he's had, the casual way they come and go. Some lasting longer than others, none prompting more than mild regret when they said goodbye, or when he did. None leaving more than a faint footprint on his heart, quickly erased.

He has yet to find his Annie.

They finish breakfast and clear up. By the time they're about to leave for church, Steph still hasn't appeared. 'Should we check up on her?' Annie wonders.

'I'll go,' Eddie says. He pours a glass of juice and climbs the stairs and taps on her door. When there's no response, he calls, 'Steph? You OK?'

Nothing. He's wondering whether to tap again when the door is cracked open. She wears an oversized grey T-shirt that comes to mid-thigh. Her hair is mussed, making it look even heavier. Her eyes are smudged in black: he recalls her tears. Thin red lines criss-cross a path through one cheek, giving it a flushed appearance. No hint of a smile.

Still pretty, though.

'Morning.' He offers her the glass. 'Freshly squeezed.'

She takes it silently.

'We're just heading out to mass now.'

'Did I ...?' She stops, frowning.

'Nothing happened,' he says quickly. 'No worries.'

'God ... I was out of it.'

'You were fine.'

'I – I'm sorry if I said —'

'You really didn't. There's pancake batter,' he says. 'It's in the fridge.'

She closes her eyes. 'If it's all the same to you, I'd rather some painkillers. Never again.'

He grins. 'The demon drink – been there, done that. Hope you feel better soon. You'll probably find something in the bathroom.'

'Thanks. See you later.' She steps back and closes the door.

He leaves her to it and rejoins the others.

Steph

SHE LISTENS TO THE THUMP OF HIS FEET ON THE stairs. She leans against the wall, a palm clamped to her forehead. What happened between them last night? Her memory is muddied. She recalls stumbling on the stairs, and his arm around her – and crying, yes, she definitely cried. Shit.

She hears voices in the hall. Did she make a public fool of herself before she came upstairs? Maybe they're delighted she didn't put in an appearance for breakfast. She waits until they move from the hall and transfer to the path below her bedroom window, and the front door is shut behind them. She traces

them down the path – a chuckle from one of the men, Julia's rich laugh, Annie's mock-indignant protest: 'I said *nothing* of the sort!'

When the sound of them has faded she crosses to the window and sees them walking in a huddle down the street, Matt and Julia leading, the other two following. Annie's arm tucked into the crook of Eddie's elbow, her head tilted up to look at him.

She shouldn't have come. She's made him mad for nothing. It was crazy anyway, to come all that way just for a weekend – no, just for a single day really. Three nights away from Gareth, since tonight will be spent in a hostel in Athens, her flight from France getting in too late for the last ferry to the island.

He'll punish her for this. He's already punishing her by ignoring her calls and messages, and she'll get the silent treatment for days when she gets back. Christmas will be ruined.

Or he might do worse than silence.

No, he won't do worse. He promised it wouldn't happen again.

But he always promises.

Her head is pounding. She has no idea how much wine she drank, her glass refilled whenever a bottle was going around. Red wine too, when she's learnt that she should always stick to white. She lifts the glass Eddie brought up – a small shake in her hand – and downs the juice. It's not nearly enough to slake her thirst, or banish the horrible taste in her mouth.

She goes to the bathroom, where she cringes at the sight of herself in the mirror above the sink. The only chink of light she

can see is that Gareth didn't witness her getting drunk. On the one occasion when Steph had had too much, early on in their relationship, he abandoned her at the *taverna* and left her to return alone to the olive mill. When she fumbled her way into their bed he turned away, and was distant with her for a couple of days after, giving monosyllabic responses to her questions but otherwise ignoring her. Making her feel wretched, convincing her that she'd ruined everything.

Drunkenness is not attractive, he said, when she pleaded with him to let it go. It shows a lack of judgement, particularly in a woman, and it's undignified. Please try to remember that – and she was so relieved, so glad he wasn't sending her packing, that she burst into tears and swore it wouldn't happen again.

And it hasn't, it didn't, until last night. The first time in almost two years that she's over-indulged, wanting to blot out her misery over Gareth's silent condemnation – but Jesus, she shouldn't have chosen the day of Annie's wedding to do it. Nice of Eddie to play it down though, when she's pretty sure she made a fool of herself with him. Nice of him not to tease her, or try to make her feel bad.

She pulls her T-shirt, Gareth's T-shirt, over her head and stands under the shower until she's used up every drop of Annie's hot water. She scrubs her teeth and gargles with someone else's mouthwash. She rummages in the cabinet below the sink and finds paracetamol and takes three, cupping water from the tap to wash them down.

Back in her room she pulls a comb through her wet hair until the worst of the tangles are sorted. Her fringe needs cutting –

she used to do it herself until Gareth took over, telling her she wasn't getting it straight. He does a better job, she has to admit, even if he never takes off enough – but she doubts she'll feel like asking him when she gets back.

She takes her phone from the pillow: still nothing. She gets dressed and trails downstairs, her stomach lurching at the cloying smell of fried something or other that rises to meet her. What did Eddie say? Pancakes. On a normal morning, maybe. Definitely not today.

She pushes open the kitchen window a fraction, needing some fresh air. She fills the kettle and plugs it in. She finds more orange juice and gulps it down. She drops a teabag into a cup, then changes her mind and puts two bags into the pot. One cup won't be nearly enough.

She sits at the table, head in hands, and thinks about the house being sold, and the thought brings the same lurch of dismay as it did when Annie broke the news to them two nights ago, and she wonders why. It's not as if she was planning to come back anytime soon, or anytime at all – so why should the thought of this house not being here for her anymore seem like such a major deal?

Can it be that this house, for all her wayward behaviour, her refusal to fit in while she lived in it, was actually the only place she ever felt … truly safe, and valued? Can that be it?

The kettle boils. She makes tea and sips it. As the minutes tick by the painkillers kick in, taking the sharpness from her headache. She thinks of the drive to the airport with Julia later, and all that will follow it: the wait in the departure lounge, the

flight, more waiting, another flight, a bus from the airport in Athens to the city centre, where she'll have to hunt about to locate the hostel she's booked. Her gloom deepens.

The sound of the front door knocker, an enthusiastic volley of thuds, sends a jolt through her. Can't be the mass-goers: they'd let themselves in. Probably someone calling to wish the newly-weds well, someone who couldn't make the wedding yesterday. She won't answer it: the last thing she needs now is a forced-cheery conversation.

Another volley. Go away, she says in her head. Leave me alone – and just when she thinks whoever it is has given up, a sharp rap on the open window behind her makes her jump again.

'Yoo-hoo – only me!'

Her heart sinks. She turns to see Cora beaming in at her. 'You must have been miles away – I was banging at the front door! You might as well let me in the back way now.' She vanishes, leaving Steph with little choice but to go out and open the door.

'I met the others at mass,' she says, walking past Steph, peeling off a scarf as she goes, shrugging out of her coat. 'They're gone back with Father Dennis for coffee. I said I'd drop by here and see were you still alive. Will we have a cuppa?' Throwing coat and scarf onto a chair, bringing the kettle to the tap without waiting for a yes or a no.

'You didn't need to come,' Steph says, praying the others won't be long. What on earth is she doing here? 'I met Eddie earlier. I was talking to him.'

Cora plugs in the kettle. 'Did you say tea or coffee? I think coffee for me.'

'I've just had tea.'

'Two coffees so. Instant will do, won't it?' Unscrewing the jar, spooning granules into mugs. 'Although you're probably used to fancy Greek coffee now, are you?'

When Steph makes no reply Cora turns, the spoon still in her hand. She looks at Steph, who stares back.

'OK,' Cora says. She replaces the lid on the coffee jar. She drops the spoon into one of the mugs. She crosses her arms and leans against the sink. 'Here's the thing,' she says evenly. 'All day yesterday you had a sulky face on you, and you're no better now. What's your problem?'

The words, so unexpected, bring a rush of heat to Steph's cheeks. 'What? What's my *problem*?'

Cora's measured tone doesn't change. 'You came here for Annie's wedding. She wanted you here, she thought you'd enjoy it, but from what I can see you'd rather be anywhere else. I'm just wondering why you bothered coming.'

The injustice of it stings. 'You have no idea,' Steph says forcefully. 'You don't know anything!'

'I know you were a nightmare when you lived here,' Cora replies steadily. 'You broke Annie's heart. I know you had it tough, I know all that, but I was hoping you'd have grown up a bit by now, and realised that the world throws you curveballs sometimes, and you have to get over them. Looks like I was wrong.'

To her horror, Steph feels the threat of tears. She won't cry,

won't give her the satisfaction. She curls her hands into fists, digging her nails into her palms. 'You don't know,' she repeats, hearing the traitorous wobble in her voice. 'You have no right to talk to me like this.'

Cora sits at the table, across from Steph. She laces her fingers together. 'Child,' she says, 'let me explain something to you. Me and Annie go back a long way. We met when we were eighteen, and just starting college. You won't know any of this, because in all the years you lived under her roof, you never even tried to get to know her. She would have walked over broken glass for you, but you either couldn't or wouldn't see it. She's the best person, the kindest and most loyal friend I know, and even though you never gave her a single reason to, she loves you, she does, because that's Annie. And because I love Annie, I want to understand what your problem is, for her sake, so why don't you tell me?'

Tell her. Tell her about the father who deserted her, who walked away and left her with Mam, and came back too late to be forgiven, because the damage was done. Tell her that she'd lashed out at Annie because all the hurt and rage inside her had to come out somehow, and Annie was the one who was there. Tell her that she'd left Ireland the minute she could, the second she could, because all she wanted was to wipe out her past, all of it, because she hadn't figured out how to separate the bad from the good.

Tell her about Gareth, who loves her, who saved her. Tell her about her great fear that in coming here, she has destroyed everything they have.

Not a chance.

'You wouldn't understand,' she says, and walks from the room, and gives herself the small satisfaction of slamming the door behind her.

Annie

'FOR A NEWLY-WED,' JULIA REMARKS, 'YOU'VE GONE pretty quiet. You hardly said a word at Father Dennis's house.'

'No, no, I'm fine.' Annie lifts an arm to draw it across her streaming eyes before passing the chopping board of diced onion to Julia. 'I'm really happy. I'm just going to miss you all when you go. It was so good to have the three of you back.'

'You don't fool me,' Julia replies, tipping the onion into the waiting frying pan. 'I know you too well. And I have a pretty good idea what's wrong.' She looks searchingly at Annie. 'It's having to sell up, isn't it?'

Annie sighs. 'Nothing gets past you. It's silly to let it upset me like this. I have to get over it.'

'It's not a bit silly. This house has been your home for a long time, and you've had so many experiences here. You have a big emotional tie with it.'

'Yes ...' Annie takes eggs from the pottery chicken on the worktop. 'There's been a bid, Julia, a good bid. The estate agent texted me yesterday morning. It makes perfect sense to sell, I know that – I'm just ... oh, I'm just fed up about it.'

'I know you are.' Julia lowers the gas under the onions.

'I feel like I'm letting Brenda down.'

'Well, there's no reason you should. I know I never met Brenda, but from what you tell me, it sounds like she'd totally understand.'

They're making lunchtime omelettes, the last meal they're to have together. Eddie is upstairs stripping beds, Matt has gone home to let Peadar get back to his own place, and Steph ...

She went off in a huff, Cora reported when they got back from the priest's house. I was just having a word with her.

Cora means well, she always does – but sometimes Annie wishes she wasn't quite so plain-spoken. Where did she go? she asked, and Cora said she thought upstairs, but Steph's room was empty when Annie checked, and now, half an hour later, Cora's headed home and there's still no sign of Steph. She'll be back, she'll have to be, if she wants to get a lift to the airport with Julia at three – but has she had anything at all to eat this morning? The pancake batter they left her was untouched, and no sign of anything else gone.

'What if Matt and Ruthie moved here?'

Annie pulls herself out of her thoughts. 'Sorry?'

'Could they not come to live here, instead of you going there? Wouldn't it be better for Ruthie to be in the middle of the village, and not stuck out where she is now? They could sell that house, and the money from the sale would pay for this place to be renovated.'

Annie cracks eggs into a bowl. 'I know it sounds like the ideal solution, and don't think it didn't occur to me, but it's not a runner. Matt would happily move in here, but Ruthie is the problem. She's never been good with change of any kind – even little ones make her anxious. That's why Peadar had to stay with her last night – she didn't want to sleep at his place, not even when we explained it was just for the one night. Can you imagine how traumatised she'd be if she had to move house?'

She washes the onion tang from her hands. 'It's not important,' she says, 'in the grand scheme of things. I'll get over it. Now tell me what you're planning for Christmas.'

To her relief, Steph shows up eventually. She walks into the kitchen just as the omelettes are being served. 'There you are,' Annie says, paying no attention at all to the puffy, pink-rimmed eyes, the absence of a smile. 'I was getting worried. Take a seat.'

She sits and is fed, and remains subdued for the duration of the meal. By unspoken consent they accommodate her, putting no pressure on her to join in the conversation.

'Will you give me a hand with the washing-up?' Annie asks her afterwards, and Julia and Eddie, bless them, take their cues and disappear.

'I'm sorry,' she says, before Annie has a chance to speak. 'I didn't mean to … I know I haven't been the best company this weekend.'

'Don't be silly,' Annie replies, gathering plates. 'I'm just glad you made it.'

'Are you?' She stares at Annie. 'Are you really? This is your weekend, your birthday and your wedding, and I've pretty much ruined it.'

'Of course you haven't. You haven't ruined anything. I loved yesterday, every minute of it – and I was delighted you were here.' Annie deposits the plates on the draining board and goes to embrace her, but Steph backs away.

'No,' she says. 'Don't. I shouldn't have come, I should have stayed away.' Biting her lip, tears close again. 'And I'm sorry I won't read my father's letter. I know you want me to but I can't, Annie. I just can't.'

'That's OK. I won't mention it again. Just remember it's here, if you ever change your mind.'

In response, Steph picks up the tea towel. Annie runs water, adds washing up liquid. 'I'm just sorry you're sad – and I'm sorry Cora upset you earlier. She can be very direct.'

'She must have thought you were mad, asking me to come.'

Annie can't deny this. What are you thinking? Cora asked, and there was nothing Annie could say to convince her that Steph should be invited. 'Look, love – Cora means well, but she doesn't always get it right.' She pauses. Is it the right time? Maybe it is.

'Steph, I'd like to tell you something,' she says, flicking the

water to make suds. 'Something that happened to me. Is that OK?'

Steph gives a tiny nod.

'Years ago, when Cora and I were in college, I got into trouble.' Steph looks at her.

'I got pregnant,' Annie goes on. 'When I told the father, he didn't want to know, and my family didn't want to be involved either. Cora stood by me, she was the only one – we shared a house at the time – and I think since then she's never broken the habit of looking out for me.'

She watches Steph digest this new knowledge.

'What about the baby? Did you have it adopted?'

'The baby died,' she says briskly, beginning on the plates. 'There was a problem during the birth, with the umbilical cord. It was nobody's fault, just something that happened. He didn't live long, just a little while.'

'Oh God. What did you do?'

'I kept going,' she says, 'because I had to. I left college – I didn't have the heart to stay. I thought I might go back, but … it never happened. I got a job right here in this house, I helped run a playschool, and when the owner of the house died some time later, she left it to me in her will. And then,' placing plates one after another into the slots of the draining rack, 'I got the idea that I might like to be a foster mother.'

Steph dries a plate silently, reaches for another. 'I never knew.'

'No.' Annie finds a smile. 'I didn't normally share my life story with my foster children.'

Steph attempts to smile back, and almost makes it. 'I'm sorry I was so awful while I lived here. I'm really sorry I caused you so much worry.'

'You weren't easy, that's true – but we got through it, didn't we?'

'I wondered,' Steph says slowly, 'when you told me you'd given up fostering, in the first letter you wrote to Greece, I wondered if I'd been responsible, but I was afraid to ask.'

Annie's face changes. 'Oh, Steph. Oh, you poor girl. You didn't put me off fostering, far from it. In fact, I always felt proud when I thought of you. You were a challenge, certainly, but I never resented you, not for a minute. I felt I did the best I could for you.'

Steph nods. 'You did. You were so good to me, and I never once said thanks.'

'But you did,' Annie says softly. 'You said it when you wrote to me. You have no idea how relieved I was to get that first letter, how worried I'd been about you. And look at you now, coming all this way for me, and bringing me a beautiful gift!'

Something, some shadow, crosses Steph's face. 'So what made you give up fostering?'

'Oh, I was just getting too old for running around after little children, that's all.'

'Really? Was that really it?'

'Absolutely.'

They finish the dishes, and Annie gives a quick sweep to the floor. 'Right,' she says, wiping her hands. 'I need to go and do a bit of packing.'

'I forgot, you're leaving today too. I wish—' Steph breaks off.

'You wish what?' Annie asks, but she gives a shrug.

'Doesn't matter. I'm going to sit in the garden for a bit.'

'Put my coat on,' Annie says automatically, and gets a ghost of a smile for that. Upstairs she adds the last of her bits and pieces to the last of her bags, the rest already stowed in her car. Not everything will go to Matt's today, of course. They'll do it in stages, empty the house over the next few weeks. She'll take her time saying goodbye to it.

She crosses the floor to the window and looks down at Steph, sitting alone on one of the garden chairs, swaddled in Annie's coat. I wish, she said, and left it unfinished. What does she wish? Annie would love to know, would love to unravel her, sort out all her kinks, or try to.

She places a call to Matt, suddenly needing to hear his voice.

'Hello, you,' he says.

'Hello.' The world settling a bit. Her mind taking a long, slow breath at the sound of him. 'How are things?' she asks.

'Good. We had beans on toast for lunch.'

Occasionally, the thought crosses her mind that he married her for her cooking. Between them, he and Ruthie can just about boil an egg and fry a sausage. 'I've finished packing,' she tells him.

'Have you?' Pause. 'And what are you at now?'

'I'm just looking out the window. They'll be leaving soon.'

'They will. They'll be back again though.'

They will – well, Julia will, when she can, and Eddie will pop over like he does when he's home. Steph might reappear at some

stage – but it won't be the same. When any of them show up, they'll have to come to Matt's house. They'll always be welcome there, and of course it'll be Annie's house too, but they'll think of it as Matt's, where they have no connection. She voices none of this aloud.

'I love you, Annie McCarthy,' he says, and it's the balm she needs to hear.

'I know you do. I'll be over around five.'

'Drive safe.'

'Yessir.'

They're not taking a honeymoon, not a proper one, because of Ruthie, who would be upset if her father went missing for more than one night. But on Christmas Day, if the snow doesn't make a repeat appearance and scupper their plans, the three of them and Peadar will pack up the car and come here, to this house. They'll cook dinner – well, Annie will – and while it's cooking they'll open presents, and afterwards they'll pull crackers and play charades and watch something Christmassy on the telly.

And all the way through, every single minute of it, Annie will try very hard not to think of it as a last Christmas, but as a first.

Annie, then

EVERYONE WAS NICE TO HER. THEY WERE SO NICE SHE could hardly bear it.

'It won't fit you yet,' Cora said. 'Give it a few weeks.' It was a dress she'd found at a market stall in France, sky blue soft cotton with a print of red sailboats. She also brought chocolate, and handmade lavender soap wrapped in mauve tissue paper and tied with a ribbon, and a bottle of wine that had come from a local vineyard. She sat with Annie in their courtyard and read aloud from *The Thorn Birds*, which she'd picked up in the airport

258

on her way home from France, and passed Annie a tissue silently whenever one was called for.

'It's a horrible thing,' their neighbour Margaret said, arriving unexpectedly at the house a few days after Annie had got home from hospital, sending Cora scuttling to the kitchen in search of refreshments. 'A horrible, horrible thing,' Margaret repeated, presenting Annie with half a dozen newspaper-wrapped pink roses from her garden, sitting on the edge of the couch, wearing her usual disapproving expression.

'No woman should have to go through it, but you're young and strong, and it'll make you stronger. No tea, thank you – I don't believe in eating or drinking between meals. I hope you're not thinking of giving up your college course.' This was directed at Annie, who inhaled the wonderful scent of the roses and wished she didn't have to talk to anyone.

'I'm going to take a year off.'

'What on earth for? You have another six weeks, haven't you, before you're due back?'

'I – I just feel I need some time.' Hanging on to the scent, willing the woman to go – and, mercifully, Margaret rose to her feet.

'Just don't throw your life away, that's all I'm saying.'

'… Thank you. Thank you for the flowers.'

'You can defer the rest of your course,' the college registrar said, when Annie finally found the strength to make an appointment, and told him that she needed to take some time out. He didn't ask for a reason. Maybe he didn't have to: maybe her devastation was written on her face. 'You can get in touch

next April to confirm that you're returning in September. Any more than one year away will need to be negotiated, but with your academic and teaching practice record, you shouldn't have a problem.' She heard the kindness in his voice beneath the official words, and clung to it.

'You can come home,' her mother said, 'anytime you want. Don't feel you can't. Nothing will be said. Nobody will say anything to upset you.' Patting Annie's hand before accepting a glass of lemonade from Cora. Flapping at her face with a leaflet she'd pulled from her handbag. 'Phew, it's hot.'

It *was* hot. It was the hottest summer in living memory, every day an unbroken stretch of cloudless blue sky and sunshine. Limerick was emptied out, half its population gone to Kilkee or Ballybunion. The Shannon was drying up, showing its base of mud and silt and stones at every low tide. Householders were urged to spare water, to limit use of hosepipes and paddling pools. Ice-cream vans were heard roaming the streets on the hour, sending Cora hurrying out for two cones, chiming tunes that Annie dimly recognised but hadn't the energy or interest to identify.

'I'm going to take some time off,' she said. 'A year, maybe more.'

Her mother frowned. 'Annie, are you sure that's wise? College would be a good distraction – and you were doing so well. Your Christmas results were marvellous, and I'm sure the next will be too.'

'I can't,' Annie said. 'Not now.'

She couldn't go back there in a few weeks, resume her life as if

nothing had happened. She couldn't stick to the same track, she needed to get off it. 'I can defer things for a year – I've spoken with the registrar.'

'Well, if your mind is made up, I suppose we'll have to accept it. But you'll need to find a job of some kind. It won't do you any good moping about the place. Will you come home to us?'

'I will, if that's OK.'

What choice did she have? She couldn't stay in Limerick, couldn't expect her parents, or Ivan, to go on funding accommodation she no longer needed. And Billy was at home, buried with Annie's grandparents in the local cemetery. They'd done that for her: they'd organised it with Father O'Grady, the parish priest. He'd said mass in the house, just he and Annie and her parents and Ivan present, and afterwards the five of them had driven to the cemetery outside the village and lowered the tiny white box into the ground.

People knew. She realised they must all know. The man who'd dug the grave would have said it to his wife, or to someone. Word would have spread, the way it always did. But everyone stayed away that day, out of a wish to respect their privacy, or out of disapproval.

She'd written to Jason. She had to let him know. *Your son was born last Monday, and died shortly afterwards.* There was no less blunt way of putting it, or none that she could think of. She told him that Billy had been buried with her people in Clare, but gave no further details. Her letter went unacknowledged; she tried hard not to care, but it added another layer to her pain.

She was preparing to leave, packing her case for departure on the following day, when Cora called up the stairs that she had a visitor.

'I hope you don't mind me showing up,' Matt said. 'I would have phoned if I could.'

He looked good. His hair was shorter, and he'd lost a bit of belly weight. He was coloured a reddish brown from the sun. The blue T-shirt was new. *Queen Jazz Tour 1978–79*, it said.

She introduced him to Cora, who offered lemonade. 'Sounds good,' he said. They took their glasses out to the courtyard, Cora disappearing to make a phone call from the box on the next street.

'I knew,' he said, 'when I wrote to you. Your mother told my mother. She swore me to secrecy, and I haven't said anything.'

She saw no sign of censure in his face. She saw only concern.

He shuffled his feet a bit. He looked at his lemonade but didn't drink it. He glanced back up at her. 'I just wanted to see that you were OK, and to say … I'm sorry it happened to you, Annie.'

She nodded, unable to speak. She remembered them sitting out here months before, when she was terrified of what might lie ahead. She was acutely aware of her post-pregnancy shape, how she had yet to regain her figure, or somewhere close to it. She wished she was wearing something other than elasticated trousers and a big shirt. She wished she looked even a little prettier.

'Can I do anything?' he asked. 'Is there anything you need?'

'… No. Thank you.'

'Will you stay in the college?'

'Not for the moment. I'm going to go home for a while.'

He nodded. He took a long breath, let it out again. 'It kills me,' he said, 'to see you like this. I'd throttle that man if I could.'

The words prompted a tiny smile. 'Thanks, Matt.'

He lifted the glass and drank. She watched the bob of his Adam's apple, saw the white lines that ran across his throat, narrow as biro strokes, where the sun had missed.

He drew a hand across his mouth. 'There's something else, Annie,' he said. 'I don't know if you heard, but I've been seeing a girl from work. Mary.'

'I heard something,' she said. She'd forgotten about Mary.

'Well, I've actually asked her to marry me.' The red in his face darkening a little. 'We're thinking of the spring for the wedding.'

Married. Matt McCarthy getting married.

'Congratulations,' she said. 'That's great.'

'I just wanted ... Well, I didn't want you hearing it from some—' He broke off, frowning into the glass. 'We haven't gone public yet, so you might keep it under your hat for the moment.'

'I will.'

He left soon afterwards, saying he'd see her when she got home. 'Mind yourself,' he said, putting his arms around her briefly on the doorstep, and she closed her eyes for a second and breathed him in.

'You won't get rid of me that easily,' Cora said the following day, when Annie stood, packed and ready to go. 'I'll come and visit, whether you want me to or not.'

'You know I want you to. As soon as you can.'

'I promise. I'll let you settle in, and then I'll arrive. Tell your mother to put clean sheets on the spare bed.' She put a hand on Annie's shoulder. 'You'll be OK, my friend. You will really. You probably don't believe it now, but you will, because you'll have to be.'

'A part of me is gone, Cora.'

'I know that.'

'I can't imagine ever ...'

'I know, but you will. It'll get better, it won't hurt so much. Time heals – that's what everyone says, and they can't all be wrong. And when you come back next year I'll boot out the new tenant, no bother.'

Annie was being replaced in the house by a girl from Sligo who was due to move in shortly before the college reopened. She thought back to her own arrival at the house, eleven months earlier. She remembered the sun shining, and Cora coming to the door in shorts. She recalled her excitement, the feeling that her real life was beginning.

Back home, Billy was never mentioned. Her daily trips to the cemetery after breakfast were undertaken alone. Her parents weren't unkind though, her mother taking her to the library in Ennis, and offering lifts anywhere else Annie wanted to go; her father coming in from work with a bar of chocolate, or a roll of the toffees she used to like. Both of them trying, with their small kindnesses, to show that she was forgiven.

She helped out at home, taking over from her mother every few nights to cook the spaghetti bolognese and chicken curry

dishes that she and Cora had experimented with until they got them right, doing the laundry and ironing without being asked, cleaning windows, mopping floors. Getting through the days, saving her tears for the dark.

She knew she'd have to get a job, a paying job, soon. Her parents put no pressure on her, but she couldn't expect to go on living there without contributing to the household. She thought about asking at the Ennis café where she'd worked over previous summers. She'd enjoyed it – the owners were nice. And it needn't be forever, just until she figured out what she wanted to do long term.

When it came down to it though, it felt too overwhelming, too big a step to take. Soon, when she was more ready.

The locals she met were friendly but cautious. Nobody asked awkward questions; nobody wondered aloud why she'd quit college. Her friends sympathised quietly, and left it at that. Matt introduced her one night in the pub to Mary, who was dark-haired and friendly, and wore a small diamond ring.

A fortnight or so after her return to the village, she was heading to the lake with her book one afternoon when she encountered a familiar figure on the road.

'Annie, it's good to see you. I heard you were home to us.'

'Miss Galvin.' Annie tried to recall when they'd last met. January, was it, or February? Did she know? She must know.

'I thought I told you to call me Brenda.' A gentle smile, no sign of disapproval in her face. You'll do us proud, she'd said, roughly a year ago. Presenting Annie with a pretty pen, telling her she was born to be a teacher. I'm so happy for you, she'd said.

She must be sixty, about that. Never married, still teaching in the local primary school. Living in the farmhouse on the edge of the village where she'd grown up, alone there since her parents had died, cancer claiming one, heart disease the other.

'Do you mind if I walk with you?' she asked, and Annie said no, and the teacher fell into step with her. The earlier fierce heat of summer had dissipated, leaving a cloudier warmth in its wake that threw up sudden light showers, and occasional thunderstorms.

'I heard what happened,' Miss Galvin – Brenda – said. 'I'm so sorry, Annie. It must have been unbearable for you.'

Her words caused an inner dissolving, a crumbling that Annie had to fight to suppress. Sympathy invariably brought her to the rim of tears.

'I believe you're taking some time off from college.'

It must be all around the village, Annie thought. They must be talking about her over the teacups. 'I … Yes, a year.' But probably more. Almost definitely more.

'You must do what feels right, Annie. Follow where your heart leads.'

'But I did that! I did exactly that, and look where it got me!' It burst out of her without warning, appalling her. 'I'm sorry,' she said. 'I didn't mean—'

'Don't apologise, Annie. Don't ever apologise for speaking the truth. I'm the one who should be sorry – my advice was well meant, but I can see how it might not have been the most appropriate.'

'No, it's – I'm just a bit … all over the place right now.'

'Of course.'

Silence fell between them. A tractor puttered: Annie searched and found it, two fields over.

'Actually, I'm glad I met you, Annie. I was going to call to you … There's something I've been thinking about, and I wanted to discuss it with you.'

Annie waited. A car approached, a finger lifting from the steering wheel in greeting. She waved to Jackie Walsh, who lived out Matt's direction.

'The thing is,' Brenda went on, 'I'm afraid I've been given some bad news lately.'

Annie looked at her.

'I have cancer, Annie. My doctor tells me I have two years, or maybe not that much.'

'Oh …'

Miss Galvin, Brenda, whose suggestion it had been to have teenage Annie offer her services at her old school each June, after the secondary schools had closed for the summer, and before her waitressing job kicked in. Annie had accompanied the children on their school tour, and lent a hand with sports day, and helped out behind the scenes for the end-of-term concert. Brenda had seen Annie's potential, and nurtured it. This will get you well in here, she'd said. When a job comes up, they'll think of you.

And now she was dying.

Annie was numb, dumbstruck. She kept walking, kept putting one foot in front of the other, but inside she was reeling with the news.

'I'm taking early retirement from the school. I'd be able to keep going for another while – in fact, I feel quite well, just less energy than usual – but I can't guarantee how long this will last, and I'd hate to have to leave in the middle of the year. That wouldn't be fair to anyone.'

'Have you – are you going to have treatment?'

She shook her head. 'I've said no to it. I don't want to prolong the inevitable really. Just pain management, when I need it.'

'I ... don't know what to say.'

Brenda touched her arm briefly. 'Sorry, Annie – I know you have enough on your plate right now. The reason I'm telling you – and I haven't said it to many, not yet – is that I have an idea I'd like to run by you.' She paused. 'I have this – I suppose you'd call it a notion – of starting a playschool in my house.'

'A – playschool?' So unexpected. The last thing she thought she'd hear.

'Well, I'm really going to miss the children, and I need something to occupy me. I've made some discreet enquiries, and I think there would be a few takers. But I'd be ... wary of undertaking it on my own, so I was wondering if you'd be interested in being my – well, I suppose you'd call it my business partner.'

A playschool, in Brenda's old farmhouse. Annie had been in it a few times, helping her old teacher to cart end-of-term paraphernalia home from the school at the end of each academic year. The house, old-fashioned as it was, had always struck her as a wholesome, welcoming place.

On the face of it, there was nothing she disliked about the

proposal. It would be something to do, and it would involve children. It would also help Brenda.

'You'd be paid, of course. It would be an official arrangement. I'd have no idea how long it could continue, but you'll probably be heading back to college next year, so ...'

She let it drift off. Not planning beyond a year, Annie thought. Not in a position to make any longer-term plans.

'Think about it,' Brenda said. 'Take a few days. I'd need to start putting the word out soon, to give people a bit of notice.'

'There's nothing to think about,' Annie said. 'I'd love it.'

Brenda stopped walking. 'Are you sure?'

'Yes.'

'Well, I'm delighted. I don't know of anyone else I would rather work with. I know you'll be wonderful.' She glanced back in the direction they'd come from. 'I might actually turn around here' – and Annie saw the drawn look in her face then, the tiredness in it although their walk had been short. 'Will you call to the house, maybe tomorrow afternoon, and we can talk some more about it?'

'Yes.'

They fixed on a time, and Brenda left her. Annie walked on to the lake, and sat and tried to read her book, and failed. But for the first time since she'd lost Billy, she felt the tiniest spark of hope.

Julia

SHE WAITS UNTIL THEY'VE SAID GOODBYE TO ANNIE and Eddie, until they've driven through the village and left it behind them, until they've covered about half the distance that lies between Annie's house and Ennis.

And then, as they drive past fields that are still blotched with Friday night's snow, as the light is just beginning to leave the sky, as a misty drizzle starts to settle on the windscreen, she switches on the wipers and says, 'You looking forward to going back?'

Keeping her eyes on the road. Sensing more than seeing

Steph turning towards her. Hearing the telling silence that follows her question. 'Is everything OK, Steph?' Giving a lightning glance, but Steph's expression is hard to read in the half-light.

'It's … complicated. I don't really want to talk about it.'

'Fair enough.' Another mile goes by as Peggy Lee, she thinks, sings of frosted window panes and painted candy canes. They cross a little humpbacked bridge, and pass a thatched pub directly beyond it with a single reindeer perched on its roof, and a scatter of large houses after that. She switches on headlights. The drizzle continues, a steady fall.

'Have you … got a partner?'

The question takes her by surprise. Ahead of them she sees the orange glow of the streetlights that herald Ennis's outskirts. When will the two of them meet again? Maybe never – and Steph is returning to what sounds like a remote Greek island. Maybe the truth can be told.

'I love someone,' she says, 'but he's not mine.'

Silence.

'He's married. I've been having an affair with him for five years, off and on. I try, every so often, to break up with him, but … I always end up going back. He promises to leave his wife, but it hasn't happened yet.' She laughs, or tries to. 'Believe me, I can hear how pathetic it sounds.'

The relief, though. The sheer relief of saying it aloud, of admitting it to someone else. Her aunt Karen doesn't know anything – Julia has managed to keep them apart. Annie knows, but not about the married bit. Lucien suspects, but they've never

had a conversation about it. Nobody knows the full story – or nobody did, until now. Who would have thought she'd confide in Steph, of all people?

They're on the bypass now, cars flying past them. She's cautious, not used to driving on the left – not that she's driven much on either side of the road in the past few years. Julia M doesn't drive: Julia M gets driven.

'Do you think he will? Leave his wife, I mean.'

Steph's voice comes out of the darkness. Julia slips down a gear, and another, as they approach a roundabout. A few stars pop out in the sky.

'No,' she says. 'I don't think he'll leave her. I think he loves me, but …'

Around the roundabout, out the far side. Another approaches, and a sign for the airport. Julia follows it.

'My partner slaps me around.'

A small rustle as she shifts in her seat. Julia throws her a glance, but she's turned to look out her window.

'He didn't want me to come this weekend. He wanted me to wait until he could come with me. He's … controlling. I had to sneak away when he was asleep. I haven't heard from him since I left. I've called and texted and left messages, but he's ignored them all.'

She's silent for so long after that, a full minute, longer, that Julia thinks nothing more is coming – but then it does.

'He saved my life two years ago. Literally, I mean – I got into difficulties in the sea. I was caught in a current, and he rescued me. He's a writer – well, he wrote one novel, years before I met

him, and it was successful, and then he wrote another, I don't think it did so well – to be honest, I didn't really understand either of them – but now he runs writing retreats in the winter, in the converted olive mill where he lives, where we live. In the tourist season I work in a pottery shop while he writes, or tries to. He says you can't force the muse.' Pause. 'He has a temper. I don't think he means it, when he hits me. He's always sorry after.'

They leave the motorway and take the dual carriageway that leads to the airport. More stars blink on. The moon slides into view, pale and small.

'He's older than me, a lot older. He's divorced, he has grown-up kids in the UK, a son and a daughter. I haven't met them, but he told me they don't approve of me. It amuses him, I think. He can be … a bit cruel sometimes.'

The road to the airport is long and straight, the land flat on either side. Ahead of them, a plane descends. Their flight maybe, arriving from Paris.

'He has the same accent as my mum – she was English too. When he talks, it reminds me of her.'

'What happened to her?'

'She killed herself when I was twelve. She took an overdose. She was an addict. I loved her though.'

All delivered, every sad, shocking word of it, without a hint of emotion. An abusive partner, a mother with an addiction. No mention of a father.

They drive past a security checkpoint, which is unmanned. The departures building is ahead on the left. Julia slows and pulls into the kerb.

'Listen,' she says, 'I have to give back the car, so I'm going to drop you here, OK?'

Steph opens the door and gets out without a word. Julia pops the boot open and watches in her rear-view mirror as Steph retrieves her rucksack.

She slides down the passenger window and leans across. 'We've got time for a drink before the flight,' she says. 'We can talk or not, whatever you want. See you inside, right?'

'Yeah.'

'I won't be long. Wait for me by the check-in desk' – but when she gets to the desk ten minutes later there's no sign of Steph, and she's not to be found in the bar, or the restaurant, or the departure lounge.

And when Julia finally boards the plane, she scans the rows of seats and doesn't find her there either.

Eddie

🌲🌲🌲

'THANKS AGAIN FOR THE CAKE,' SHE SAYS. OVER THE course of the weekend she must have thanked him half a dozen times.

'No worries,' he says. 'Happy to do it. Sorry about the top tier.'

'What sorry? Didn't we eat it?'

They're standing in the hall. The Jeep is packed up, everything set for his departure, but both of them are lingering over the goodbye.

'You won't feel it till you're home again.'

'I won't.' He's spending Christmas in London, his penalty for taking this weekend off. Working right up to closing time on Christmas Eve, back to work two days later. Returning to Ireland at the end of the month, just in time to ring in the New Year with his family.

'We could do with a café in the village,' Annie says. 'A little bistro, or tea rooms or whatever. It's great to have Ollie in the chipper, but it would be nice to have an alternative too. The pubs do sandwiches, but not everyone wants to go into a pub. Anytime you get tired of your fancy London job, you can come back here and open one.'

He laughs. 'You never know. I'll keep it in mind.' He pulls on his jacket, locates his gloves in the pockets.

'Tell Francey I said hello,' Annie says, reaching up to fuss with his collar. 'She might sit in when you come to see me again.'

'She'd like that.'

The prospect of another stay with his family brings mixed feelings, as it always does. Just three left in the house now, his father and Francey and his stepsister Evie, sixteen since September. When he shows up she'll take her attention just long enough from her phone screen to acknowledge his arrival, and ignore him after that. Sometimes he wonders if she remembers his name.

His siblings, the ones still living close to home, are busy with their own growing families, but they'll drop around to see him at some stage over the few days he's there, or he'll visit them. He gets on well enough with them, he supposes, much as he gets on with his colleagues in the caff, or his flatmate Colin.

It's ironic that out of all his family, the one person he really looks forward to seeing is the woman with whom he shares no blood ties.

'Are things any better with your father?' Annie asks. 'Do you mind me asking?'

She met his father precisely once, when he and Francey came to reclaim Eddie. 'No, I don't mind. Things are OK. We get on OK.' Which is true enough, if getting on OK means not arguing, not falling out about anything. Hard to argue if you don't talk all that much, and if your talk scratches the surface only. Hard to fall out with someone you never really connected with.

'I'd better get going,' he says eventually. 'I'm on the last ferry, so I can't afford to miss it.'

She hugs him. She puts her hands on his shoulders and stands on tiptoe to plant a kiss on each of his cheeks. 'Come and see me when you're back,' she orders, 'with or without Francey. Stay the night if you want – there's lots of room at Matt's.'

'I'll do my best,' he promises. 'Thanks for a great weekend.' He climbs into the Jeep and drives off, and she stands at the gate waving until he rounds the bend at the end of the street.

Fifteen minutes later, a mile outside Ennis, the rain starts in earnest. His wipers move in jerky arcs as he approaches the spot outside the town where he stopped for Steph two nights earlier.

She's complicated. He never got her story. She put her number into his phone yesterday, after she'd had enough wine to cause a sparkle in her eye, and before she'd had too much, and the

sparkle had dimmed. If you ever come to Greece, she said, look me up. We'll find you a bed for the night. Ring me, she said, so I'll have your number if I ever get to London, so he placed a call, even though her phone was upstairs.

He thinks of the invitation she issued at her bedroom door. I'm lonely, she said. I need someone. I want someone. The wine talking – or the truth coming out. Maybe all wasn't as it should be in Greece.

Half past four. She and Julia will be waiting to board their flight. Eddie's never been to Paris, or to Greece. Holidays didn't feature in his childhood, his father too busy with work, Francey with cooking and cleaning for the children she'd inherited, no time to have her own until Eddie was into his teens, and the older ones drifting away. Or maybe that was just how it had worked out. Maybe she would have welcomed her own earlier, but they hadn't come. Forty-two when Evie was born and no more after her, and again he has no idea if that was by accident or design.

The rain continues as he crosses the country, washing away the last of the snow. He maintains a careful speed as he skirts logs of water, or drives cautiously through the ones he can't avoid, remembering his near-miss on the English motorway.

He thinks of returning to his place of work tomorrow. He pictures the next couple of days, full of pre-Christmas bustle and flurry. The staff parties and gangs of friends and family get-togethers, the rush to get meals onto tables, the heat and the noise, the endless uncorking of bottles and refilling of

water jugs, the steam and sizzle and frayed tempers in the kitchen.

Your fancy London job, Annie called it.

He conjures up an image of the village street, with Ollie's little chipper wedged between one of the pubs and the supermarket. We could do with a little bistro, Annie said. Or tea rooms, which wouldn't really be him, but he likes the idea of an eatery in the village. He might even be tempted to throw away the current dream, and make a new one come true – but cafés, even small village ones, need money behind them, and Eddie makes barely enough to live on in London.

He drives on, switching radio stations as coverage wavers. Somewhere between Tipperary and Clonmel, an hour and a half after leaving Annie's, his phone rings in the bag he's dumped on the passenger seat. He ignores it, and the call is followed by the beep of a voicemail. When he stops for petrol in Clonmel he plays the message.

It's me, it's Steph. I, um … Well, give me a call, if you want to.

Steph. She must be landed already in Paris, killing time in the airport before her next flight. He thought it would take a bit longer to get there. He fills his tank and pays, and pulls the Jeep to the side of the filling station to call her back.

'It's me. I was driving, just got your message. Everything OK?'

'Yeah … I just thought I'd ring you. To fill you in.'

Speaking quietly, almost murmuring. Forcing him to press the phone to his ear.

'Where are you? Are you in France?'

'No. I'm actually still in Ireland.'

'What? Was the flight delayed?'

'The flight's gone,' she says. 'At least, I presume it has. I'm not at the airport anymore.'

He sits up straighter. 'You're not? Where are you?'

'… I'm on the way back to Annie's.'

'You're *what*? Why? I mean, why didn't you go?'

'Well,' she says. A silence follows. He waits. 'It wasn't right. Greece. I realised it's not the right place for me.'

'Wow.' He watches a man with a coat held above his head half running across the garage forecourt and vanishing through the sliding doors of the store. 'So you're not going back? I mean, ever?'

'Well … no. I don't think so.'

'And you, what – just decided that when you got to the airport?'

'Well, sort of. Or maybe on the way.' She laughs – or maybe it's not a laugh. 'I know how crazy that sounds.'

He doesn't contradict her. 'So how are you getting back to Annie's?'

'Same way as before. I was ages waiting for a lift, and then I had to wait for another one in Ennis, just like the last time, but now I'm almost there.'

'And what happens next?'

A beat passes, two beats. 'I don't know,' she says. 'I haven't a clue, but … I'll figure it out.'

Oddly, he believes her. She strikes him as a fighter, a

survivor. He wonders what exactly she's turning her back on, and what suddenly decided her.

'Eddie,' she says then. 'You know what you told me yesterday? About your job, I mean.'

He's instantly wary. Again he regrets opening his mouth. 'What about it?'

'I think,' she says slowly, 'it sounds like you're not in the right place either. I just – I don't know, maybe I'm wrong, maybe it's none of my business. But I wanted to tell you what I've done, just in case …'

Just in case you decide to do it too. Just in case you feel like throwing everything away in a moment of complete madness. He doesn't know what to say to that.

'The thing is,' she goes on, 'even though everything is uncertain now, and I have a lot of stuff to sort out, I know I've done the right thing. I just feel it.' And for the first time, she does sound sure.

'I'm glad to hear it.'

'Well, I'd better let you go.'

'I might see you,' he says quickly. 'I'm coming back to Ireland on the thirtieth. I'm going to stay with my family in Limerick over the New Year, just for a few days. I told Annie I'd drop over to see her at some stage. You might still be around.'

'Sure. I'd like that. Safe trip, Eddie. Keep in touch.'

And for the rest of his journey, for the duration of the rather choppy ferry crossing, and the long trek through Wales and England, right up to when he pulls into his parking space in

front of the apartment block, stiff and tired, he thinks about how terrifying it would be to hand in his notice at the caff, and tell Colin he was moving out, and pack up the Jeep and just … go.

How terrifying, and how exhilarating.

Steph

WHAT HAS SHE DONE?

'Thanks very much,' she says, opening the door. 'Thanks a lot.' Climbing out, pulling her rucksack after her. 'Happy Christmas to you both.'

What has she done?

When the car has pulled away she hitches the rucksack onto one shoulder and crosses the road to Annie's house. She stands in the rain at the small gate and takes a deep breath, and then another. The house is in darkness, its façade thrown into soft intermittent light by the flashing bulbs on the neighbours' holly

bush that she remembers from the night of her and Eddie's arrival. She knew Annie would more than likely have left, but she might still have a way in.

What has she done?

She pushes open the gate and walks up the path, her damp jeans clinging uncomfortably to her legs. Half an hour standing in the rain at Shannon, another twenty minutes outside Ennis. She turns left at the front door and passes the sitting room window, and turns again at the corner of the house. She makes her way in darkness down the side passage and around to the back. On the patio she crouches to shift the piece of broken slab that's propped by the wall next to a drainpipe – and there is the spare back door key, still in its old hiding place.

What has she done?

Eddie thinks she's mad. He didn't say it but he does – he must. She's not entirely sure why she felt compelled to call him and tell him what she'd done. And she shouldn't have said that bit about him being in the wrong place too. He probably didn't appreciate her giving him advice, with her own life so muddled-up.

She slides the key into the lock and turns it, and opens the door. She steps into the absolute silence of the empty house. Already the air feels chillier, after what must be just a couple of hours since Annie's departure. She feels her way along the wall to the kitchen, not wanting to turn on a light and alarm neighbours who won't be expecting to see any sign of life here tonight. Not until she's phoned Annie at least, and let her know that she's back.

The kitchen, always so cosy, holds onto some of its warmth. She blots the worst of the rain from her hair with the small towel hanging by the sink. She peels off her wet jacket and takes out her phone and scrolls through her contacts until she finds Annie.

'It's me,' she says. 'It's Steph.'

'Steph? Where are you, pet? Are you landed in France? Is everything alright?'

'I – Annie, everything's –' She breaks off, frowning, suddenly at a loss. What? Everything's what, exactly?

'Steph, what's going on?' Annie's voice takes on a new sharpness. 'Are you hurt? Was there an accident?'

'No.' She closes her eyes. 'I'm fine, I'm not hurt. I didn't go, Annie,' she says all in a rush. 'I came back.'

'*What?* Back where?'

'Back to your house. I let myself in with the spare key.'

'But – why did you not go? What happened? Did you forget something?'

'No, nothing happened,' she says. 'I just couldn't go. I was at the airport and I just – decided. I knew I couldn't.'

'So how did you get back? Tell me you didn't hitch again, Steph.'

She opens her eyes, finds a chair in the gloom and sinks into it. 'I'm sorry – but I'm back now, I'm safe. Please can I stay here, just for a few days?'

'Of *course* you can stay, you know that – but you must come to this house, we have lots –'

'No.' She grips the phone. 'No, Annie, I'd prefer to stay here,

285

in your house. Can I, please? I – I think I need to be alone, just to get my head around it. It wouldn't be for long, honestly.'

'For goodness sake, you can stay as long as you want – but there's no food there, I emptied the fridge. I'll bring you over some dinner, we can have—'

'Annie,' she says, 'I don't want food. I'm really not hungry, but I am very tired. Thank you for the offer, honestly, but all I want to do now is go to bed.'

'Well, in that case, I'll leave you alone – oh, but the house must be freezing!'

'No, it's fine, I'm—'

'There's a fan heater in my room – get it and bring it to yours. And fill a hot-water bottle, and you'll need clean sheets, they're in the hot press. Can I not come over and help?'

'No, you can't. I'll find everything I need, don't worry about me.' She stops. 'Actually,' she says, 'there is one thing you could do.'

'What's that?'

'Could you get in touch with Julia at some stage and let her know? I – left the airport while she was giving back her car. I feel bad that I didn't wait to tell her.'

'Of course I will. I can do that.'

'Thanks, Annie. You're not mad at me?'

'No, pet, I'm not – why would I be mad at you? I am a bit worried though.'

'Don't be,' she says. 'There's no need. I'm OK, Annie – or I will be.' Will she?

'Well, get yourself to bed then and we'll talk tomorrow. Oh,

and turn on the heat the minute you get up in the morning – there's no timer on it, but you know where it is, don't you?'

'I do.'

'Ring me when you wake then, and I'll pop over. Have a good sleep.'

Steph thanks her and hangs up. She drops her head wearily onto her forearms, wondering if she has the energy to climb the stairs.

I can't do it. Just like that, it had come to her. Standing at the check-in desk behind a couple and their baby, it had hit her with a certainty that had caught her breath for several seconds. *I can't go back to him.*

But it wasn't just like that, was it? It had been a slow, creeping realisation that she'd refused to acknowledge – until yesterday, sitting in the church pew and seeing how Matt looked at Annie, and knowing, *knowing*, that Gareth would never look at her in that way, that he'd never cherish her the way Matt cherished his bride.

And it wasn't even just the wedding. It was Annie gathering her into her arms on arrival, and her own tears that she could see now were ones of relief. Relief to be back in the place where she'd always known she was accepted without question, with no expectation. It was Cora this morning, telling her that Annie loved her.

But still she hung on, still she refused to admit what was staring her in the face – until Julia, of all people, had made it possible to voice it aloud. Julia, with her astonishing revelation in the car – who would have guessed the famous singer was

having an affair, was in love with a married man? It was Julia who had paved the way for Steph, had allowed her to speak her own truth.

She'd hardly been aware of Julia driving away. She'd walked into the departures building like someone asleep – and there in the queue she'd come to her senses, and turned everything on its head.

Eventually she gets to her feet. She boils the kettle and fills one of the hot-water bottles that live under the sink. She trudges up the stairs, legs like lead. In the room she regards as hers she drops her bag onto the floor and strips off her damp clothes. She pulls Gareth's T-shirt from her bag and puts it on. She hasn't the energy to find bed linen, or even to go to Annie's room for the fan heater.

She crawls under the blankets and curls into a tight ball, hot-water bottle cradled in her arms. Tomorrow she'll write to Gareth. She'll put it in a letter, so she can make sure it comes out right. He might try to phone her tomorrow when she doesn't show up, but she won't answer, because if she does she'll hear his voice, and she doesn't trust herself enough to let that happen.

In the letter she'll tell him she doesn't want any of the stuff she left there. He probably wouldn't send it if she asked, and this way she won't give him the chance to say no. She'll say she needs to feel loved, and she never did with him, or not for a long time. She might say more, or she might leave it at that.

And later, maybe in the New Year, when she's hopefully

sorted out some kind of a job, she might ask Annie for her father's letter. She might finally be ready to face that truth too.

She closes her eyes. She sneezes twice, and cries a little, and tries to sleep.

Annie

'I WASN'T HAPPY ABOUT HER, MATT. FROM THE minute she arrived I wasn't a bit happy. She was distracted – she wasn't *content*. She wasn't at ease in herself. I was disappointed: from her letters it sounded like she'd sorted herself out – well, I hoped she had, but it's hard to get at the truth from letters, isn't it? Then I thought maybe it was just being back in Ireland, back in my house where she'd always been so … muddled, and angry about everything. I was afraid it might have mixed her up again, brought back all the chaos she grew up with, and I was blaming myself for having invited her – but now I'm thinking it wasn't that at all.'

They sit together by the fire, dinner over, Ruthie gone to bed. The television is on at a low volume, a children's choir singing carols. Such pure voices, like small angels – but since Steph's call, she can't pay them the same attention.

'I could see she was still bottling everything up, like she always did – and now she's gone and skipped away from the airport and come running right back here, and I just don't know what I can do to help her.'

'You don't need to do anything,' Matt points out mildly. 'She's an adult – and hasn't she been fending for herself since she left you, and doing OK?'

He doesn't get it. She doesn't expect him to. He doesn't know Steph like she does. He didn't care for her, or try to, for six years.

'I feel … protective of her, Matt. She left here with pretty much nothing to her name – a small bit of cash I gave her, and the bit she got from the agency, and a list of hostels in London. I begged her not to go, I pleaded with her, but her mind was made up. I made her promise to ring me if she ran into any kind of trouble. I told her I'd wire her money to fly back if it came to it.'

'So you did all you could. And you never got that call, so she made out alright.'

Six months – or was it more – without a word from her. Annie remembers the nights she'd lain awake after Steph had gone, worried out of her mind about the girl. Forget about her, Cora said, she's not your responsibility anymore – but Annie couldn't forget. Why hadn't Steph used the envelopes Annie had slipped into her rucksack? All she had to do was put a stamp on them.

Even if she sent them back empty, at least Annie would know she was still alive.

And then, finally, the first letter arrived from Germany, and the next, a couple of months later, from Italy, and then Croatia. She was still on the move, still getting as far from Ireland, and from Annie, as she could. A single page was all she wrote, giving precious little information and no return address, but they were such a relief.

And after another few countries, and another few letters, she got to Greece, where she flitted around the islands before eventually staying put. *I've met a man*, she wrote. *He's English, and gorgeous. His name is Gareth, and he's a writer, and I'm mad about him.* And for a while, it seemed she was really happy at last.

She moved in with him, and Annie was finally given an address, and could write back to her. The letters were full of him: he was funny, and sophisticated, and highly educated. He was far cleverer than she was; he was teaching her so much. He was turning her into a reader – *imagine, Annie!* He was this and he was that, and all was well. Steph was helping with the writing holidays he hosted at their home, and working in a pottery shop to support them both when the retreats finished for the season, so he could get on with his own writing.

That last caused a little qualm in Annie – should Steph be the sole breadwinner? Couldn't he find some part-time work, and write around it? But she said nothing, not wanting to dampen any of Steph's enthusiasm, and apparent happiness.

And then, so slowly and so gradually that Annie didn't notice

it for some time, her mentions of him grew further and further apart. The letters grew shorter too. She was busy, Annie told herself. All was well.

But it wasn't, was it? All wasn't well, not when she's suddenly decided against returning to him. I knew I couldn't, she'd said on the phone, and Annie had had to stop herself asking more. Leave her alone, let her sort it out without interference. Tomorrow they can talk.

'I must give Julia a call,' Annie says, reaching for her phone. 'She should be home by now.'

Julia *is* home. 'Thanks for letting me know,' she says. 'I was pretty sure she wasn't on the flight. I debated ringing you, but I didn't want to worry you. I wonder what she'll do now.'

'I'd love to keep her here,' Annie says. 'I said she could come to Matt's, but she wanted to stay in my house. I wish I could leave her there for as long as she needs to stay – but at least she can have it for the next while.'

'Annie, she told me something in the car,' Julia says. 'I don't know if she said it to you.'

'What? What did she say?'

'She said that the man in Greece hit her.'

'Oh. Oh, no.'

'She didn't tell you?'

'No. Oh, poor Steph. Poor child.'

'So it's good,' Julia says, 'that she's not going back to him. Let's hope she doesn't have second thoughts.'

'Yes ...'

'By the way,' Julia says then, 'you wouldn't have an address for Peadar, would you? I just thought I should thank him for the photo of Henry the horse.'

Ah.

'I do have his address. He'd be delighted to hear from you. I'll text it to you.'

And she does, along with his mobile number. Matt's eldest son has had his share of women, and possibly he's been responsible for a few broken hearts along the way, but Annie's fond of him. He's good to Ruthie, and close to Matt.

And Julia would be perfect for him.

She'll do what she can at this end. She'll give Peadar a little nudge, like she nudged Dan and Cora. She thinks she might have a flair for it.

And if she puts her mind to it, she can surely find a nice young man for Steph too.

She turns to regard her new husband, who's watching the children on the screen. She won't say anything: he'd only tell her to stay out of other people's love lives and mind her own business.

He wouldn't understand that it *is* her business. Men, she's found, can be a bit slow like that.

Annie, then

△△△

WHEN WORD GOT OUT THAT THE PLAYSCHOOL WAS
on the way, people pitched in to help. Matt McCarthy installed
a sandpit out the back of Brenda's house, and Ivan rigged up
a swing that hung from one of the beech trees at the bottom of
the garden. A carpenter who often worked with Annie's father
fashioned miniature benches and tables to match, and donations
of toys arrived by the boxful.

Cora thought it was a great idea. Cora, as promised, had
been a faithful visitor to Annie's house, spending a night there
every few weekends throughout the year. It's not the same

without you in Limerick, she told Annie. The new girl is grand, but she snores like a foghorn – I can hear her clearly from my room – and she doesn't like the smell of onion so I have to keep every window open when I cook with it. I'm counting the days, Annie, till you come back. This will keep you going nicely until then.

They opened on the third of September, a few days after the primary school started back after the summer. Their intake was small, just seven little three-year-olds, two of whom kicked and sulked and wept for the first half an hour and then settled, one on Brenda's lap, a thumb stuck firmly in his mouth, the other surrounded by the collection of dolls Brenda and Annie had amassed.

They operated from half past nine until half past one each weekday, co-ordinating with the school infant timetable to facilitate drop-off and collection. There was a dressing-up box and heaps of toys, and paper and crayons, and jigsaws. They had story times and puppet shows and singsongs. They planted apple pips in pots, and stirred Rice Krispies into melted chocolate, and just before the Christmas break Santa himself dropped by, with a postman's satchel full of small treasures.

On birthdays Annie's mother would provide a homemade cake, and Annie and Brenda would book Ollie Barrett, who had just taken over in his father's chipper, to deliver sausages and chips enough to feed their little gathering, and Annie would take photographs of the festivities and get them developed in Ennis, and add them to the scrapbook she was filling.

On fine days the children would play outside, making castles

out of sand and taking turns on Ivan's swing, and chasing and running races and throwing sponge balls into a bucket. After Halloween two more children joined, and in January they took in their tenth and final child.

Right from the start, Annie loved it. She adored the children, all offspring of various local families, all of whose parents and grandparents she knew. She relished the challenge of keeping them occupied, and sorting out the inevitable squabbles. She even liked clearing up afterwards, restoring order to Brenda's house.

And Brenda did what she could, which turned out to be not very much at all. Mostly she sat on a wing chair in a corner of the kitchen, and read from picture books to anyone who wanted to listen. By April, even this was a struggle, and Annie would take over when she saw the colour draining from her friend's face, and would pass her any child who was in need of a nap, and who wouldn't require any more than a space on Brenda's lap.

Over Easter, Matt McCarthy got married in Kilkenny. Annie went to the wedding with her parents, and stood on the church steps for photographs, and smiled when the photographer told them to say 'cheese', and wondered, just for an instant, if she would ever stand at an altar and promise in front of a congregation to love someone for the rest of her days. She doubted it.

At the reception, Matt took her onto the floor for a dance. 'How are you, Annie?' he asked, and she said, truthfully, that she was doing alright. 'I'm glad to hear it,' he said, his new

wedding ring catching the light when he raised his arm to twirl her around.

In June, with just a couple of weeks left until the holidays, Brenda said, 'You'll be starting college again in a few months,' and Annie knew the time had come.

'I contacted them at Easter and gave up my place,' she said, knowing the disappointment it would cause, but unable to prevent it. Walking through the college gates again, trying to take up where she'd left off, simply wasn't an option, because she knew it would bring everything flooding back. College was now part of the life she'd left behind, part of the miserable year she was doing her best to forget.

Brenda's face fell. 'Oh, Annie – I don't believe it. If anyone was born to teach, you were. You must go back. It might be difficult, but you must. Write and say you've changed your mind.'

'Brenda,' Annie replied quietly, 'the day might come when I want to go back, but it's not here yet.'

Brenda was silent for a bit. Annie waited for what she sensed, or knew, was to come – and it came.

'We can't continue with the playschool in the autumn, Annie. I'm not able for more.'

'I figured as much,' Annie replied, 'so I have another plan.' And she put it to the woman whose friendship she'd come to treasure over the months they'd worked together, the woman who had reached out to a grieving Annie and given meaning to her life again, who had always shown her endless kindness. Brenda protested, as Annie had known she would, but Annie persisted, and reasoned, and finally talked her round.

July came, and with it what should have been Billy's first birthday. Annie spent the morning in bed, her head full of the tiny creature she'd brought into being, and lost. She got up in time to welcome Cora, who'd taken her bicycle on the train from Galway to Ennis and cycled the rest of the way to the village. Cora was a godsend, chatting brightly to Annie's mother all through lunch, taking the focus off Annie, who was swamped in too much grief to do more than poke at her slice of quiche.

Afterwards the two friends walked to the cemetery, encountering on the way a man who stopped his tractor when he spotted them. 'Annie!' he called down. 'I have spuds for your mother – she said she'd take some off my hands. I'll drop them over later.'

'Great – thanks Dan.'

'Any spuds for a Galway girl?' Cora called up. 'I'm staying the night at Annie's, I could take delivery there' – and he grinned and told her he'd see what he could do.

'Not bad looking,' Cora remarked when he was gone. 'Is he available?'

'He is actually.'

They kept going to the cemetery, where Annie wept at the graveside, and Cora stood by and let her. When she was emptied out, when she had found a kind of sad peace, they sat on a bench under a tree and uncorked the bottle of wine Cora had hidden in her bag, and emptied it bit by bit into two plastic cups.

By now Annie had told Cora that she wasn't going back to college. Cora had objected, of course, but Annie's mind was

made up. Now she told her what her new plans were, and Cora listened as she always did.

'Are you certain about this, Annie?'

'Absolutely. It's what I want to do.'

Cora sighed. 'You know best. I'd love to strangle Jason O'Donnell, though' – and Annie was reminded of Matt saying much the same thing when he'd called to the house after Billy had died.

'I'll get you a teaching job in the school here when you qualify,' she promised Cora. 'We can move in together again. It'll be like old times.'

Cora refilled their cups. 'That sounds like a plan.'

'Might even find you a husband. What about Dan with the spuds?'

'I'll consider him carefully,' Cora promised.

The following week, Annie told her parents that she would be moving shortly into Brenda's house. 'She's getting to the stage where she needs someone with her,' she said. 'I'm going to be her carer. We've sorted it all out, and she'll be paying me the going rate.'

They'd known for some time that Annie wasn't returning to college – they'd had that argument, and lost it – but this bit was new.

'Annie, do you know what you're taking on?' her mother asked, and Annie lied and said yes. How could she know, never having done it before? What she did know was that she wanted to, and that was all that mattered.

In early August the new routine began. Brenda moved

downstairs into the sitting room where a bed had been installed, and spent much of her time there. Annie would come and go, bringing food and drink and medication, reading parts of the paper aloud or simply listening to Brenda's beloved Beatles on the record player while Brenda, full of painkillers, drifted in and out of sleep.

In September, a young woman at the other end of the village opened a playschool. When Annie heard of it she packed up toys and costumes and delivered them there, and arranged for someone to come and collect the little benches and tables. She and Brenda had no further use for them; they might as well go where they were needed.

And then, out of nowhere, she was visited by a new sorrow. In the first week of February, Annie's father was getting out of his van after a day's wallpapering in the parish priest's house when he sank to his knees in the driveway, and toppled over. A couple passing by on the road just then witnessed his collapse and rushed in to tell Annie's mother to phone an ambulance, but by the time it arrived he'd left them. They buried him in the same plot as Billy, and Annie's feeling of loss for both of them was softened by the thought of grandfather and grandson cradled together on some other plane.

More months passed. Brenda lasted in the house till May, when both of them had to admit that the time had come for a hospice – and one morning in early June, as Annie sat by her bedside, her old teacher and cherished friend slipped away peacefully.

On the day of her funeral the entire village school lined up

along the street to applaud as the hearse drove by. The church was full: pretty much everyone for miles around had been a pupil of Brenda's at some stage, or was the parent of a pupil – and six months after that, Annie was summoned to the office of a solicitor in Ennis and given the news that the house that had belonged to Brenda now belonged to her.

Brenda had willed her the house. The possibility had never once occurred to her. As she sat silenced by the news, the solicitor passed an envelope across his desk. 'She also requested that this be given to you,' he said. The letter inside was written in spidery, wobbling lines, and dated three months before Brenda's death.

My dear Annie
This must be short, because my hand is betraying me and won't co-operate. I am leaving you the only real gift I have, to say thank you for all you are doing, and have done, for me. I know you will find a good use for it.
Be happy, dear friend,
Brenda

She left the solicitor's office and walked the streets slowly to the river. It was a week to Christmas, and everyone but herself seemed to be in a rush. She stood looking down at the moving water, knowing that she had reached another crossroads. When the cold moved her on she went to the bus station and waited for the next bus home, her mind filled with memories.

The opening day of the playschool, the timid little faces of their new arrivals. Brenda telling a story, the children seated

before her on their specially made benches. Matt prancing about the kitchen in his Santa suit, singing 'Jingle Bells' off-key. The red leatherette chair in which Annie had sat as she held her friend's hand in the final hour of her life.

And further back, the little white box that had carried Annie's son to his place of rest, her mother's arm around her shoulders as they followed it to the graveside.

The bus arrived, and brought her to the village. She got out and walked the short distance to Brenda's house. Her house – except it didn't yet feel like hers. She turned the key in the front door, like she had done so many times before. She stood in the hall and wondered what came next. Not another playschool, not with the one at the far end of the street. There wasn't enough business for two in the area.

The front door knocker sounded, causing an answering thump in her heart. Who could that be?

Matt McCarthy stood on the doorstep. 'I spotted you heading in here,' he said.

'Brenda left it to me,' she told him. No harm: the whole place would know soon enough. 'She left me her house, Matt. I've just heard.'

He nodded slowly. 'Makes sense,' he said. 'You were very good to her.'

'Still, I never for a second thought she'd do that. I hope nobody will think that was why I looked after her.'

'Jesus, Annie,' he said, looking genuinely shocked, 'as if anyone would think that of you.'

He'd always thought highly of her. She remembered

dreading him hearing of her pregnancy, knowing how his opinion of her must change – but he'd never given a sign that he held it against her. 'How's the new arrival behaving himself?' she asked. His son had been born a few weeks earlier. Peadar they'd called him, after his paternal grandfather. Ruth was the name they'd had ready for a girl, after Matt's mother.

He grinned. 'Grand. No sleep yet, but we'll survive.' He pulled an envelope from his pocket. 'Here, this came for you today, care of the post office. I was going to drop it in tomorrow.'

She took it and glanced at it. She thanked him, and waved him off. She brought the letter into the kitchen and looked at the handwriting that hadn't changed in over two years.

She'd seen him once, maybe a year ago, in Dublin. She'd gone up with her mother to the January sales, and they'd split up to go their separate ways for an hour. Annie emerged from a shop at the top of Grafton Street and there he was, in conversation with another man as they waited to cross the street. She stepped back into the doorway and took in the brown trousers and grey jacket, the hair long enough now to curl over his collar. His shoes, white runners, could have been cleaner. His companion said something that made Jason throw back his head: his laugh sounded precisely the same, and made her wheel abruptly and re-enter the shop. When she came out again, he was gone.

Almost two and a half years he'd waited to make contact. What could he possibly have to say now that she wanted to hear?

She stood, uncertain – and then she quickly slit it open, and pulled out the sheet of paper. She unfolded it, and something fluttered to the ground.

She scanned the words. It didn't take long.

Annie
I'm so sorry. I behaved abominably. Please accept the attached as a token of my deep regret.
I hope you're OK. I hope this reaches you.
Jason

She crouched and picked up the cheque, and read two hundred pounds.

Two hundred pounds to say sorry for abandoning her, for leaving her to bear the worst pain alone. Two hundred pounds to ease his conscience, and rid himself of her.

She tore it, and tore it again, and again. She put the pieces into his envelope along with the letter, and balled everything up. She shoved it into her bag, to be disposed of in the first bin she met.

She left the house and made her way home in the twilight.

Julia

SHE'D WORRIED ALL THE WAY TO CHARLES DE Gaulle, and through passport control and baggage reclaim, all the time searching for Steph but not finding her, for once paying little heed to the whispers and elbow nudges her presence gave rise to along the way. She'd continued to worry as her taxi had sped up the motorway and through the city streets to her apartment.

She couldn't call Annie and tell her that Steph had disappeared – what could Annie do but worry as well? She'd wait till morning, and if she'd heard nothing by then she'd

have to think again. But how could she hear anything? She and Steph had been going to exchange numbers so Julia could let her know about the Athens concert, but they'd both forgotten, so Steph had no way of getting in touch with her. Why couldn't she have waited in the airport, and told Julia what she was planning?

My partner slaps me around, she'd said – but a few minutes later she was making excuses for him, saying he didn't mean it when he hit her, saying he was always sorry after. Was she so in need of any kind of relationship that she was willing to put up with someone physically abusing her?

Julia wished she hadn't told her about Jean-Luc. It felt good to share it, even to admit aloud the hopelessness of it, but Steph, she thought now, was the last person she should have confided in. Steph, a near stranger, who'd walked into an airport terminal and vanished.

She wouldn't try to sell the story for money, would she? Julia had given no names, no details. She could deny everything – but would anyone even check it with her before splashing it across the front of a newspaper? Julia M and a married man – they'd lap it up. She'd be even more hounded than she already is.

Round and round her thoughts had travelled – and then her phone rang and she expected it to be Jean-Luc but it was Annie, letting her know that Steph was there, that she'd made her way back to the house. And now Julia has showered and is dressed in pyjamas, and has poured a cognac nightcap, and is digesting this news.

She feels guilty for her earlier suspicions. For all her complications, Steph doesn't strike her as vindictive, or self-serving. And she certainly wasn't thinking of Julia when she fled the airport; she was simply running to safety. Maybe confiding in Julia helped her to see her situation more clearly, and to realise how wrong it was.

I'd like to keep her here, Annie said on the phone – and Julia thinks it might be the best place for Steph too, in the short term at least. She might not have been ready for the succour Annie's house offered her before, but maybe it's exactly the refuge she needs now.

Except that it's being sold – and by the sound of it, it won't be on the market for too much longer. Annie might dilly and dally about the offer that's been put on it, but she'll have to be practical and accept that she must let it go if she wants to save it from ruin.

Julia swirls the remains of her drink, picturing the big sprawling house in her mind's eye. Her phone rings again, and this time it's the call she was expecting.

'*Chérie*, how are you?' he asks. 'How was your weekend?'

Julia tells him, and listens to him saying what she knew he'd say – that he won't see her before Christmas, that it's impossible.

'Not to worry,' she says. 'Come when you can, and we can talk.'

Because there must be talk. Because Steph isn't the only one who needs to face up to reality.

Twenty minutes later, as she's climbing into bed, her phone

beeps to signal an incoming text. Lucien maybe, checking to see if she's returned.

But it's not Lucien, it's Annie again, sending Peadar's address as promised – and adding his mobile number, which Julia hadn't asked for. She opens her bag and finds the photo of Henry, and reads again the note on the reverse. *It was nice to meet you yesterday. Peadar tells me you have a lovely voice.* From Peadar, not from Henry. Taking the trouble to find the snap, writing the words on the reverse, figuring out how to have it delivered to her.

They hadn't talked much in Annie's house, after she'd returned from the church on Henry's back. He'd been commandeered by locals, and by his family, for much of the time. She'd glimpsed him across the room now and then – and once they'd caught one another's glance, and he'd grinned and raised his teacup. He'd found her before he left, and said goodbye, and that he hoped to see her again. The kind of thing that's said just to be polite.

She'll write to him tomorrow, just to be polite too. She'll find a little card, nothing fancy. She'll keep it short and casual, like he did.

Or …

It's a few minutes after ten in Ireland, not too late. She picks up her phone and opens a text box.

Hello to Henry from France. Thank you for your photo, very nice, and thanks for taking me back to Annie's house – Julia

She adds a smiley emoji and inputs the number and sends it off before she can change her mind – and as she replaces her phone on the nightstand, something happens.

One glorious night the world turned white,
Pushing all my dark away,
Taking wolves and bringing horses
Sending me a sunny day.

She sings it, the tune already there, light and happy and magical. She moves to the piano and plays softly, and sings it again, capturing it. She adds a verse, and another verse. In half an hour it's complete and it's perfect, and it's called 'Song For Henry', and it's the new song for her tour.

And ten minutes after that, as she's on the point of falling asleep, her phone beeps again.

Thanks for my first text message. The other horses will be mad jealous.
Don't leave it too long to come back – Henry

She smiles. She sleeps, with music in her heart.

One year later,
Christmas Day

Everyone

EDDIE FOLDS NAPKINS, HUMMING ALONG TO THE song that plays on the radio.

'I hate that one,' she says, kissing him to shut him up, so he resumes humming when the kiss is over, to make her do it again.

'It's a waltz,' he tells her, and he catches her and whirls her around the big table that still belongs to Annie. 'See?'

They're going to have dinner in the kitchen, because the café tables are too small for the crowd he's feeding, eleven in total – and anyway, the kitchen is cosier at this time of year.

'What else can I do?' she asks, and he tells her she can whip cream for the plum pudding, because Annie said Ruthie won't touch brandy butter. The kitchen smells of roasting turkey, and the onions in his stuffing, and the cinnamon-clove tang of the ham he baked last evening that's now reheating in the smaller oven.

The timer pings. He sets aside the napkins and lifts out the turkey, and while it's resting under foil he gets to work on the parboiled sprouts that he's going to halve and fry in butter, along with some flaked almonds and crispy bacon.

'Eddie.'

He turns. She's holding out a cracker. 'Pull,' she says.

'They're for the table.'

'There's enough on the table. I've counted. Pull this one.'

He pulls, and the cracker rips apart, and an object flies out and lands with a small plastic clatter on the floor. 'A key-ring!' she exclaims, pouncing on it. He loves how she finds delight in the littlest things. He loves how happy she is, and he quietly takes some credit for that – but of course it's not all down to him.

Brenda's, Annie said, when they were casting about for a name for the café. Could we call it that? I'd like her to be remembered – so Brenda's Café it became, named for the woman who owned it years before Eddie came to live in it.

The café is where the dining room and old parlour used to be, the wall that divided them knocked through, the side window replaced with a pair of glass patio doors that can be flung wide

on warm summer days, allowing customers the option of sitting in the newly created courtyard if they prefer.

There have been other changes too. You must decide what needs to be done in the kitchen, Annie told Eddie. The chef must have it the way he wants – but he hasn't altered too much. Some new appliances and equipment, the back scullery turned into a modern larder, the old chipped sink replaced.

A village café never featured in his plans. When he dreamt about where he wanted to work it was always in a city. Tucked into a little leafy alley maybe, didn't have to be on the main drag, but gaining a reputation under his stewardship so people took the trouble to find it. Ivy-covered, he thought. Steps up to the front door, big plate windows. Serving meals in the evening, and maybe lunches too at weekends. Relentlessly chic, with a fearless, exciting menu.

This couldn't be more different. Here they offer daytime food from Monday to Thursday, with evening meals served only at weekends. There wouldn't be a demand for more than that, with a population of fewer than four hundred between the village and its surrounds, and Ollie's chipper needing to stay afloat too. The menu isn't as fearless as Eddie would like either, with no great call for quinoa salads, or sushi, or artichoke on pizzas – but his chicken fajitas and blue-cheese burgers have big followings, and he regularly runs out of seafood chowder and sticky spare ribs.

'Cream whipped.'

He turns again to look at her. To drink her in, to marvel that he's finally found someone capable of breaking his heart, and

that he's fairly certain she's not going to do it.

She laughs. 'You've got your soppy face on again.' She inspects the resting turkey and pronounces it satisfactory. She works as a waitress in the café, along with Paula and Trish, who moved into the house at the start of the summer, just as the café was about to open. Both turned eighteen, both just out of fostering and with no place to go. Found, of course, by Annie, who'd made enquiries with the agency she'd worked for as a foster mother. They'll help out, she told Eddie, in return for their keep, and so they do. Paula has also found time to paint every room in the house since her arrival, and Trish is responsible for the courtyard planting.

Sometimes he's frightened by how happy he feels.

'Penny for them,' Steph says, not that he ever has to tell her what he's thinking. He's such an open book.

I'm leaving my job, he'd said. Back at the beginning of January, when Steph was still holed up in Annie's house, and Annie was still not saying yes to the bid that had been put on it. I've handed in my notice, he told them. Home for a few days to ring in the New Year with his family, taking time out, like he'd said he would, to visit Annie, and Steph.

What will you do? Annie asked him.

I'm going to move back to Ireland. I've had enough of London. It was great, but I've had enough.

You'll be back in Ireland – wonderful! So you'll look for a new job here?

Yeah, that's the plan – and while he was still working out his month's notice in London, Julia phoned Annie from Sweden, where she was in the middle of her tour, and put a proposition to her. And the very next day, Matt showed up at the house and told Steph he was there to take down the 'for sale' sign.

And after that, everything changed.

You must stay, Annie said to Steph. You must be part of all this – so Steph stayed, and moved in with Matt and Annie and Ruthie while the renovations were going on, while Annie's house was getting the care and attention it needed, thanks to Julia, who had decided that it was a worthwhile project for some of her earnings. And it wasn't long before the café idea was dreamt up, and Eddie became another part of all this.

And at the end of April, when Annie's house was habitable again Steph moved back in, and Eddie packed in the part-time job he'd found in a Limerick restaurant and moved into Annie's house too, so he could oversee the furnishing of the café wing. And a week or so after that Julia came home from France for good, and based herself at Annie's house while she looked around for someplace to buy in the locality, and shortly after that Trish and Paula joined them, and all the bedrooms in the house were full again.

And maybe it was inevitable, maybe it was ordained or predestined or whatever, but one day Steph looked at Eddie and understood that somewhere along the way he had come to be important to her, and sensed that maybe she'd become important to him too.

Gareth hadn't answered her letter. He hadn't called, or texted, or written back. He'd simply moved on without her – and she can't deny that it hurt, his cruel wiping out of their past, but it also proved that she'd done the right thing, and helped her to move on too. The day she deleted his number from her phone she went for a long, fast solitary walk, and when she got to a place where she was fairly sure nobody at all could hear her, she shouted all the things she needed to say to him, and walking home she felt better.

And something else happened.

I don't know if you'll ever see this, her father had written in the letter she finally found the strength to read. *Annie tells me you never opened any of my presents but I'm trying again, because I need you to know the truth of what happened.*

One truth was that he hadn't walked out on them, like Mum had told her.

She left me when you were six months old, and took you with her. We hadn't been getting on well; there was blame on both sides there. We weren't right for one another, and it made sense for us to split up, but the last thing I wanted was to lose you. I begged her to let me have access, but she told me she was going back to England with you, and she refused to give me a contact address. I should have gone to the courts, forced her to let me go on seeing you, but I couldn't face the battle I knew it would entail, and I'll never forgive myself for that.

And he did try to get her back, but Steph wouldn't let him.

318

It was only after she died that I discovered you'd never gone to England, and that you'd been taken into care. My name was on your birth cert, but by the time they tracked me down – I was living in Northern Ireland – you'd been sent to Annie's. I couldn't believe it when I was told how bad the situation with your mum was – I swear I would never have let her take you if I'd suspected she was an addict, or on the way to becoming one. We both liked to smoke a little, but that was as far as it went for me, and for her too then. I am so sorry that you went through so much. When I got in touch with Annie and you refused to meet me, or even to talk to me on the phone, I was devastated. You know I kept trying, and it broke my heart that you continued to have nothing to do with me. I never gave up hoping that you'd change your mind one day, and give me a chance to explain, and to apologise.

And now you're eighteen and free to live wherever you want. I'm back living in Galway because my father died last spring and my mother was alone there. I called to Annie's last week, hoping to get an address for you, hoping that maybe now you were out of fostering you might agree to meet me, but she told me you've left Ireland, and she doesn't know where you've gone. I asked if I could write to you one last time and leave it with her, in case you make contact with her again, and she's promised to save it for you, so here it is – and here I am, still hoping.

I don't know what your mum told you about me. I remember that she wasn't always a truthful person, and I'm guessing she may not have painted a good picture of me,

but I hope you'll believe what I'm telling you, because every word of it is true. I'm including my email address and my phone number. If you ever want to look me up I'll be waiting. I didn't handle things right, I know that, and I feel so bad about it, but I will always hope that you get in touch. That will never change.

And for six years Annie had kept his letter, and finally Steph had read it, and re-read it, and thought about it.

And then, her heart in her mouth, she sent him an email.

She told me you'd left us. She said you were with someone else and had a new family, and you didn't want to have anything to do with me, and I believed her because I was a kid and she was my mum. It was tough growing up with her, but if you didn't know about it I suppose I can't blame you.

Can we meet?

And, since then, Steph has a father – who hadn't got together with someone else, and who doesn't have more children – and a grandmother called Connie, who held Steph's face between her hands the first time they met, and who somehow thinks Steph is the best thing since sliced bread, and her father and her grandmother have both been invited for Christmas dinner, and should arrive shortly.

And now Eddie has moved into Annie's old room to be with Steph – and about four months ago Julia moved out of Annie's house, because something else happened there.

Just then the kitchen door opens, and speak of the devil.

✻❀✻

'We let ourselves in,' Julia says. 'Smells good.'

'Hi there,' Steph says, pretty in a red dress. So much prettier since she got that mane of hair properly cut. 'Happy Christmas. The others are inside – we're just waiting now for my dad and gran. Eddie, will you get them some champagne?'

Julia was going to wait until Steph noticed, but she suddenly can't. She holds out her left hand, pretty much shoves it into Steph's face, and Steph's hands fly to her cheeks. 'Oh, my *God*!'

Will you? Peadar asked, not going down on one knee because that's tricky on horseback, and Julia said of course she would. And he took her hand, which was already resting on his waist because she was sitting behind him on Henry's back, and she felt him slipping a ring onto her finger. He told her it had been his mother's engagement ring, and said they could replace it with another if Julia wanted, but Julia doesn't want. It's small and sweet and perfect.

Hard to believe how much has changed in little over a year. A year last Monday since they met for the first time outside the church where Annie and Matt had just got married. Eleven months or so since Julia had sat in a Swedish hotel room, two hours before she was due on stage, and called Annie.

I've been looking for an investment, she said, and I think I've found it. I want to pay for the renovations to your house, so you don't have to sell it.

*

Annie, predictably, was flabbergasted. Julia! You can't go spending your money on me!

Of course I can. I can do whatever I want with it, and I want to do this. Don't you want to keep the house?

Well, yes, I'd love that, but—

And now that you don't need to live in it anymore, couldn't we think of another use for it? Maybe it could be turned into a small guesthouse, or, I don't know … a retreat for writers like Steph was running with that man in Greece. Something like that, maybe.

And because Annie still protested at the thought of Julia financing it, Julia had to come clean.

I'm giving it up, she said. All of this, all the touring, and the publicity. I hate it, Annie. I never wanted it. I want to move somewhere quieter, where I can go on writing and recording songs. I want to come home, Annie. I want to buy a place in Ireland, and it would be great if I could take a room in your house, use it as my base until I found my own house.

She could just buy Annie's house, of course. She could simply buy it and have it done up and move in. The possibility had thrown itself up while she was casting around, and looking at her idea from all its sides – but Annie's house wasn't what she wanted. It was too big for her: it would feel wrong to have just one person living there.

It took a while to convince Annie, to make her understand that this was what Julia really wanted. And after that, once Annie agreed, the rest just … happened.

I have to let you go, she told Jean-Luc. I need someone who

puts me first. I want someone who wants me as much as I want him.

Of course he tried to change her mind. He made renewed promises, he swore he would tell his wife he wanted a divorce. She thought of all the other promises he'd broken, all the times she'd said goodbye, only to relent and come back to him. I have to let you go, she repeated, and it was unbearable but she did it.

At the end of the tour she took Lucien out to dinner and told him of her decision, and endured his shock and his dismayed objections, and his predictions that her career would collapse without touring.

Do you want me to find a new manager? she asked, and he looked appalled and said of course not. I'll still write songs, she told him, and I'll perform in smaller venues, mostly in Ireland, and maybe in the UK.

But Julia, he said, you are a world-famous star. Your fans will want to see you.

My fans will have to come to Ireland, she replied, if they want to see me. Otherwise they can listen to my music.

And your producer? Jean-Luc is based here. How will it work, with you in Ireland? You'll have to travel here when you want to record.

Jean-Luc and I have parted company, she told him. Believe it or not, there are producers and studios in Ireland. You'll love it over there, Lucien. You might even decide to move there too. She told him this would make her happier than she'd been in a long time, and he sighed, and shrugged in that most Gallic of ways. Julia, he said, in that case, how can I argue? She paid

the bill and kissed him on both cheeks, and walked from the restaurant with a lighter step.

Over the following days and weeks she had more telephone conversations with Annie, who told her that Steph wanted to be part of whatever the house turned into, and that Eddie had quit his job in London and was looking for work as a chef in Ireland. And before the end of that particular conversation, one of them, she couldn't remember which, mooted the idea of a café with Eddie at the helm, and the house renovations took on a new focus.

While she waited for them to be completed she put her apartment on the market. She made enquiries among her musician friends and found a recording studio in Galway whose director proclaimed himself more than happy to meet with her when she returned to Ireland. With Lucien's reluctant help, she issued a press statement to the effect that she was taking a step back from touring, but would continue to make music.

Within a month of it being put up for sale the penthouse apartment was bought by a film director and his wife. Julia's aunt Karen told her she'd miss her, and promised to visit as soon as Julia was settled in Ireland.

And she wrote songs. She wrote song after song, the music and the words and the happiness flowing out of her, unstemmed, and it's all undoubtedly her best work. A delighted Lucien is planning a double-CD release in the spring.

And every few days she would send a text to Henry the horse, little nonsense messages about nothing at all, and Henry would text back with his own bits of nonsense.

And sometimes, it wasn't really nonsense.

Henry, I have decided to move back to Ireland. Please keep an eye out for houses for sale – Julia

Julia, Peadar and I are very happy to hear it. Peadar will make a list of suitable properties, and I will give my best whinny when I see you – Henry

That was how they began, she and Peadar. They coaxed something small into being then, ready to bloom when she finally moved back to Ireland in May, and Peadar called to Annie's house not long afterwards with a trailer-load of blocks he'd chopped from a fallen tree, and ended up staying for dinner with Julia and Eddie and Steph.

And five months after that, when he and she had got to a place where they were secure, and sure of one another, he suggested that she move in with him. And yesterday he asked her to marry him, and she can't wait for them to tell Annie and Matt, and Ruthie.

'Better show our faces inside,' she says, when Steph has finished enthusing over the ring, and Eddie has poured two glasses of champagne. 'We haven't told the others yet.'

'I've got to see this,' Steph says, untying Annie's old apron, so the three of them head for the sitting room, leaving Eddie with the sprouts. Julia opens the door, and looks past Matt and Ruthie and Trish and Paula, and finds Annie.

Something has happened.

She knows this, she sees this, even before a radiant Julia displays the ring, and prompts a general hullabaloo that involves hugs and kisses and handshakes and back-slapping – and just as that's dying down someone knocks on the front door, and Steph leaves the room to admit her father and grandmother, and Annie settles back onto the couch with a feeling of immense satisfaction.

Her three special chicks, all sorted, or getting there. Julia's romance she takes some credit for – although admittedly those two would probably have got there without her help, so ridiculously perfectly suited are they – but Eddie and Steph was a complete surprise. How could she have missed it? How had she never thought to put that pair together? There she was, trying to come up with some suitable young man for Steph, and he was under her nose all the time. Never mind: they did it all by themselves, in their own way – and of course she *did* help, if unwittingly, by offering Eddie a job in the café and bringing him back into Steph's orbit.

She watches Steph help her grandmother into a chair. How the girl has blossomed. How the act of coming to terms with her past, and travelling into the future with people who belong to her, has taken the lost, hunted look from her face and replaced it with easeful calm. She's at peace now, and truly able to love – and in Eddie she's chosen a most deserving recipient of that love. Really, things could hardly have worked out better.

'You're looking mighty pleased with yourself.'

She turns to regard the man who understands her, who sees when her old sorrow returns, as it still does now and again, and who holds her until it passes.

Monday was their first wedding anniversary, and her sixty-first birthday. The day was cold and dry so they bundled into coats and she took him for a walk while Ruthie was painting pine cones and wrapping presents with Julia. Remember? she asked, when they got to the place where she'd popped the question, and he laughed and said would he ever forget.

For her birthday he got her the necklace she'd admired in an Ennis jeweller's window last month. He needs a bit of help with presents, but he's good at picking up hints. Tomorrow they're having a big get-together with his children and their families, but today they're here at Annie's, her beloved house that's in safe hands now. And Brenda, who made it all possible, is being remembered in the café's name.

She looks across at Trish, who's starting a job with a market gardener in January, and Paula, who's already begun an online course in interior design. When they move on, as they inevitably will, Annie will find others to replace them, others coming out of foster care who need a breather, some safe place where they can come to terms with their independence and figure out their calling.

They raise glasses and drink a toast to the newly engaged couple, and a minute or so later Eddie puts his head around the door.

'Dinner's ready,' he announces, and the small crowd begins to move. When the room has emptied out Matt adds a little coal to the fire, and Annie puts up the fireguard. He offers her a hand: she takes it.

'Happy Christmas, Annie McCarthy.'

'Happy Christmas, Matt McCarthy.'

They follow the others to the kitchen.

Annie, then

WHAT HAD POSSESSED HER? WHAT IN THE LORD Almighty's name had made her think she could do this? Who had allowed her to do this? They had no right, no right at all to let her believe she was capable.

'I can't do it,' she said.

'Of course you can,' Cora replied calmly. Cora, who'd begun working in the local school in September, after graduating from college. Cora, who'd been seeing Dan Flaherty now for over a year, Annie having made sure she bumped into him

accidentally on purpose any time she was around, until he took the hint and asked her out.

'Cora, what do I know about bringing up a child – especially one who's just lost both her parents? I haven't a clue.' Chewing on a thumbnail until Cora pulled it away from her mouth.

'Now listen to me, Annie O'Reilly. You would have made a spectacular primary teacher if that had gone according to plan. You made a spectacular preschool teacher – remember those references for the fostering agency from the parents? Do you think they were making them up?'

'They were just being—'

'Shut up. You really think you would have got the go-ahead from the agency if they didn't think you could do it? You will make a spectacular foster mother. I know this, and I'm never wrong about anything. Ask Dan.'

'Cora, be serious.'

'I *am* serious. You're just nervous because it's the unknown, and because you can't see what everyone else sees about you. You're kind and you're loving, and that's all any child needs. You'll be great.'

Annie checked the clock on the wall for the millionth time. 'They'll be here any minute,' she said, feeling another heart-leap of fright. You're getting a girl, Cathy from the agency had told her on the phone. Just gone three years old. Parents killed the previous week in a road accident. No relatives able to accommodate her, Cathy said, an aunt in Paris who'd taken time off in the immediate aftermath of the accident but needed

to return to her job now, no capacity to look after a small child.

A three-year-old girl being placed in Annie's care, Annie wholly responsible for minding her and feeding her and keeping her alive. She'd be dead in a week, having choked on a toffee or been strangled by the cord of a blind, or run over by a car when Annie's back was turned, or savaged by one of the village dogs who'd never done it before, but you never knew.

She got up and paced the floor, thumb drifting back to her mouth. Three years old, both parents gone. How did a child cope with that? Annie's father's sudden death the previous year had been crushing, but Annie was an adult, able to process it and deal with it. This poor child must be wild with grief. She needed a counsellor, not a foster parent who'd be making it up as she went along.

The knocker thumped. Annie started violently.

Cora stood. 'Come on, we'll go together. Annie, you can do this. I have faith in you.'

'I can't. I'm going to be sick.'

'You're not, and you can. Think of Brenda' – and it was exactly what she needed. Brenda would have approved. Brenda would have had faith in her too.

She walked out to the hall and made the endless journey to the front door, Cora steady as a rock beside her. She reached up and turned the knob.

'There you are!' Cathy said brightly. 'We've been looking forward to meeting you, haven't we, love?' Looking down at

the small child whose hand she was holding, the child with enormous dark eyes, who was fixing Annie with a solemn stare. Pink coat a size too big, white shoes with pink laces. Brushed brown hair, a clip shaped like a butterfly pushed in on either side. A soft toy of some kind, a teddy or a rabbit, pressed to her chest.

Annie dropped to her knees. 'Hello,' she said softly. 'My name is Annie, and I'm very happy to meet you. I've been wishing so hard that I had a little girl in my house, and here you are at last.'

The child blinked.

'We're having sausages for dinner. Do you like those?'

A tiny nod.

'Oh good, me too.' She paused. 'What's your name?'

And then, in a whisper so small she barely heard it: 'Julia.'

Acknowledgements

A big thank you as ever to all who had any hand, act or part in getting this book from first idea to last full stop:

- All at Hachette Books Ireland, in particular Ciara Doorley, who can officially read my mind at this stage;
- My invaluable agent Sallyanne Sweeney, who always has my back;
- Copy-editor Hazel and proofreader Aonghus, both consummate professionals;
- My parents and siblings, greatly supportive as ever;
- My research assistants Mags, Patsy, Orla, Sadhbh, Kirby and Judi, thanks so much for your help;
- Book bloggers for early reviews and spreading of the word;
- Anyone who's shared or retweeted my pre-book blather online – it hasn't gone unnoticed.

Thanks in particular to my faithful readers, without whom I would have gone belly-up years ago, and welcome to the newcomers – I hope I justify your faith in me.

Roisin Meaney

THE RESTAURANT

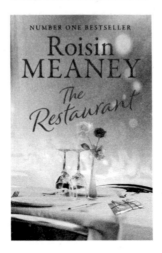

'Meaney leaves you wanting to know more about the characters and what they do next, almost as if they have become friends'
Irish Independent

When Emily's heart was broken by the love of her life, she never imagined that she would find herself, just two years later, running a small restaurant in what used to be her grandmother's tiny hat shop. The Food of Love offers diners the possibility of friendship (and maybe more) as well as a delicious meal. And even though Emily has sworn off romance forever, it doesn't stop her hoping for happiness for her regulars, like widower Bill who hides a troubling secret, single mum Heather who ran away from home as a teenager, and gentle Astrid whose past is darker than any of her friends know.

Then, out of the blue, Emily receives a letter from her ex. He's returning home to Ireland and wants to see her. Is Emily brave enough to give love a second chance – or wise enough to figure out where it's truly to be found?

Also available as an ebook and audiobook

Roisin Meaney

THE BIRTHDAY PARTY

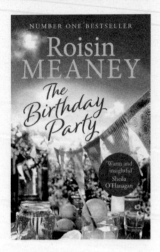

'Meaney is utterly credible, utterly authentic, utterly irresistible'
Irish Independent

Summer is in full swing on Roone, an island off the west coast of Ireland, and preparations are underway for a big birthday party at the local hotel. But before then, love and friendship will be tested ...

Who is the stranger who arrives at Imelda's door, just weeks after her world falls to pieces?

How long can Eve hide her secret from Andy?

And will Nell and Laura's friendship survive the storm that's about to hit the island?

Also available as an ebook and audiobook

Revisit the island of Roone in *One Summer*,
After the Wedding and *I'll Be Home for Christmas*

Roisin Meaney

THE REUNION

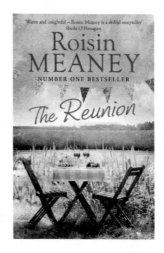

It's their twenty-year school reunion but the Plunkett sisters have their own reasons for not wanting to attend ...

Caroline, now a successful knitwear designer, spends her time flying between her business in England and her lover in Italy. As far as she's concerned, her school days, and what happened to her the year she left, should stay in the past.

Eleanor, meanwhile, is unrecognisable from the fun-loving girl she was in school. With a son who is barely speaking to her, and a husband keeping a secret from her, revisiting the past is the last thing on her mind.

But when an unexpected letter arrives for Caroline in the weeks before the reunion, memories are stirred.

Will the sisters find the courage to return to the town where they grew up and face what they've been running from all these years?

The Reunion is a moving story about secrets, sisters and finding a way to open your heart.

Also available as an ebook

Roisin Meaney

THE ANNIVERSARY

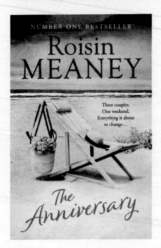

It's the bank holiday weekend and the Cunningham family are escaping to their holiday home by the sea, as they've done every summer for many years.

Except that now, parents Lily and Charlie are waiting for their divorce papers to come through – and have their new partners in tow.

Their daughter Poll is there with her boyfriend and is determined to make known her feelings for Chloë, her father's new love. While her brother Thomas also has feelings for Chloë – of a very different nature …

And amid all the drama, everyone has forgotten that this weekend also happens to be Lily and Charlie's wedding anniversary.

Will any of the couples survive the weekend intact?

Also available as an ebook and audiobook

In loving memory of Colm O'Mahony, a sweetheart